REMNANT'S HOPE

Tales of Resonance

Hugo Jackson

Inspired
Quill

Published by Inspired Quill: June 2025

First Edition

Content Warning: This book contains mentions of physical assault and abuse, war, death, hospitalisation, bullying and soldier brutality.

Chief Editor: Sara-Jayne Slack
Cover Design: Katie Hofgard (patreon.com/Eskiworks)
Additional thanks to: ChocolateRaisinFury
Typeset in Garamond

Paperback ISBN: 978-1-913117-15-3
eBook ISBN: 978-1-913117-16-0
Print Edition

Printed in the United Kingdom
1 2 3 4 5 6 7 8 9 10

Inspired Quill Publishing, UK
Business Reg. No. 7592847
www.inspired-quill.com

Praise for Hugo Jackson

"[Legacy] is very satisfying. Jackson brings a complex and colorful anthro world to life. His descriptions are full of lush detail."
—Fred Patten, *Dogpatch Press*

"I can't say enough good things about this book. The writing is great. The world is fascinating. The heroes are intriguing and lovable. The villains are terrifying, and the fight scenes are written as if by a fight choreographer. I loved it. A perfect book for adults, teens, and children alike."
—M. Shaw, *Amazon Reviewer*

"I loved it! This book honestly gave me a huge nostalgia rush — a lot happens once things start rolling. [...] A fun fantasy romp with a great cast of heroes."
—David Popovich, *Bookworm Reviews (Youtube)*

"Overall, a very well written story that kept me entertained from start to finish. Every once in a while, you stumble across an amazing gem, and this is one of those."
—J. Poole, Bestselling *Author of* The Bakkian Chronicles

"[Fracture is] An epic anthro-fantasy [...where] Jackson tenders relatable albeit convoluted motivations, heart-rending tragedy and an all-too-familiar feeling of unease in this dismal chapter of our heroes' history, closing as friends old and new commit themselves to a brighter future for all Eeres. Eagerly anticipating RUIN'S DAWN!"
—Mark J. Engels, *Author of* Always Gray in Winter

Thoroughly enjoyed reading it. Such a rich, detailed world, a compelling cast of characters, and thrills aplenty.
—Mark Cantrell, *Author of* Citizen Zero

For the ones who fight
Even when it seems
That the world is ending

Thank you.

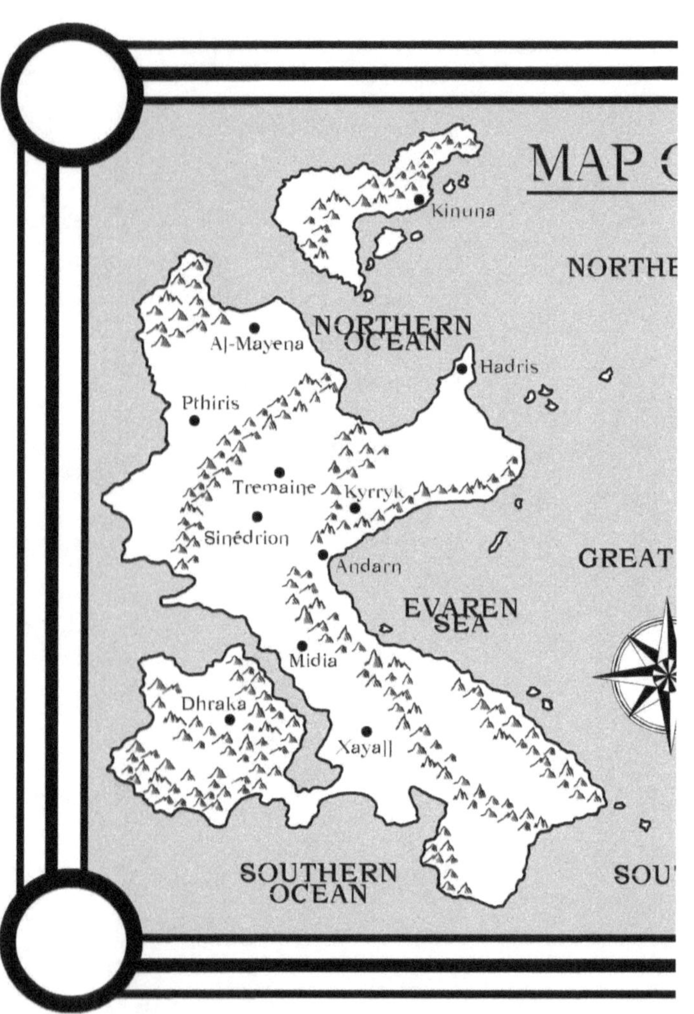

MAP O
NORTHE
Kinuna
NORTHERN OCEAN
Al-Mayena
Hadris
Pthiris
Tremaine
Kyrryk
Sinédrion
Andarn
GREAT
EVAREN SEA
Midia
Dhraka
Xayall
SOUTHERN OCEAN
SOU

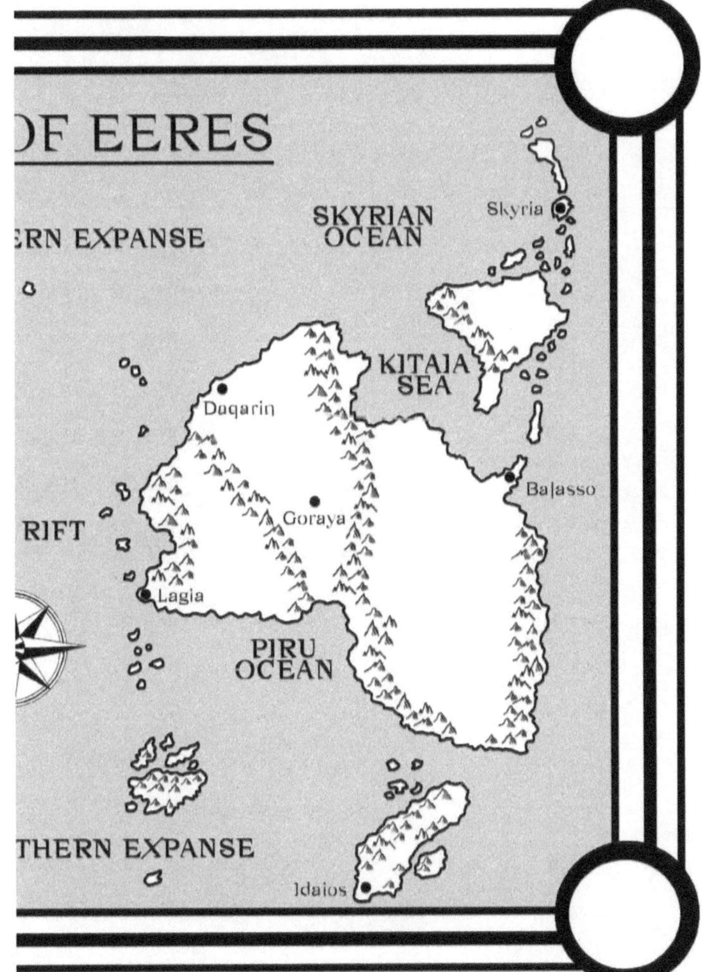

OF EERES
ERN EXPANSE
SKYRIAN OCEAN
Skyria
KITAIA SEA
Daqarin
Balasso
RIFT
Goraya
Lagia
PIRU OCEAN
THERN EXPANSE
Idaios

Table of Contents

THROUGH THE FIRE

Chapter One

Golden planets spun on metal axes. The orrery, proud centrepiece of Xayall's library, was well-maintained, and thankfully had escaped damage in the siege. Books and scrolls had been ransacked during Dhraka's brief occupation, and disrupted again when Thrain's delegation had been 'auditing' Xayall's archives and Faria's capability as Empress. The building itself had escaped the siege relatively unscathed, although a good number of its documents appeared to be missing. It would take a long while yet to determine how much was gone and how many secrets may have been stripped away to be sold or advantaged.

Kier gazed up at the array of shining metal planets adorned with constellations and landmasses, still as enthralled as he had been the first day he saw it. The gleaming bodies of the moon, sun, and their planet Eeres glinted in the light from the tall, arched windows, all embossed with lustrous detail. The gentle rhythmic clicks and rumbles of the mechanisms echoed quietly in the grand room. It calmed and inspired him; an influence he needed especially now, being reunited with Bayer and also having to face the prospect of negotiating protection with Jed Othera of the Senate. All while the violent ousting of Shadow's Claw, the insidious group who attempted a brutal insurrection against the Senate, still rang in their ears. His shoulders relaxed and his breathing slowed as he let it match the slow, rolling noises of the clockwork system. If he allowed himself to drift too far, he'd fall asleep underneath it again. In truth it was his favourite place to sleep, were it not for the embarrassment of being woken by guards or scholars, most of whom had accepted his sporadic moments of fatigue, even if he still berated himself for them.

Worst of all was a few weeks back when, as acting Representative, he'd overslept. He'd been awoken by a slew of soldiers bursting into the room in a hurry to locate him. It had been a very awkward and humbling explanation to the ambassadorial detachment of Tremaine guards, and doubly so to Osiris.

His face still flushed when he thought about it.

The fox's ear flicked; his crystal earrings gently chimed against each other. The door opened far behind him, bringing a cool pressure sweeping into the library chamber, and a soft smile lit his face.

The wonderfully familiar ocelot Bayer strode in, robes sweeping the air as he moved. His pace was a little slower than he was used to, still unfamiliar with the finery that adorned him as a delegate of his home sovereign. It wasn't excessive, but still felt uncharacteristic of his history as a warrior. It was like being swaddled, but was apparently necessary to appear 'legitimate' to the upper echelons of other sovereigns to whom he needed to appeal.

"Thought you'd be hiding here," Bayer called, his tail drifting behind him in a lazy flick. "I half thought you'd be invisible, though."

Kier shook his head with a wry smile. "It's not invisibility. But no, my head's hurting a little too much right now."

"The meeting with Jed wasn't *that* bad, was it?"

Kier flicked his head back. "No, it... was what I expected. I'm just tired. I haven't turned everything off for a while," he huffed, indicating his eyes, and resisting the urge to massage them. "This place makes me feel... grounded. Maintaining a sovereign is one thing. Rebuilding it, and the Senate by proxy, is a whole other monster. We... I mean, you and Faria –could have a greater voice than ever, and that's amazing. I want the changes we make to last. Neither of us were trained for this, and I'm much more Faria's guard than her advisor."

Bayer walked up to the fox and laid his left arm across his shoulders. "You know how I feel about politics, and here I am running from one broken city with nothing but promises to keep a second from falling to pieces."

"You'll have more than a promise by the time you leave, I prom—er, well, I mean..."

Bayer let out a deep chuckle.

Kier's exasperated sigh bounced around the ceiling. "Don't even try, I'm a lost cause."

"My tail you are," Bayer snorted, swinging down to sit under the orrery's slowly shifting frame. "You've saved my life twice now. At least."

The fox shrugged. "Didn't save your arm though."

Bayer gave him a glare under his eyebrows, taking his remaining arm from Kier's shoulders to pull at the robes on his right, as if asserting to himself that his limb was still gone. "Don't start projecting guilt onto a situation that wasn't yours to be part of. This was a result of my choice, my battle," he warned, in a quietly admonishing tone. Gently he placed his hand on Kier's, his expression softening slightly. "You needed to be here with Faria. I don't have any regrets, and I won't be pitied for what I lost when I have so much yet to do."

Kier nodded, the fur at his cheeks flushing slightly. "I can't dispute that. You saved the Senate, after all. Maybe you and Faria should compare notes." He jostled, giving his companion a playful nudge with his elbow.

The ocelot delicately sat at the base of the orrery and gestured for Kier to join him. The fox curled his bushy tail to the side and took a spot next to him, idly cradling it in his paw.

"She still takes the flag on that one." Bayer replied. "I did very little, comparatively." He flicked some dust from his claws, with a brief grimace. "By her strength Eeres still turns, and we exist to pick up the pieces and stand guard so it doesn't happen again."

Kier nodded in agreement, rubbing the back of his neck.

"You can let your resonance go for a while if you need to," Bayer offered softly. "I won't let anything happen."

Kier's paws furled for a second. "No, I should... m-maybe later," he mumbled. "Thank you."

They absorbed the quiet for a few moments, while the room rumbled with the constant ambience of the mechanism behind them. A planet swept overhead and they watched it pass together. Kier caught himself looking at Bayer afterwards, and quickly glanced away. A cautious look back suggested he was safe from being noticed as Bayer looked deep in thought, his eyes soft, focusing somewhere in the middle-distance. It was strangely the most relaxed Kier had seen him in a long time. His expression seemed peaceful, or at least a newly focused, in a way that lifted his spirits above the discord he had been in a few months earlier.

Kier released his tail and leant back on his paws. Aisles of high shelves radiated out from across the orrery's circular plinth in a wide arc before them, punctuated by grand stone pillars. Most were half-empty, a grim reminder of the work yet to do and the knowledge lost and scattered. Elsewhere shelves and scrolls were still being repaired, replaced, reordered, salvaged, or rewritten as best they could after being torn apart by Vionaika's whirlwind pillaging to find hints of Nazreal, and Thrain's disingenuous attempts to steal information. It was comforting to see the shelves being stocked again, bit by bit, after so much disruption. It felt like a return to stability and knowledge over greedy ignorance. Kier had fond memories of this part of the library, especially with Bayer.

"Enyart would already be forcing you to train your other hand by now," he said.

"As you mention it," the ocelot replied, "I asked Raede if she knew him – she was in Pthiris. She hadn't heard of him. Maybe he changed his name, or left Pthiris, or didn't actually intend to go back in the first place…"

Kier wrinkled his snout. "He was very… impassive. I don't think he revealed a single thing about himself all through training. The stone in the water, right?"

Bayer shrugged. "I'm still not sure it was a good metaphor, but I can see what he meant by it more clearly now."

Kier tapped his claws together. "Yeah… Even if he wasn't the most comforting mentor… we might not be alive right now if not for him. Nor Faria."

Chapter Two

Before the civil war, Kyrryk was a small and picturesque sovereign, with smooth hills towering over acres of farmland, and banks of long grass perfect for hiding in on sleepy summer days. It rained considerably, but the people had adapted to grow great yields of water-loving fruits, and farmed ample quantities of fish. A modest amount of metal sat underneath Kyrryk as well, and so several mines and quarries resounded in the low valleys with the workers' busy activities.

Like most others, farming and fishing were the backbone of Bayer's village, located in the nation's south-eastern valleys. Strategically placed near a river, with wide fields perfect for seasonal crops and bordered by ditches that freed them from flooding in the heavy rains, his village rarely went hungry, and could trade well with others. Most of this was unknown to him as a child because his parents, and the village overall with its relatively moderate size of thirty or so families, provided for him dutifully, but his family always talked of the importance of good nature and sharing as a pathway to later prosperity. Mostly he just wanted to play, although he did help with duties, and began to take pride in his ability to contribute, sometimes offering his catch of the day or fruit gatherings to his neighbours or giving them to his mother as a gift if they were considered surplus. He walked alongside his father at the river's edge, carrying a small handcart with caught fish, and some spare spears and nets. He beamed with awe whenever his father gestured for them to stop to expertly lance something in the water and add it to the barrow. This time it was a large pike, almost too big for Bayer's proportionate wagon.

They had been out late that day. After dinner his parents had gathered with the older villagers and talked for a long time; he wasn't allowed to be there, so he spent most of the early evening spearing a small woven toy with his favourite stick. His parents had ushered him directly to bed when they returned, and the next day were strangely sombre. Bayer hadn't been able to find out why, even when following his Dad on their next day's trail.

"But it's important, isn't it?"

"Very," his father replied deeply. "With luck, you'll never know anything that comes to pass."

Bayer ran to catch up. "But I want to know! I want to be important too!"

His father held his impatience. "You are important, Bayer. But not old enough to help. I won't speak of it further."

Bayer tried, and true to his word, his father either did not reply or simply repeated the same curt denials. The young ocelot sank into petulant silence, kicking stones whenever he could, aiming for them to land just closely enough to his father that he might notice them and his anguish, but not close enough to hit him. At one point a stone looked like it would crash right into his father's heel but it bounced aside at the last instant. Bayer was ready to hide in the rushes if he actually hurt his father, and after that point calmed himself until their journey back to the village.

When they reached the village's communal food preparation area, under the large thatched hut near the gathering circle, he saw a much greater number of fish and animals than usual for the village's meal.

"Is it a celebration?" he asked.

"No. Just supper."

The fish gutters weren't singing their usual rhythmic ballads. Instead they conducted their instinctive slicing with a disquieting sobriety. Bayer shuffled quietly around to try and see if the fish gave him a clue as to their sombre outlook, but he gathered nothing but warding stares and a sense of apprehension deeper than was comfortable. Shying away, he decided to retreat home to see his infant brother Tyl, cradled by his mother. Bayer sat next to her as she played games on the cub's nose, tickled his chest, or poked his spots, and he giggled appreciatively.

"Has he been good?" Bayer asked.

His mother gave him a smile. "He's been fine. I'm more concerned whether *you* were good."

Bayer sat proudly on his knees. "I helped Dad carry all the fish."

"I heard you were asking a lot of questions," she replied, raising a suspicious eyebrow.

He froze. "Um, yes, but only for a little while." Then he leant forward, balling his paws into fists on his thighs. "I wanted to know! Something's going on."

She sighed, cradling Tyl. "There is, Bayer. Your father's leaving tonight, along with some other elders, to help some villages nearby."

Bayer tilted his head. "Help them?"

She sighed again, glancing briefly at the doorway. "There's trouble. Your father's going to stop it. He shouldn't be gone for long."

"Oh." Bayer fell quiet and looked at the floor. "Does he need me to carry his fish?"

"He won't be taking fish, Bayer sweet."

"But… isn't he going to eat?"

She shook her head, and something in her smile worried Bayer. It wasn't her usual smile. "He should be given everything he needs when he gets there."

Bayer sat, quietly at first, then started rocking on his haunches and glancing around the room. Outside, the noises of preparation grew and more voices were converging near the large ring-shaped mound at the heart of the village, in the centre of which was a large, low fire. After a short time, a group of older villagers marched past their door and took their places sitting at the mound – usually divided by family units, but sometimes folks would sit in groups they worked with, and children assembled in a circle closest to the fire pit to keep them warmer. Bayer helped his mother to her feet and they joined the circle. A short word of thanks to the land and the foragers was usually offered at every meal but this time when the leader, a grizzled but alert panther, stood before his assembly, he wore a very different expression.

"We are ever grateful for the love and fortune we have received here. Every day we rise with the sun, forage within our means, and rest with our loved ones. We have been blessed with fortune and wisdom that has kept us from great loss, and have exchanged good favours with the surrounding villages and lords to keep a steady and productive peace."

He looked to each villager in turn as he spoke. "Today, we held a meeting. Kyrryk is falling to unrest. While we have long been insulated from the conflicts of others, the rumbling of drums creeps closer, and soon we will no longer be able to ignore it. Today we give thanks and praise to our brave protectors, who have volunteered to assist the lord to our north in exchange for safety. While our great desire was to stay within our village sanctuary, the danger is growing quickly. Today, we hope that each of us will be protected, both within and without, at home and while journeying, and that any loved one's absence will be swift. We ask that this food we consume, granted to us by the land, gives us strength to protect ourselves and our loved ones, that we may always live to protect, and thank, and grow."

His speech was met with low murmurs of solemn approval, with many concerned looks exchanged across the circle of flame. Food was brought from the table and shared around. Bayer eagerly took a large piece of fish, ready to devour it, but paused and held it for a while. He looked to his mother.

"Should… should I take a smaller bit? Because, if they're leaving, then they need more of it."

His mother placed an arm around his shoulder and pulled him to her side. "I need you strong too, my love. They'll eat what they need. Don't feel guilty."

He nodded, and took a small bite. Across the circle his father gave a wan, weary smile.

Bayer sat by the fire all evening, feeling the warmth ripple through his fur and watching the light play softly across the faces and bodies of his village. It didn't seem very different to normal, except everyone seemed… closer, almost. It reminded him of when he followed his mother around when something scared him, or he kept his brother in sight because he could tell he was imminently to cry or fall over. As families returned to their wooden shacks, the fire began to die. Before it ceased completely, and Bayer's head grew heavier without the light of the flames to keep him awake. His mother gently pulled him up into a sleep-addled stagger back to his nest of blankets and wool. He didn't even remember lying down before sleep took him.

When he awoke, it was daylight. The quiet struck him instantly.

He sprang to his knees, ears twitching, tail flicking slowly about him.

"Are you all right, Bayer?" his mother's voice was soft, and a little distant. He looked round to see her weaving a thick belt out of wax-coated yarn, with an array of rotating tablets strung between two poles.

He stood up. "Something's strange."

She twisted the tablets, causing the yarn threaded through them to interlock so she could pass the weft across the next line. "Nothing's strange, Bayer; they've just gone."

Bayer looked through the open door. The stillness hung around his head like a veil. "Already? But… Dad… I was asleep…"

She took in a long, tremulous breath. "He loves you, Bayer. And he believes in you. He needs you to be strong, and take on some of his jobs while he's gone. Can you do that?" She knelt down to him and stroked his arm. The pads on her hands were warm and rough. "Make him proud. He'll want to know all of the things you've done while he's been away."

She gently ruffled the fur at his cheek, and tilted her head with a smile. "You will grow so much."

Bayer grabbed his muzzle to suppress a small cry, and nodded at his mother. Her eyes glistened, and in an instant she pulled him into a tight embrace.

Chapter Three

The village lost more than they'd hoped.

After the initial tribute of thirty bodies, twenty more were sent as soldiers, leaving the rest struggling to keep food stocked. On top of this, a cart with an armed, mounted escort in yellow plated armour arrived at least twice a week to take bundles of fish and vegetable crops. Everything was becoming harder to find. The fish upstream were fewer and further between, and they had to search dangerously close to other villages or gated feudal lands to catch anything worthwhile. Some had talked about hiding supplies from the armoured convoy, or even stealing from some of the nearby lords, but it would risk them becoming an even more vulnerable target.

Bayer's new tasks were varied, and harder than his father always made them appear. Bayer cut himself repeatedly while fixing fences, stripped patches of fur from his hands while binding rope to make nets, and was chased by a boar in the fields. The fatiguing trudge home was always a time to search for the splinters that had sunk into his paw. He usually found them all, but sometimes had to ask his mother for help. He felt tired always, never fulfilled, never refreshed, and with a constant shadow over him even on bright days. He was not strong, and he knew it.

Worse, he felt *they* all knew it too.

While nobody scolded him outright for his pained exclamations or noisy mistakes, the tired eyes of his guardians and the diminishing sun that warned of their task yet unfinished judged his ineptitude without a single word. He returned to his mother each night unwilling to talk of the bad things that happened each day, wanting only to make her proud with stories of success or prowess, or retellings of the compliments he may have received. But they were becoming fewer and fewer. Sometimes he wouldn't say anything at all, and instead grilled her about what she did and how Tyl was. Bayer had energy to play some days, but most of the time he'd fall asleep immediately after eating, or while his mother tried to demonstrate tablet weaving to him. He knew it was necessary, because his boots and forearms were bound with the beautiful woven textiles she'd made for him that were slowly becoming ragged and covered in slubs, but any time he tried to focus on it, he collapsed into sleep after a few rows.

On good days he went fishing. It didn't matter what the weather was like – any day he was asked or could persuade the guardians to let him fish was one he looked forward to, because that was what he'd enjoyed doing with his father most. He was going to catch enough fish for the whole village in one day, he'd proclaimed at first, often, and loudly. Occasionally he wasn't able to swap duties with someone else so resorted to sneaking into a fishing party, and would receive stern words or a march back to his assignment when he was discovered. His mother had to tell him the importance of sharing work, even if certain tasks were difficult. Begrudgingly he agreed, but volunteered to fish every morning regardless.

On an overcast day that threatened rain in its pulsing cool

air, as he stood on the bank with his sharpened, glistening spear, and thought about his father's return. The weeks had grown short with the days long, extended by the increasing sense of claustrophobia from those who kept taking their supplies. Bayer heard some of the villagers whispering about leaving, or asking for help, and being hastily hissed down for it. 'Too dangerous', apparently. He'd been afraid to ask what was happening; the grim looks on their faces had been enough to warn him not to risk a question. When he was fishing, he could forget the feeling that the sky was getting closer. Steadily raising his spear, he watched a fish shimmer its way down the current.

A low sound in the distance caught his attention. He and the other villagers turned to it, somewhere beyond a nearby mountain. The echoing burst rolled through the valley, followed by a cold, empty silence. The leader of the party, a female puma called Kodi, hissed to another villager, who scurried away in the direction of the noise. Kodi disappeared ahead for a minute or so, then re-emerged from the foliage beside them, giving an 'all clear' gesture for the rest to keep fishing.

Bayer's fish had gone. His heart pounded, and the tip of his spear wavered in his grip.

A short while and a meagre amount of fish later, Kodi's subordinate returned. They exchanged quiet words, then gave a signal. Everyone bundled up their catch and hurried back to the village.

Bayer hadn't been allowed to hear what was happening. The village, anyone not old enough to wield a spear, had been rounded up into one of the larger houses and were being cared for by a trio of the older (and scarier, by most kits' accounts) mothers. When the remaining parents came to collect their children, it was already dark, and many had to be pried from deep within woollen blankets. Bayer had deliberately stayed awake, intent on monitoring the parents' reactions, and to ensure he wouldn't miss the chance to ask his mother about it while it was still fresh in his mind.

When she entered, he quickly scooped his brother into his arms and handed him to her. She smiled wryly, knowing her son's determination.

"Wait till we get home," she said quickly, just as he started to open his mouth.

The second that she shut the door to their home, he whirled around expectantly. He was not expecting to see her so ashen.

"Tomorrow, before light, you will go with Kodi to the next village and ask them for help."

"But... am I old enough?"

A flash of panic crossed her eyes – Bayer recognised it as the same look she bore when trying to avoid answering his questions. "You are one of the oldest of the kits, and need to show the village your strength and dedication. We will be leaving this place soon. We aren't safe."

Bayer stepped towards her, fur bristling. "What about Dad? Will he know where to find us?"

"He... He'll know. Don't worry about that now, Bayer. Just get some sleep. You'll be awake before long."

He did not sleep.

He lay still, not responding to his mother when she laid a gentle paw on his side. Even in the woollen sheets a chill ran down his body when he thought about her words. They weren't safe? What about his father? Was he all right? Was he in the village already? He squeezed his eyes shut and forced memories of his family to play in his mind. He envisioned all of the things he promised himself or his brother that they would do together, and dreamed himself as a strong and wily warrior capable of outmanoeuvring any threat to his village. He repeated these dreams over and over until his mother gently roused him.

"Time to go, sweet. Kodi will protect you."

Bayer's breath was heavy in the hot, misty morning; not just from lack of sleep, but the emotions boiling under his ribs, feeling like they would explode out of him. His mother had dressed him in his newest robes of black, brown and white. He didn't bear look at her for fear of crying, and he had to be strong today if he was to come back and show her how successful he'd been. She took him in her arms as the group of eleven made to leave, carrying with them a cartload of supplies to offer as tribute. He hugged her tightly back, then turned sharply and traipsed into the haze.

It was a few hours of meandering dirt pathways and forest trails, taking strange routes away from the wider roads. A few times Kodi had stopped them dead in the brush, and told them to get down. Bayer had strained his eyes to see through the leaves, and saw groups of spearfolk walking along the road. He dared not breathe, not even understanding why they were avoiding them. His legs ached, and his ears stung hot with his worry. He desperately wanted to be home.

The next village looked in almost as dire shape as his own. The inhabitants were wary of their approach, but seemed to relax once they realised Bayer's community had no weapons.

Much to his surprise, the neighbouring village invited all of the visiting party to their biggest house when they arrived. Bayer sat quietly on the worn wooden floor while greetings were made, tributes paid, and plans discussed. His thoughts kept wandering between the journey home, his father, and his family, so he missed most of the conversation going on around him. He heard snippets about the 'approaching war', and 'many having already been lost', but the longer he tried to pay attention, the sleepier and less focused he became.

He awoke with a start, as the cheetah he'd fallen asleep on moved to stand up. Bayer wiped his mouth, bowed clumsily at the hosts, and followed his villagers outside. The haze had lifted, replaced by a faint smell of smoke. Bayer scanned about to see what this village liked to cook, but saw no sign of fires. A little disappointed that he'd apparently slept through the offerings of food at the meeting, he kept close to Kodi's side as they began the journey home.

Thankfully, the empty cart being made hauling it back much faster. Bayer could still smell the fires of the new village an hour or two after leaving. He wondered if it had saturated his clothes somehow. It unnerved him; no matter how many times he beat or rubbed his arm bindings, he couldn't remove the smell.

The closer they got to home, the stronger it became.

When they were a valley over from his village, the smell became unbearable. A slow silence fell across the group. Even the plants they brushed through seemed quiet, either reverent or terrified. Bayer kept his eyes on the destination.

Against the sky, he was the first to see the thick, ghostly plume of smoke.

Right where his village stood.

He sprang into a run. Kodi bounded past him at incredible speed, rounding the path and darting through the trees faster than he could see. The cheetah and a lynx passed him as well; his breath ripped from his throat with each pounding stride he took. His head felt ready to explode; he could barely keep sight of where he was running, he tore across the ground so fast.

He felt the heat the moment he broke onto the path above

the village. An orange and black inferno raged below. Bursts of ash flew past his face. Everything was aflame; the walls, the houses, the crops. Charred, blackened shapes lay in the grass beyond the entrances. He saw Kodi and her two assistants darting around the periphery, shielding their eyes, trying to find survivors. Bayer stumbled forwards. He knew where his house was, but he couldn't see it. He tried to strain through the smoke but his eyes burnt with the heat. He ran to the gate, feeling the flames searing his fur even before he touched it.

"Mum!" he called into the blaze. He took another step and a force grabbed his arm, tearing him from his feet and whisking him into the trees.

"Leave it," Kodi hissed. Bayer pulled and scratched at her arm.

"Let me go!" he yelled.

"No, Bayer!" she barked, ignoring the gouges he scraped in her wrist.

"I won't leave them! Mum!" he cried. Kodi's grip was strong; he sank his teeth into her. She grabbed him by the scruff of his neck and threw him down, then dropped to her knees and pinned him down with her arm.

"Bayer, be *quiet!*"

He felt her blood dripping across his neck. He wrestled for a second, then saw she had a wound across the top of her chest. A clean, swift cut, from a blade. She glanced up for a second, then dropped to the ground next to him.

"I'm sorry, Bayer," she whispered. "Just stay low. Breathe as quietly as you can. We're not safe yet."

A rush of dizziness swept over Bayer. The smell of the smoke, the pressing heat, the deafening roar of the fire, all of it rose to a crescendo.

He passed out.

Chapter Four

Ash covered the ground. Bayer awoke with his nose in the dirt, and a bundle of grass and leaves piled in front of his snout. Kodi was next to him, binding her wounds with twine and scraps of scavenged cloth.

He stepped towards the village. A deathly grey mist clung to the air.

"Has… has it stopped?" he trembled.

She kept padding leaves onto her chest, weaving grass across the stems. "Fire lives under the ash. You'll get burnt if you're not careful where you step."

He dug his claws into his pads. "I need to see… I want them to be all right."

Kodi pulled herself to a stand. "I'll be with you. The soldiers have left, but it's not safe to be alone."

"Soldiers?" Bayer led her carefully through the undergrowth.

She winced as she tightened the woven leaf bandage across her chest. "They stayed to kill the survivors."

Fear roiled up and down Bayer's spine. Weren't soldiers supposed to protect people?

They reached the black, crumbling remains of their gates.

Smoke drifted from the ashes like spectres. The air was thick and humid, and carried the acidic smell deep into his lungs. Bayer covered his mouth but his breath came so fast that he heaved into a coughing fit. Kodi went to grab him but he wrested himself away and lumbered forwards, wiping his eyes. He could make out the old pathways, even with the houses being little more than crumbling black frames now. Some had collapsed. But his muscle memory knew the well-trodden paths so closely that not even dead soot could disguise them.

Skeletal huts faded into view as he walked. They terrified him. He knew them all, and he could feel screams of despair within the charred wooden bones of each remnant he passed. He kept his gaze ahead, hoping even in spite of the devastation that his hut would still be there. It had to be there. They *had* to be there.

He didn't see it at first.

He knew where it was supposed to be, but… when he looked down, he realised he was already within it.

The ghost of his hut surrounded him. Black shards of wood penetrated the ash at jagged angles. Chips of ash-caked pottery poked through the fire's thick carpet. Seeing what remained of his house brought on the coldest of fears, and a dreadful electric emptiness that hung behind his head. His breath stolen from him, he slowly turned around to see if any faint clue had been left as to where his family had run.

There was an irregular mound near the far wall, where his brother's bed had been. He stepped closer to break the layers of lingering smoke between it and him.

He froze. Piercing the dust of that huddled misshapen form, with jagged, bony protrusions, were three charred arrow shafts. In an instant, that horrible, unforgettable shape became his living terror.

They were dead.

He collapsed to his knees, and screamed. He reached a quaking arm forward to touch his mother's body but Kodi grabbed him away and pulled him over her shoulder before his fingers could reach her. He watched their charred forms disappear in the smoke and wailed, beating Kodi's back as she took him away. He clawed at passing struts to escape her grip but they crumbled to charcoal in his hands. He screamed to go to them, to help his mother, to bury them both.

Kodi refused, and kept running.

The next village they travelled to was deserted, no doubt fearing the same fate. Bayer had finally stopped resisting and followed Kodi, albeit barely; a reluctant shadow. He kept stopping along the path in brief catatonias, debating whether to continue or drop to the floor and die, but when he felt about to fall he instinctively set a paw forward and kept walking, just in enough time to not lose sight of Kodi. He had said nothing, and while she hunted for food scraps and a spear within the village grounds, he swayed desolately by the gates.

The next few days he spent in an aching, listless silence. There were no more words for him. He barely ate, and cried when he did. Kodi often threatened to give up and warned he would die if he didn't pull together, but she kept him going forward regardless. He wouldn't have blamed her if she left, and in a way he expected her to. He would have abandoned his own body if he could, but instead he was doomed to survive in a world with no home, and no love for him.

While they sat against a long brick wall on a dusty afternoon, a steady march shook the air.

Soldiers.

A parade of troops in shimmering white armour strode

down the path to the lash of drums, riding lizard steeds with heads held high. The precision, the power, the size of the formation made Bayer tremble with a strange sense of terror and anticipation. Cast in more metal than he had ever seen, they seemed like otherworldly creatures, glimmering in the misty, thick air.

Kodi gripped his shoulder. "Careful. They're from Andarn."

He barely heard her. He'd never seen an army before, but stories had been told for years of great powers that marched from one end of the land to the other, eliminating dark forces with every step. Before the fire they roamed through his dreams every night, weaving tales of epic battles, with him at the forefront of all of their fantastical strength, the champion of hope and protector of the good.

He tore away from Kodi, bursting across the grassy ditch that separated them from the road the army marched on. Instinctively some soldiers reached for their weapons. He ignored the blades but kept approaching, shaking, tail flicking madly around him.

"Will you save us?" he shouted, trying to keep pace.

The nearest soldier, a marmot, shoved him away. "Keep back!"

Another, a young deer, broke from his formation and handed Bayer a small sweet potato roll from his knapsack. "We'll try. Stay safe."

"I want my home back. Can I help? I'll go with you!"

The deer shook his head. "No, not here, not now. Go somewhere safe."

He straightened and quick-stepped back to his position. Bayer watched the battalion file by. The sounds of their footfall were like a drum that beat the land, shaking life from beneath its surface which had sunk deep beneath it under the war.

The other soldiers didn't stop, nor look at him. They simply marched onwards, unrelenting, undaunted. He watched until the last of them disappeared in the haze of the previous day's rain, and felt the weight of his loss burn behind his eyes.

Bayer followed Kodi from town to village and camp to trail for several weeks as they tried to find food or work in exchange for shelter. Some refused to even look through the gates at their arrival, and many other places were still ravaged by war, barely able to support themselves, let alone transient refugees. Over time the distant battle cries ceased, and more and more wounded Kyrryk soldiers could be found wandering the dirt pathways, muttering or groaning. There was not much on offer for anyone, and too many displaced folk for any one place to hold. Some roads they tried to traverse were met with armed soldiers, or harried travellers frantically fleeing in the opposite direction, yelling terse warnings of danger ahead. At one point they reached the edge of the sovereign and were turned away as they had 'no reason to be there'. Neither recognised the armour the guards were wearing.

They had nowhere to stay, and nowhere to go.

The northernmost township was relatively undamaged by conflict, but as such was deluged by lost villagers as the state's remaining safe haven. Kodi pushed through the crowd, gripping Bayer firmly by the wrist to make sure he didn't get lost in the crush. A large tavern swarmed with people around its doors, apparently turned into a conscription centre. Kodi looked back to her charge. The emaciated, dirty ocelot in torn robes gazed back in a sort of confused daze.

"Stay outside," she said firmly. "I'm going to find out

where we can be safe, or at least protected. Don't move without me."

Bayer planted himself by the wall as she wrestled her way through the doorway. Another crush of people brought the crowd edging closer to Bayer. They were loud, and some were growling and snarling with impatience. He shuffled away, pulling his tail close. The bindings on his right arm kept slipping where Kodi's grip had stretched them, and every time he tried to adjust them the weave loosened a little more. Looking at the angular diamonds in orange and black brought him straight back to memories of his mother, but he was too tired and nervous of the swelling crowd to cry. The pit of emptiness still yawed in his stomach.

An opossum's tail whipped across his face as its owner clambered to the door. Twice, three times it flicked him. He pushed it away, his fur riling up around his neck and cheeks. It hit him again. Bayer's claws flicked for a second, then he stopped himself. He had to wait for—

It hit him again, in the eye this time.

He bit it as hard as he could. Blood spurted from the pink leathery skin, and a piercing howl erupted in front of him. The sound roused Bayer from his rage; the incandescent face of the opossum, mouth wide with needle teeth, rounded on him. He rolled away from its furious claws and careened around the back of the tavern. The alley was dark but ahead was a large cart laden with supplies. Hearing the opossum drawing closer, he sprinted to it and leapt inside, nestling behind a barrel. He hauled a canvas bag over his head and froze in place, ears ringing with panic.

A set of quick footpads thudding by stopped the breath in his throat. Low, rhythmic growls pierced the symphony of voices beyond. Bayer silently, slowly, tilted his head to look through the weave in the bag's untidy seam.

The possum paced around, nostrils flared, claws arched. As he turned back to the cart, three figures in ragged cloaks approached him.

"What're you doing back here?" came a low growl.

"Some brat filth bit my tail to shreds, look at it!"

One of the larger figures, a tiger, tilted his head. "Doesn't look that bad to me. Why'd they bite you? You doing something to 'em?"

The opossum scoffed. "I didn't do anything, but I damn well will when I get my hands on that damn cub!"

The third figure, hidden by his cloak, but very bulky, grabbed the opossum by the shoulder. Bayer saw a flash of white armour on his wrist. "Don't make threats you can't keep."

He paused. Bayer could see his head tracking around, surveying the alley. "I don't see any cub. Why are you here?"

"Here for our supplies, are you?" the second soldier had a darkness in his voice that turned the shadows cold against Bayer's fur. "There's no tolerance for thieves or traitors here."

"Get your hands off me!" the opossum hissed, pushing the soldier away. "I'm no thief! Those are our supplies in the first place, and you're not even from our sove—"

He didn't get to finish. The first soldier's hood flew back, revealing a heavily-scarred badger, as he rounded a vicious wide punch to the opossum's jaw. The emaciated marsupial crumpled to the floor immediately.

"I told you it was dangerous," he rumbled, before standing over him to lay another punch to him. There was a weak groan for mercy underneath him.

"Scrounging mongrel."

The others stood on the back of the opossum's legs, and

soon he wasn't making noises of protest anymore. Bayer watched in horror as blood and teeth flew from the creature's mouth. Bayer was the one that bit his tail. The opossum didn't do anything at all, except chase him.

In their violent movements, Bayer saw white armour on all of them. These spectral-dressed officers, far from being the heroic saviours he dreamed of, enacted brutality he'd never seen before. He watched their sickening betrayal in the darkness with wide, furious eyes. Bayer's head swirled.

Soldiers were supposed to protect people.

They invaded his land.

They took his village's supplies.

They refused to help him.

It had to be a mistake.

Someone must have lied to them about who the enemy was, or they were imposters using stolen armour, or… something else. Their cruelty terrified him, but what scared him further was the searing thought that the people he saw as liberators could be more capable of evil than those of his own sovereign.

Worse still, he could only cower in the darkness. While every inch of him burned with the desire to intervene, to scream at them for being so needlessly cruel when it had been his fault the possum was even there in the first place, all he did was sit under the canvas in tremulous silence.

Kyrryk had been destroyed all around him in battles he'd only heard across valleys or been told horrors of, and all he had done was run.

He wanted help. He needed help. Everyone did; to restore their home and make it safe and calm. To rebuild villages, reunite families. They had the power, he *knew* it. He could see it hewn into their armour, the ability to conquer any evil.

Why weren't they using their power to protect those without?

They dropped the opossum to the ground. Maybe he was still moving; Bayer couldn't tell whether it was the pulsing light of the distant torches, or wild, terrified focus tricking his eyes. He stared through the dark, searching for signs of life. The horror of the opossum's death being caused by his irritated panic drilled into his conscience. He desperately hoped the creature would move again.

Two of the soldiers slipped back to the tavern while the other turned his back to the cart. Bayer cursed his fragility, his fear. He couldn't move, or they'd know the opossum was telling the truth, and they might do the same to him. He waited in the cart, staring at the limp and bloody mess a few feet away, and the harbinger of his injuries only a few feet further than that. What could he do?

Then a noise and a jolt from the front of the vehicle stunned him to silence. A few seconds later, it started moving, away from the soldier and his prey. Bayer scrabbled at the barrels but they wobbled and swayed on the uneven planks and kept crushing his paw when he tried to clamber between them; they were too heavy and he was too weak to shift them aside.

He sat back against the crates and hugged his knees, trembling. The symphony of desperate voices at the tavern disappeared into the darkness, and somewhere among them was Kodi's. Something in him compelled him to shout his legs into life and jump back to her, but he was too tired, too shaken.

The glow of the township fires faded to a tiny flicker, then disappeared behind the dark mass of a passing hillside, and he was left in cold, rumbling darkness. His mind battled to reconcile the hopes for the army's protection in his mind with the fresh, bloody memory of their savage beatings. Too enervated to cry out, and filled with the dread that another brutal soldier may yet be mere inches from him, he curled up on the floor and shut his eyes tight, trying to force the fears away from his racing mind.

I'm sorry Kodi. Please be safe.

Chapter Five

Bayer awoke to the rattling of metal. The floor beneath him shook, the barrels either side of him lurched dramatically, threatening to crush his head where he'd fallen between them. He scrambled upright and shoved a tipped crate aside to see where in Kyrryk he was.

The bright grey sky blinded him. He blinked desperately and shoved his palms into his eyes to wipe the dry sleep from them. When his vision adjusted, he was in a landscape he'd never seen before. Trees unfamiliar to Kyrryk swept by. Twisting hills and thick forest on a distant mountain range were completely different to the landscape of his home. He shrank back against the barrels once more. Would Kodi be worried? Would she be safer without him burdening her? Would there be anyone to take care of him, wherever he was going?

Tucked in his sleeve, and barely kept in place by his bindings, was the last piece of food Kodi had managed to give him, a stale oat-and-vegetable cake, part crushed by him sleeping on it. He cradled the crumbs in his paws and ate them carefully, knowing each tiny scrap was energy he may never see again. The wild and erratic jostling of the cart threatened to tip him over, but he managed to finish it with minimal loss. He shook his sleeve of the inedibly miniscule crumbs caked to his fur and rebound his wrist, before settling back against the barrel. His tongue was rough, and his eyes painfully dry. He could feel his paw pads stretch when he moved them. He needed water, but everything around him in the cart sounded heavy, and very undrinkable.

Eventually the vehicle began to slow its pace, and around him he could hear more rattling wheels and low tones of pedestrian travellers. He chanced a peek through the slats again. Converging crowds of people were drawing to the side of the cart, flowing together in an uneven tide on the road. Soon the traffic ground to a punishing crawl, while the noise of other carts, creatures of burden, travellers, performers, merchants, all rose to an undulating din. It was almost as noisy as the tavern in Kyrryk, only without the thread of fear edging its varying tones. It was lighter for the most part, aside from the distal barking of traffic direction by some booming authority.

A shadow passed overhead – a giant archway, baring the teeth of a fierce and forbidding portcullis. Behind the shoulders of the pedestrians pressed almost equally as close to the other side of the wood, he caught a glimpse of something in the arch's shadowy gatehouse. He crammed his face between the stalwart barrels for a wider view.

His chest filled with hollow dread at the gleam of white armour.

Not just one soldier. A whole company of the white-clad army. As the cart breached the other side of the gatehouse he saw more soldiers marching the streets. His ears flattened, and he began pulling at his pads with his claws.

He was in the wrong place.

He shifted his body to the end of the cart and pressed his

feet against the rear gate. In a flash, he pushed himself up, sliding his legs through the gap he'd entered. He twisted his body over the wooden slat and dropped to his feet. Unwilling to stay conspicuous, terrified of the eyes around him, he ran for a side street and careened to its end, before rounding a corner and skidding to a walk, barely controlled by fear. It was all he could do for camouflage.

High and faceless walls stood in pale indifference at every turn; it took Bayer a few seconds of straining upwards to see where they ended against the sky. Following the wood-and-slate lattice of rooftops stretching either side of him, fear pricked his fur once again as he found himself an unintentional stray in this faceless reality of stone, devoid of green, with the sky above the only clue that it was connected in any way to the world he knew before.

For the next few hours he did nothing but walk, taking in the alien foreboding of his surroundings. The old, sometimes sagging geometry of buildings placed too close together, or built on land that shouldn't have been disturbed, unsettled him where his world had been so full of nature and wood, with respect to the contours and features of the land they lived upon. He'd never walked this far without seeing grass, and all of the trees he encountered were surrounded by decaying fences or sad, slowly warping brickwork.

The people around him seemed indifferent to his wandering. Nobody questioned him; they seemed accustomed to vagrant children, apparently. He tried not to catch anyone's eye, though. Occasionally he was followed a short way by curious soldiers, but Bayer quickened his pace whenever they drew near and darted between close groups of civilians to get out of sight. Around every corner were more people, a never-ending stream of every kind of creature he could think of, except one to help him.

After a time exhaustion took him, and he sat down heavily on the wide steps to a building with a large double door. Inside was distant noise, a low, rumbling murmur that undulated and paused, then rose again. It sounded like laughter, or music, perhaps. He listened for a while, staring up at the slowly drifting clouds. The noise washed over him, and he felt the emptiness in his stomach begin to grow.

"Hey, get lost."

It took him a second to realise he was being talked to. He looked across to where the voice had come from, to see a fennec and a tenrec glaring at him, flicking their claws. The fennec was the one who'd warned him.

"Get out, theatre is our spot."

Bayer glanced about, and shrugged. "There's a lot of room," he said quietly. "I'm tired."

"Well, go be tired somewhere else!" the tenrec hissed, pointing a wild claw at the streets beyond.

Bayer frowned. "I don't get it, what do you—"

The doors swung open, and dozens of creatures piled out of the building, laughing, talking, swarming the steps. The two young animals darted to their side of the steps and held up their paws, begging at the exiting revellers. Bayer just watched them pass in a daze, but not before someone pressed a coin into his hand and closed his fingers over it. Another tossed a small fleck of silver his way, but it flew past his shoulder and landed among the trample of feet. Between waves of passers-by he saw the glares of the other two. More people threw Bayer coins, and one handed him a dried meat stick. He ate it immediately, keeping a wary eye aimed at the kits opposite, who were thankfully focused on themselves.

Almost as quickly as it appeared, the throng vanished, and

Bayer was left standing in front of the theatre, face to face with the feral urchins who were already eyeing up his score. He shoved the change into the pouch on his belt and stood up. The fennec and tenrec tensed, ears forward, tails flattened.

Bayer sprang from the steps and bolted; he could hear their footsteps matching his. He ducked under people, dodged behind dresses and carts as fast as he could, heading towards the city's huge outer walls. The crowds grew more dense the closer he got. He weaved and pushed but the tenrec's ragged breath was still over his shoulder.

Something swiped at his shirt. Claws tore his sleeve, but he wrenched his arm away. With a panicked glance he saw the fennec – in a quick grab Bayer wrenched him forwards and down, slamming his nose into the cobblestones. Bayer leapt away, bursting through the crowd till he almost ran muzzle-first into another carriage, a simple, enclosed passenger cart rolling its way out of the city. He shadowed it for a few seconds, and when it began to accelerate, he leapt onto the tailboard, gripping the wood tightly as it carried him through the gatehouse.

He didn't see either of his pursuers again; hopefully the bloodied nose or chipped teeth would be enough of a deterrent. He gave a silent whistle of relief as he arranged himself on the carriage's meagre tailboard, watching the manic, white city disappear behind the trees. The pouch jingled at the bumps in the road. He poured out a few coins and turned them over in his paws.

He had no idea where to use these.

This carriage ride was rougher than the first. The road bumped, swayed, and meandered much more than the path to the white city, and the board he perched on was so narrow it dug into his thighs, leaving him stiff and squirming for a comfortable position. A wrong move would cast him into the rough, dry mud below and leave him even more lost.

The forest bordering the road grew denser and greener, with wider leaves that played across the sky like lazy fingers held up on a sunny day. Despite the comfort of the verdant leaves, the unfamiliarity of it left him twitching with apprehension. The inhabitants of the carriage could stop, and he'd have to hide or risk getting beaten or arrested. He could fall asleep and tumble into the wheels, his body dismissed as another stone in the road. They could be raided by people from the forest, and left bleeding in the dirt. He dug his claws into the wood, panting, arms rigid, pulling his seat firmly onto the platform. The faster it rode, the tighter he gripped, and the more it jolted his tail and spine.

After what seemed like hours, there was a deep, heavy bump and the carriage veered to the left. Bayer barely clung on, his fur bristling, claws aching with the force he dug them into the plank. The carriage ground to a halt, and a new terror struck him. He leapt to the ground and darted into the bushes, rolling onto his back to keep as flat as possible. The driver dismounted and stuck his head through the window at the occupants, gave a brief check of the wheels, then swept back up into the driver's seat and whipped the large reptile steed into motion. Bayer shot upright but was already too tired and sore to give chase, and instead, from his nest of crushed ferns, he watched it rattle away down the path. He was once more alone on the trail to a destination he didn't know, that could hold either hope or terror. But he had to be optimistic, regardless, just to keep moving. He gave a shaky breath, and made his way solemnly after the carriage.

He encountered a few other travellers on the road, but he dared not ask anyone for directions, in case he had to reveal where he was from and risk being herded back to the white soldiers; when anyone reached out to him he scurried ahead. The only time he approached someone was when he came to a fork in the road, as the sky drifted to the orange hues of dusk.

An armadillo knelt by a stump on the road, arranging sewing notions and delicate tools on a strip of leather that had come unfurled as they walked.

"Excuse me?" Bayer croaked, barely a whisper.

The armadillo's ear twitched. They gave a furtive glance in Bayer's direction.

Bayer cleared his throat. "Please, can you help me?"

"That depends on what you want to ask of me," the armadillo replied artlessly.

"I, er, I'm not sure where I'm supposed to go."

They looked to the dirty cub, then at the forked trail to their right.

"You came from Andarn, did you not?"

Bayer wasn't sure how to answer. *That must be the city of the white soldiers.*

"Right will take you to Midia, left to Xayall. Are you travelling alone?"

Bayer nodded.

"Ah. Then you'll want to go to Xayall. You'll end up in better care there."

Bayer pulled at his claws. "Is it far?"

"It's not bad. If you walked all night, you'd get there by next sunset. It'll be a better journey if you rested now, though."

"Thank you," Bayer replied quietly, looking down, his ears flattened.

Something fell at his feet. A small linen-wrapped package lay before him, and a modest water flask. Gently he picked the package up, and unwrapped it to find some oat biscuits.

"I guess you can eat them," the armadillo grunted, pushing on their knees to rise to a hunched standing position. "Won't be upset if you can't, but don't get sick. Maybe you can trade 'em for real food if you have to."

Bayer nodded, his voice caught by a lump in his throat. He didn't look up, hoping that by staring at the food in his hand that the traveller wouldn't see him crying.

The armadillo picked up a small, gnarled walking cane from beside the stump and shuffled along the right fork, towards Midia. "Anyway, be safe, wherever you end up."

Once they were out of view, Bayer completely drained the water flask into his mouth, drips of it melding with his tears. He looked around a little for any sign of more people, but the armadillo had faded into the encroaching forest dusk and there appeared to be no more travellers nearby. He was okay with that, for now.

He hunched over on the stump and laid his head on it, looking down the road he was supposed to take.

"I hope you're a good place," he whispered, wrapping his arms around the stump, and falling into an exhausted slumber.

Bayer woke with a start to voices above him. At some point in the night he'd fallen off the stump and crawled into the grass, and standing around him in the pale morning sun was a group of concerned marmots, all dressed in the same robes. They reached down as he woke, but he kicked himself away, pushed between two of them, and sprinted along the path. He chanced a quick look over his shoulder; two were laughing, another tried briefly to pursue him, and the rest shared bemused shrugs. He gave an apologetic half-wave, but continued his run till they were completely out of sight.

He ate while he walked, the dry crunch of the oatcakes reminding him that even with the gift of the flask how little he'd had to drink over the last few days. His mouth felt like an empty riverbed, and the crumbs all but rattled down his throat when he swallowed. At least the forest gave him some form of peace over his walk, and at a resting post some hours down the track was a small well, which he gleefully took several flaskfuls of water from. He didn't even care that he looked like a slavering beast when he drank; he wanted to absorb it all immediately. He waited there for at least an hour, letting the water flow into him (and out of him, having to escape to a friendly tree a few times).

Forest creatures of various kinds chittered, harped, and sang in the distance. Bayer would have had a greater stomach for it if he wasn't so sore from an uncomfortable journey and heavy rest, but it was still a world untouched by the memories that lit a dark fire in his chest.

On his second night he slept further away from the road, in a low divot that had some overhanging roots which felt like the rafters of his old home when he crawled beneath them.

The next day he woke damp from dewdrops, and cold. He began at a slow pace and meandered between spots of sunlight to try and warm up. The weeks of dirt in his clothes made the weight of the water even heavier, cloying at his fur.

Eventually, as he dried, he even began to enjoy the peace in between subtly evading the travellers passing him in either direction. And, finally, he caught sight of something between the trees. As the path crested the edge of a low valley, a shining spire stood tall above the forest. He steeled his focus on that tower, with its wing-like pinnacles cradling the sky. His breath caught in his throat, his ears burned, and his paws began to tremble in anticipation.

Descending the valley road, he began to see fields, farms, water mills, small farmer's huts like the ones near his village.

The familiarity to his home in this quiet, new forest felt uncanny. Eerie.

He swayed uneasily. The nearby tree branch rocked as he fell against it, shaking.

What had he done? Where was he? Why did he leave?

He clasped his head in his hands and fell to a crouch as he willed the ground to consume him, make him disappear. This wasn't home. This was a mistake. This was too different, and too similar. He needed to go back. Kodi would have protected him. Maybe she needed to be protected. Maybe she was looking for him. Or maybe she didn't care anymore. Visions of his scorched home bled into his mind. His right foot twitched, his mouth formed into a rasping snarl, and he dug his claws so deep into his head that a rivulet of blood ran down his cheek.

"Just go away," he whispered, to everything.

There he crouched for some time, harried breaths sighing deeply from him. He rocked back and forth, trying to pit the horror he had left behind against the fear of the unknown he was surrounded by; even this idyllic facsimile of his land was tainted by the creeping shadows of his memory.

After a minute or two he stopped rocking, and his fervour subsided. He couldn't go back. Even if he wanted to, he needed help – for himself and so many others, to get rid of those terrifying soldiers. Maybe… if he could save himself first, then he could save everyone else. Gradually, anxiety's fire faded and he could breathe normally again. He wiped his head, and smeared the blood on his trousers. His hands stopped shaking, and carefully he eased himself to stand, lifting his stiff neck to greet the new world with a timid gaze.

After taking a few deep, steadying breaths, Bayer stepped forward.

Chapter Six

The spire was deceptively far. Once he reached the hills he could see it as the central beacon of a city, which gleamed in the midmorning sunlight in far brighter colour than the labyrinthine city of terror he'd just escaped. In the crook of the low, wide valley, with a river flowing both around and through it, was the next place he would try to survive in. He was afraid of being turned away, but resigned himself that he may have to live as a stray outside the walls, or within one of the farmer's huts, if they allowed him to work. He could catch fish, even if it meant swimming into the city under cover of darkness. Anything to keep him alive.

"Xayall. Zai-ahl," he murmured, trying to mimic the armadillo's pronunciation. On approaching one of the city's main gates, he saw the river to be a lot wider than it looked from afar, hidden by the deceptive landscape. A long bridge, wide enough for several carriages, spanned it, manned at either end by guards in green and gold livery. At the city's gatehouse was a large gilded flag, with a fox's head over a blue shield. He stopped before the bridge to gape at it for a moment.

"Hey," came a gruff call. Bayer jumped from his staring.

He glanced fearfully at the wolf guard with charcoal fur,

who was holding a shield bigger than Bayer and a spear that looked like it could pluck the sun from the sky.

"You doing all right, kit?" the guard asked.

Bayer nodded. "Yes… I like the, um… I mean, I'm just going inside."

"Are you from the farmlands?"

Bayer thought for a second, then nodded, slowly.

The wolf gave him a look of kind reproach. "Do you know where you're going?"

Bayer nodded again. "Yes. My, er, father sent me to get… it's a thing for our granary, but not big. It's er, it's… he also gave me a letter to take, to make sure it's right. He's working hard, so he couldn't come. It's my first time, but… I think I can do it." He jingled his little pouch of coins in the hope of adding more merit to his lie.

The guard looked him up and down, then scratched his muzzle, keeping a stern eye on the ocelot cub. "You promise to be safe, and not get lost? I'll ask about you if I don't see you come out."

Bayer nodded, keeping his hands tight against his thighs to stop them from shaking. The wolf threw his thumb over his shoulder in approval, and Bayer skittered onto the bridge, giving a barely audible 'thank you' as he passed.

He stopped mid-crossing to watch a barge drift underneath him, and ran to the other side as it re-emerged from the shade. His ears flicked with excitement, and the slightest of smiles lit his face. Filled with renewed confidence, he strode underneath the gatehouse and the banner that flapped proudly in the breeze, and entered Xayall.

It was much less busy than Andarn, but still populated. There was a market square almost immediately to his right, with sandstone houses bordering it. Beyond that in any direction were more buildings, and the ever-present wings of the tower as the city's pinnacle, some way ahead through corners he couldn't yet see. He turned left past the market to explore his options.

Most of the city dwellers seemed to be preoccupied with going to market, because their paths all flowed in that direction. Once he got far enough within, there weren't many more pedestrians around, and the bustling sounds were more distant. He reached out a hand and stroked his claws along the walls, feeling grounded by having a sense of direction as his gaze wandered again to the tops of the buildings and threatened to unsettle his balance.

After a while, above the calm rush of the wind overhead, he could hear running water, and something else he had not heard in a long time: children's voices.

Letting his paw slip from the wall, he quickened his pace and ran to the source, coming to a pavement that shadowed a canal curving through the city. A small, arched bridge lay ahead of him, and on the other side of it were the children. There were three that he could see; a wolf, a cheetah and a mink, about his age or slightly older, shouting and laughing, throwing stones at something. He stepped closer to see around the bridge's wall, and saw a young fox cowering in the shadow, trying to shield himself against the hail of pebbles. Tiny, pitying mews cried from his shielded form.

Bayer's claws flexed, his jaw tightened. Heat spread up his neck, raising his hackles. The fox cried out again as a stone hit his forearm and he collapsed to all fours, beginning to make a crawl in Bayer's direction. More stones struck the back of his legs, faster and harder, attempts to halt his pace completely.

Bayer was shaking. He balled his fists.

"*HEY!*"

The mink looked at Bayer and elbowed his companions, but kept lobbing rocks.

The ocelot took another breath, quaking so much his legs almost failed to keep him standing.

He marched forwards.

"*LEAVE HIM ALONE!*" he roared.

They threw a few last stones, but seeing Bayer approach with increasing ferocity, they exchanged looks and fled, not before the wolf cast a last-minute shot towards Bayer. It skipped past his feet. Bayer stood for a few seconds between the fox and the cubs' retreat, chest heaving.

His paws wouldn't stop shaking. Gripping his dirty, worn trousers to pump some rigidity to his fingers, he turned to the fox, who still leaned against the low brick wall, rubbing his arms.

"Are you all right?" Bayer asked quietly, his voice quavering with the unstable concoction of tiredness and adrenaline coursing through his body.

The fox shook his head, letting out a short cry which he immediately stifled before turning away from Bayer.

"They're gone now," Bayer croaked, checking quickly around to make sure what he said was actually true. "You're safe."

The fox shook his head again, cradling it in his paws, staring at the floor.

Bayer knelt down to try and catch sight of his face. The fox waved his paw desperately.

"Can I see? You're hurt, right?"

The fox started to shake his head, but this time nodded partway through, panicked and confused. He leant his head against the bridge.

Before him Bayer saw shadows of his village life, and times

when he'd tried to stop older village cubs from picking on friends, and, shamefully, times when he'd been reprimanded for doing the same. He reached out to the fox, who hunched his shoulders closer to his chest.

"I want to help," the ocelot said, perhaps a little more forcefully than he intended. He gently tried to peel back the fox's paws to see the injury underneath, but the fox jerked away, gently rocking on his hindpaws.

Bayer folded his arms and stood upright, scrunching his nose. "I can't help you if I can't see it," he tutted. "And I'm not going to leave you alone, so you'd better show it to me. I'm not like those cubs, I won't make fun or hurt you. They were flipping nasty."

The fox nodded sadly, and slowly stopped rocking. His shoulders relaxed a little, enough for him to take his shirt sleeve and wipe away the tears that soaked into the fur on his muzzle. His other arm stayed pressed to his forehead. Bayer could see blood underneath it, seeping through the fox's bright orange fur in trails of crimson.

"Can you stand?" Bayer asked.

Carefully, the fox rose to his feet. Now being able to actually see Bayer, he looked him over with a studious eye that even the tears couldn't wash out. Bayer's jaw dropped.

The fox's eyes were completely silver.

"Wh-whoa!" he cried. "Your eyes!"

The fox shied away, as if hurt, still clutching his forehead.

"No, wait," Bayer protested. "They're not bad, just… I've never seen eyes that colour before. It's nice."

The fox vaguely shook his head, then shrugged. Bayer opened his mouth to say something but then stopped, unsure of what the fox had meant, or what to say next.

The fox's robes were a greatly finer cut than Bayer's, as the ocelot expected from someone living in a big golden city, but they were almost as dirty, no doubt from the scuffles, blood, and dust. The fox sniffed and rubbed his ears, running his paws over the crystal earrings he wore as if to count them. Once he'd accounted for six, his shoulders relaxed and he straightened his posture a little, but cradled the elbow of the hand he pressed to his head.

Bayer watched him for a second. "Can… you not speak?"

The fox didn't respond, but tears started welling in his eyes again.

"Were they hurting you because you can't speak?" Bayer asked again. The fox shook his head, his foot tapping the floor in ire. For a second he lifted his paw from his head wound, and Bayer saw a vicious gash left by one of the stones, just above the fox's left eye. The fox wasn't looking at him anymore, staring agitatedly into the middle-distance. A slight ringing hung in Bayer's ears.

"Well," the ocelot started, a little distracted by the noise, and the cut in front of him. His mother told him heads bled a lot, but he was desperate to find a way to stem it. "You need to get someone to look at that. I know a bit, but… I'm lost, and…" A lump swelled in his throat. "Please don't tell anyone, but I'm not from here. I had to run away."

The fox glanced at him for a second; his expression softened.

Bayer swallowed a few times, trying to banish the emotions from his throat. "You, er…" He coughed. "I'm sorry they hurt you. I… hope… I did okay."

His new friend nodded.

"I'm not normally very brave," Bayer continued, his voice cracking. "Not really. I mostly run from things. But… if… if you don't want me to help… then…"

The fox gave him a gentle tap on the arm, then patted his chest with his hand. Bayer smiled.

"Thank you," he squeaked, giving some big sniffs to try and inhale the emotions he'd just released. "So… can you tell me about this place?"

The fox shook his head again, his white crystal earrings jangling against each other.

Bayer let a small sigh of frustration hiss from his teeth. "Please? Just a little bit?"

"No, nobody likes it when I speak!" the fox cried, stunning Bayer into silence. There was no issue with the fox having a voice, evidently, but Bayer immediately caught the reason for his resignation.

"Can you… not hear properly?" Bayer asked, pointing to his ears.

The fox said nothing, but wiped his eyes of fresh tears.

Before Bayer could offer any words of comfort, the fox ducked away. Bayer turned just in time to see the stone collide with his crown. A strong, dull pain burst across his head; he yelped and cradled his forehead. More stones pelted his chest, sides, and arms.

The ringing in his ears grew louder, swamping his senses. He risked a glance to see what it was, or assess if he was passing out. As he moved, a pair of paws clasped his ears closed. The fox pushed Bayer's head down and a tremendous noise split the air, like a prolonged thunderclap. The bridge shuddered. A wave of distortion flashed across the road and the three stone-throwing irks were catapulted backwards.

As the rumble subsided and the fox released his grip, footsteps penetrated the vanishing echo in all directions. With a panicked whimper, the fox sprinted down the streets to the right. Bayer tripped over himself to follow, narrowly avoiding the grasp of a soldier in green and brown.

Bayer skidded along the pavement, scraping his shoulders on the corners of the sandstone buildings to keep up with the fox and evade the soldier that rattled ominously behind him. Hands reached out to him from startled citizens in an attempt to catch hold, emboldened by the soldier's efforts to keep up and frustrated cries to halt. They missed every time, although one clipped his ear with a swift claw.

Still good at running.

Darting across another corner he came to a wide, busy street with a long, low building surrounded by pillars directly opposite. A blur of orange slipped through the door at the top of its steps. The fox was incredibly fast to make such headway, or maybe Bayer was just exhausted.

With more traffic moving across him he snaked and dodged through, eyes fixed on the doors ahead. The guard's armour clamoured with his bulky, hindered pursuit and rapidly unravelling politeness at pedestrians who collided with him, and Elasmotherians, great reptilian beasts of burden that tensed at his approach. Bayer gave one last glance at his increasing lead and finished his serpentine path to the final stretch up the stairs.

He crashed through the door, tripping on his feet as he hit the threshold. His frantic bump and squeaking slide across the floor echoed in the huge marbled chamber.

So many heads turned his way. He froze, prostrate on his stomach, skating slowly along the polished floor on his filthy shirt. He had never seen a building like this before. Rows of seats and tables filled the area by the entrance, and further back were regiments of tall shelves, supplied with more books than he could ever hope to count.

Bayer looked around, eyes wide, still sprawled on the floor.

A sharp weasel attendant shot him a glare – he couldn't tell if it was surprise or anger, but Bayer picked himself up and hurtled towards the shelves, looking for his fox. He heard the soldier enter a few seconds later, and slid behind unwitting bodies that could mask him, pretending to engross himself in books even though he couldn't understand most of the language. He stayed silent, but his ears swivelled to track the guard's echoing, rattling footsteps around the hall, and he slunk around shelves in opposition to stay out of sight. Finally, the pacing faded. With the subtle boom of the closing doors came the signal of his escape. Bayer pushed his book onto the nearest shelf and reignited his own search.

The winding library held tomes ranging from brand new to impossibly ancient. And they were all different – how could there be so much to write about? Bayer ran his claw over some of the spines, stroked the smooth surfaces of neatly-stacked scrolls. Most of the writing in his village was done by the elders and the trainee scribes to log village histories, discoveries, maps, and family records. Stories weren't recorded – they were saved for retelling around the fire, by elders or from villagers returned from long journeys. Words were considered trustworthy for the voice they were given, where books were not – they had no voice to tell them, no emotions to read and discern, so were only suitable for facts and histories. The books around him now, and the tapestries and paintings set handsomely on the walls, sucked in his gaze. He wanted to explore them all.

His curiosity gave no help to the mounting insecurity at losing his fox as he wandered amongst the shelves, however. At times the decorous aisles stretched on for what seemed like infinity, and the thought of there being so much knowledge in a building so huge was terrifying – he couldn't even imagine how much he didn't know. Even for how wondrous its construction was, an unnatural cold touched him with every padded footfall. Something so big should not exist outside of nature.

He weaved silently past the library patrons for a long time, quick to step out of the way of moving carts or inobservant book addicts. He wanted to ask each one if they'd seen his friend, as desperation gradually wove together a ball of unsteady emotions in his chest. It may be premature to call the fox such, but it was the first thread Bayer had found that connected him to the child he was. In that fox he clung desperately to the hope that he could have some sense of normality and purpose again, instead of a wild and lonely creature threatening to permanently break. The fox was his sole hope for connection right now. Bayer needed his friend, and more than that, he needed to be needed in return. He'd been transient, distant, since last seeing his mother and brother, feeling the safety in the give-and-take of a loving world entwined with his own.

The biting fog of loneliness crept through his mind. He shook himself, gave a quiet growl in defiance of his fear and lowered his head, quickening his steps, sharpening his gaze, desperate to grasp a lifeline that would save him from his burning, aching loss.

With the first floor devoid of his quest, he raised his eyes to the lattice of balconies and walkways hugging the perimeter of the huge room. He crept gingerly up the wide, bifurcated staircase at the rear, yielding space to the scholars laden with books and scrolls on their unsteady, learned descent. At the top, he scanned past the shelves, most of which were short cul-de-sacs, and came to rows of doors with chalkboard placards on them, each adorned with white, dusty squiggles. He walked his way up to one of the doors and pressed his ear against it, hearing adult voices talking softly within. Each door he tried produced the same result; he encircled almost the entire upper floor till he came to a large set of double doors, standing ajar.

He slunk through the gap.

Within the tall, semi-circular antechamber were more shelves, this time closer together, and taller. Almost as high as the main library hall below, this room had a domed ceiling laced with golden stonework. Beyond the shelves lay a circular platform surrounded by windows, home to an enormous orrery in bronze and silver, which to Bayer, was like being presented with an entire galaxy. He stood motionless, staring at the huge metal spheres for what must have been a full minute; he didn't even notice the small figure sitting silently at its base.

A noise took Bayer by surprise; a soft, ringing thud, like knuckles on metal. Immediately he looked behind him, but seeing no one, turned back. Sat under the orrery was the fox, who, upon meeting Bayer's gaze, instantly looked down, rubbing his temple with a paw. Bayer betrayed his attempt to be calm with an enormous, teeth-baring smile. Half-running, he strode to the fox and held out a hand for him to shake, then immediately retracted it and held his hands behind his back. He gave a small, polite, bow, padding his paws together at his chest.

"Hi," he called, loudly enough to hear it echo along the smooth stone walls. He grimaced, seeing the fox flinch and close his eyes at the unexpected volume.

Bayer tugged at his shirt collar. His tail swayed uneasily behind him.

"I found you," He said, at a more modest volume, almost confidently. "You didn't have to run."

The fox's ears twitched. "Did," he grunted, looking away with one eye closed. "I'm trouble again."

Bayer kept looking up at the orrery's globes. "Do they always chase you?"

The fox shrugged. "Not always. Some days it's worse. Like when I can't… when…" He clenched his paws into fists and scrunched his eyes, his eyelids flickering rapidly. Bayer watched quietly, his own paw drawing back to his chest in concern for what looked like pain flashing across the fox's face.

"Did that noise hurt you?" Bayer whispered.

The fox shook his head, able to open his eyes normally again after a few seconds. "No. Well, yeah, but… not how you think it does. I do it so they leave me alone. They chase me cause… cause…" He tugged at the base of his ears, rubbing them forcefully. "It's not my fault I didn't know things made noises. Like burps and chairs and bodies and laughing, and things being so loud. It hurts!" he cried plaintively. "They say I'm stupid and broken and useless and nobody wants me."

Bayer twisted his knuckles together and looked at the floor, swallowing hard. "Well… I… they don't… they're just wrong, and angry. *They're* the stupid ones because they just don't know what you need. Someone wants you, I think."

The fox locked him in a shaky glare. "Then where are my Mum and Dad?"

Bayer's throat tightened; he felt his eyes welling up, but he quickly blinked them clear and gave a stalwart sniff.

"You can… you can still find friends without them," he lied. Maybe. "I just know… no-one deserves to be chased and bullied like that. So…" He scratched the back of his neck. "If they don't like you, I can be your friend, if you want."

The fox dug his claws into his palms. An open book and a pencil lay half-abandoned next to him. A set of printed letters with a few drawn in facsimiles of their shapes adorned the top of one page, then further down devolved into scrawls and scribbles, then what looked like a set of rhythmic, wavy lines.

"Why?" the fox winced.

Bayer looked around for an answer, frowning. "You're not supposed to ask why, that's rude," he scoffed. He dug a tooth into his cheek to keep his emotions from welling up again. "…I haven't got any friends. I ran… a long way, and my family's…"

The fox tapped his claws on his thighs, and meekly looked up at his guest. Big tears rolled down Bayer's muzzle, either side of the smile he projected with all of his strength. The ocelot wiped his arm across his face and let out a wavering sigh through the gritted grin. "I'm… I'm lost. So…" His voice cracked. "So I really want to be your friend. Please."

The fox looked away again, gently touching a pawpad to the cut on his head.

"You'll get in trouble too."

Bayer let out a small whimper, and had turned back to the door to leave when a paw grasped his wrist. The fox stood, head lowered slightly, giving furtive, bashful glances every few seconds.

"We match."

Bayer's brow furrowed.

He pointed at Bayer's head.

"Scar brothers. So that's good."

The stray looked confused for a second. The fox pointed at his cut, then back to Bayer's. The ocelot reached up to his brow and winced, finding a smart bruise and the warm softness of drying blood above his right eye. He grinned back at the fox, who looked away again, but was growing a smile of his own.

With his head bowed in timidity, the fox reached out his right paw.

"Kier," he whispered.

The smile pushed more tears from Bayer's eyes. "I'm

Bayer, Bayer Kanjita," he replied. They stood for a moment, shaking paws. Kier looked about at the floor, while Bayer beamed at his companion.

"I promise not to throw stones at you, ever," Bayer said boldly.

Kier nodded in reply. "Me too. And I won't run away from you, unless it's a game."

Bayer let out a small giggle, and scratched his ear. "How did you make that noise?"

Kier tensed. "What noise?"

"When they came back. You knocked them over, didn't you?"

The fox paused for a second, then reluctantly nodded. "Mmm, I did. I'm learning to hear and see better," he huffed, his foot tapping anxiously. "When I get tired I can't see very well so I trip and they laugh at me. Or my hearing goes when people are talking, or my head hurts from being tired of looking with my crystals and I have to lie down and they say I'm lying."

Bayer tilted his head quizzically.

Kier gave another fatigued grunt. "When I was born, I was almost deaf and mostly blind. They gave my crystals to help me hear," he explained, flicking his earrings with a pawpad, "and I have ones in my eyes for seeing."

"In your *eyes*?"

Kier pointed impatiently at his eyes for Bayer to look at, a difficult feat when the fox kept turning away out of bashfulness or blinking hard. Eventually, drawing very closely to the fox's face, Bayer saw it – a web of black crystal slivers implanted in Kier's eyes, giving them their metallic glean against dull grey irises. He gasped in shock.

"Whoa, cool! So those make you see, and these make you

hear?" he said, pointing at his earrings.

Kier tilted his head back, gazing at the ceiling. "Not like proper hearing. I have to… make it happen… Like… learning to walk on your hands."

"That sounds weird," he replied sympathetically.

Kier shrugged matter-of-factly. "It is. It bothers me more that it hurts when I get tired. Or that I can't always get it to work. That's when I get scared, or bullied."

"How does… it work?" Bayer asked quietly, hoping he wasn't pressing too much.

Kier seemed somewhat used to the questions, and tilted his head, demonstrating the earrings. "You can touch it. *Gently.*"

Bayer took an earring delicately in his paw. It felt like it was moving, vibrating ever so slightly, as if full of tiny soft insects.

"How do they work? Can you do other stuff?"

Kier shuffled awkwardly. "Kind of, but most of it hurts or makes me sleepy. I'm not supposed to anyway, because I could hurt someone." He suddenly smacked his fists on his thighs. "But it's okay if they hurt *me!*" he protested, storming round in a circle. "They say I'm a freak, and a teacher's pet, and throw things and trip me and make stupid loud noises in my ears, but I get told off for hitting back!" He let his breaths rip from him for a short while, then his shoulders dropped, and he clenched his paw a few times. "So that's when I make noises like that, and make them go away"

Bayer nodded sympathetically. "I'm sorry they hurt you," Bayer said quietly. "But what you can do is amazing! I've never heard anything like that."

A tiny, mischievous smile crept across the edges of Kier's lips. "I like scaring them."

"They flew through the air like dolls!" Bayer twittered. "So… can you do other stuff?"

The fox gave a bashful grunt. "I'm not very good at it all the time. But, um…" He stopped still for a moment. His eyes flared briefly, and then his entire body shimmered, faded, and vanished, leaving a trembling patch of air in front of Bayer. The ocelot leapt back in shock.

"You went invisible!"

The air flashed, and Kier reappeared, holding his temples with a wince. "No!" he groaned. "It's not invisible. I moved the light so it went around me. You just didn't see me between your eyes and the wall."

"That *is* being invisible."

"Not really."

"Yes it is!"

"Don't like being called invisible."

Bayer folded his arms. "All right, it's like… being behind a mirror that looks backwards."

Kier nodded. "Yeah, I like that better. I do that with my eye crystals, but it hurts more than the ear ones."

"Does it… always hurt?"

He nodded. "Yeah. I get used to it, but… I wish it didn't."

They stood in silence for a moment, each of them lost in their own ponderings. Bayer rubbed his arm; the size of the building felt like it was making him shrink.

His stomach rumbled; the noise startled the both of them. Bayer grinned apologetically.

"I'm hungry."

Kier nodded and walked past him to the door. Bayer watched for a few seconds, unsure of what was happening. Reaching the threshold, Kier looked back over his shoulder and waved for him to follow, and, needing no second prompt, Bayer sprinted after his friend.

Chapter Seven

The young Kier led Bayer on a trailing, circuitous route to the market from the library, wary of being seen by people who knew him. He had a small pouch of silver coins which he used to buy them both some fish skewers and sweet apple things that Bayer had never eaten before. He devoured the food within seconds. Warm, full satisfaction blossomed through his body. When Kier paid for it, he suddenly remembered the money in his own pocket from outside the terrifying theatre steps, and was quick to buy cider for them both in return for the fox's kindness (and was greatly relieved the money he'd been given was actually real). They meandered over the lower section of the city, and exchanged stories of bruisings they'd received in their misadventures. They stuck close to each other, cleaned their wounds off in the canal, and then Kier led Bayer towards the arena.

"Where do you live?" Bayer asked.

Kier scowled. "The Tor. I get made fun of for that too. They keep saying I'm rich and spoilt, but I'm not."

Bayer didn't have any indication of what the Tor was, so he just nodded. "Did your parents live there?"

"No."

"Oh. So, they're… um… where are they now?"

Kier shrugged. "Don't know. Well, um… maybe they're going on a quest that was too dangerous for me. They could be saving lives or fighting big evil creatures somewhere."

"But… what if they're not?"

"If they're not… then… they… they're horrible people and I don't need them in my life." His voice wavered. He cleared his throat and gave his head a little shake. "I don't. I have enough people here that already don't like me. They're not nice, or they're dead. Hopefully both."

Bayer stopped walking. "How can you say that?" he hissed.

Kier whirled round. "Well, they left me here alone so if they're not dead then they're not nice, 'cause if they *are* nice, then why would they abandon me? And if they're dead then I don't want them to have been nice," he said bitterly, "because nice people don't deserve to die. So that's how."

Bayer stood silently for a second. "I'm sorry."

Kier leant forwards, peering under the ocelot's hanging head. "It's okay for me, I had a long time to think about it. You've only just got here, and… went through all that."

Bayer nodded, pre-emptively wiping his eyes, and they continued walking. "So… are you just by yourself when you run away?"

"Yeah. It's better than school. I can read about adventures, and learn to do things like exploding my voice. Sometimes I get to see Aidan – he's the Empress's husband. But not very often now, 'cause they just had a baby."

"Ah. We don't really have school. We get taught things like how to use tools every day, but it's more about how we run the village and who we are."

Kier shrugged. "Sounds more fun to me. We do sums and history and writing a lot. I don't know how to fish."

"But there were so many books in your city already! Is that what they want you to do?"

"I don't know. *I* don't want to do that," Kier murmured. "I want to be a hero."

They came to a stack of crates sitting opposite the arena gates, awaiting storage. They crept behind it and peered round to the large, empty stadium.

"They don't tell you how to do that?" Bayer whispered.

"Not yet. It's just boring stuff. They don't like me so they don't let me read what I want to, which makes me tired faster," the fox replied, looking away from the people passing them in the street. "And they keep putting stuff in my eyes and testing my ears. It hurts. So... maybe if I was a hero I could show them I don't need all that."

Bayer winced at the thought of having things put in his eyes. "Do they know what you can do?"

Kier pulled Bayer across the road to hide behind the large buttress that framed the arena door. He was so used to encountering soldiers at almost every turn back in Kyrryk and the white city, their relative absence here made the labyrinth of stone walls and ornate windows even more alien to Bayer. Through the arena door came unexpected comfort, however – a wide, flat, open space. Room to breathe in, and see the sky unhindered by architecture. Behind its far wall though, he could still see Xayall's immense central tower, eminent and imposing.

"What is that?" he asked, grabbing Kier's forearm. "I could see it from the forest."

Kier pried him off. "That's the Tor, where I talked about before. I live there, and the Empress and her family do, too."

Bayer tapped his hindpaw in the sand, a mix of awe and anxiety swirling through him as he watched the clouds sweep behind it. "It's so high! Weird that you have an Empress though, 'cause this is just a city."

Kier shrugged.

"Kyrryk had a King once," Bayer continued casually. "I heard he was nine feet tall and could make fire in his paws."

The fox pouted. "Bet he couldn't."

Bayer kicked at a stone in the dust. "Yeah, well, it's just a story. And he got eaten by a monster anyway." He looked about them, scanning the empty arena. "Why are we here?"

Kier smiled, one of the biggest and most sincere smiles Bayer had see him give. "It's where I come to play. It's empty when the guards are practicing outside the city and there's no games on."

They ran into the centre of the circle. Their play started off slowly; they talked and skirted the arena walls for a few minutes, then began clambering and jumping up and down the stone seats, engaging in a series of back-and-forth races with each other, or against big, invisible monsters. Just as Bayer slipped out of Kier's grasp, with breathy laughter he turned back to the fox.

"How fast can you go?"

"I am already," Kier replied between breaths.

Bayer shook his head. "I mean, can you use your powers to go faster?"

Kier shrugged. "Don't know if they do that."

"You can make a boom, though! Can you use it to push yourself forwards, like a cannon?"

The fox looked furtively around, making sure the arena was still empty. "Um, maybe. I'll try…"

He grounded himself at their end of the oval and took in a deep breath, lowering his head and pointing his fists behind him. A low buzz hit the air; Bayer grabbed his ears in anticipation. The air blurred for a second, and a rush of wind hit him in the face as a deafening thunderclap pounded the arena. Kier disappeared from where Bayer was looking; in the same instant he reappeared in the middle of the amphitheatre.

On the ground. Unmoving. Silent.

"Kier!" Bayer sprinted to him and skidded to his knees to shake the fox awake. The doors before him swept open; three guards marched through, their steps unsettling the sand around them. The leader, a snow leopard in dark purple armour and a fluttering black demi-cloak, immediately set eyes on Bayer, who threw himself over his fox friend.

"Kier, come on, please! They're gonna take me away!"

Bayer clasped Kier's paw tightly as the snow leopard rounded on them with a ferocious, severe glare.

"It wasn't me! Help him!" Bayer pleaded, voice cracking with tears. "I'm sorry, I didn't think it would hurt him! Is he all right?"

The snow leopard knelt down and rested a paw on Kier's neck, then felt for the fox's breath.

"He's alive," he said gruffly. "What were you doing?"

Bayer stared at the big cat for a moment, eyes wide with fear. "P-playing... I-he-we... I just wanted to know how fast he could go. It was an accident – I didn't know! Please don't take him away from me!"

The commander gave him a puzzled look. "What's your name? Are you from the school?"

Bayer shook his head. "I'm Bayer Kanjita from Kyrryk. I'm lost."

"Kyrryk? What are you doing with Kier?"

"W-we were just playing!" he cried, still holding his friend's paw.

The commander studied him for a few interminable moments, then stood. "He's just passed out. Lay him on his back and raise his legs."

Nodding timorously, Bayer did as he was told, not taking his eyes from Kier's face, waiting impatiently for him to wake. In seconds, the fox's silver eyes flickered open. He raised a shaky paw to his forehead.

"I'm cold," he groaned, his focus swirling about him. It took him a moment to recognise the imposing feline soldier standing over him. He recoiled immediately, jerking his legs from Bayer's grasp and almost pulling him over on top of him.

"Commander Enyart!" he squeaked. "I, um…"

"*You*," Enyart boomed, "are troublesome, Master Lugos. Not only are you truant, but I hear you assaulted three children. Am I correct in hearing this was after they discovered you sneaking out of school, or is there some further information you would like to give me?"

Tears massed in Kier's eyes. He gripped his robes tightly. "They threw stones at me, Commander," he mumbled. Bayer nodded in support.

"They did, sir," Bayer said quietly, pointing at Kier's forehead. The snow leopard gave him a cautionary glance.

"And they threw one at Bayer, too!" Kier continued. "I'm used to being hit, but he was hurt, and I didn't like that."

Enyart knelt down to face Bayer, laying a hand on his head and stroking his thumb gently over where the stone had cut the cub's forehead.

"I see." He gave a gruff sigh. "As much as I hate to admit it, His Majesty might be correct in saying that school is not for you. You are obviously too great a liability, and even though he insisted it should be highly improbable, you've found a way to weaponise your resonance enhancements." He glared down his nose at the fox. "Trust a fox to circumvent limits put in place for his own safety."

Kier rolled over and sat up. "But where will I go?" he asked, his hands so tightly wrought that they looked inseparable.

Enyart looked over the arena. "You liked protecting your friend, didn't you?"

Kier nodded.

The snow leopard rolled his neck, evoking a dull click from his spine. "Then you'll train to be a guard. I'll be directly responsible for your education from here, seeing as your power and timidity are leading to dangerous places. You'll still take lessons with the school when I am unavailable, but this is where you will find your focus. If you insist on honing your powers in this way, I will not have them being wasted by an insipid lack of confidence."

Kier at once found his legs and stood up sharply, looking directly into the commander's steely eyes. His wobbly knees betrayed the determination in his face. "Can you train Bayer too?" he asked. Bayer felt a swell in his throat.

"What?" Enyart rumbled.

"I want Bayer to train," Kier continued. "He's lost, has no home, and he's my friend. He saved me. And he's a cat too, so maybe you'll like him more."

Bayer quaked, trying to blink back tears. Enyart was terrifying before he'd even opened his mouth, and looked like he was about to erupt into a barrage of teeth, claws and bile.

The leopard shook his head with a growling exhalation.

"Remember that I give nothing without expecting great things in return," he flared, eyes narrowing. "If either of you step out of line or miss your training even once, I will send you to opposite ends of the city. I am not a parent. I will not feed you or console you; I exist only to train you. Is that clear?"

"Yes, sir!" they chorused. The commander stepped over to

Bayer, his dark purple armour glinting in the sun.

"My name is Commander Mai Enyart, Master Kanjita. You will call me 'Commander' or 'sir', and nothing else. Do you understand?"

Bayer saluted back, grinning from ear to ear. "Yes, Commander!"

"Good. Kier, I will send you back to the school with my soldiers to collect your things, then you and Bayer will be given a room here at the barracks. You'll share rations until I can assign provisions for you. Do not dawdle."

He gave another sigh, this time with a quieter, reluctant tone. "I'll inform His Majesty the Emperor Consort of my decision. No doubt he will relish the news, and court a great many jokes at my expense."

He turned on his heel, sending his cloak sweeping over the young animals' heads, then looked back. "You can be sure that will be repaid also."

As Enyart left, they smiled at each other.

Chapter Eight

Two years passed. Kier and Bayer trained. Together, they learned combat skills with Enyart alongside the soldiers of Xayall's guard; studied scrolls and books, took lessons in the library, and explored the city in the free evenings. With help from Enyart and Aidan, Kier's resonance abilities continued to develop, helping him master his senses more clearly, and hone his focus to expand his abilities as a warrior and spy. Bayer learnt about how resonance worked in order to support him, how it affected a user's body, and what strategies to use when fighting a wielder of such a power. The two youngsters were virtually indivisible, and medicine for each other's damaged pasts. Even when they sparred lightly against each other, any injuries or arguments were soon forgotten and their camaraderie renewed.

On one quiet, sunlit afternoon, they waited in the arena for their scheduled class with the Commander. Normally they rushed to meet him and were chastised for the tiniest sliver of tardiness, or made to run laps around the arena, but this time the snow leopard was nowhere to be found. They went through their warm-up exercises and basic training routines as they always did, just in case he was lurking in the shadows to test them for dedication, but even after finishing those and having an extended practice spar with their wooden swords he was still absent.

Kier shot his friend a worried look. "Do you think he's sick?"

Bayer shook his head. "Enyart doesn't get sick. If he did he'd show up and blame it on us anyway."

"Do you think something happened?" the fox asked quietly, looking towards the Tor. The rest of the city sat in eerie quiet. "Something doesn't feel right."

The feline shrugged. "Probably." He thought for a moment, then let out a giggle. "Maybe we get to make *him* run around the barracks this time."

Kier shuddered, laughing nervously. "I bet he'd make you run double if he heard you say that."

"Yeah… and you too, just because."

"That's what I was worried about."

They started doing impressions of the impassive snow leopard, and had just broken into a raucous re-enactment of a particularly bad telling-off when a Xayall guard ran into the arena. Instantly they stopped, pulled themselves off the floor, and stood to attention. The guard, a mongoose called Gior, looked wan, sickly. Kier's tail bristled as he approached.

"Get back to your rooms, you two. There's no training today."

"What happened?" Bayer asked quietly.

"Just… go to your rooms. You'll find out soon."

Gior marched away. As he did so, Bayer and Kier both looked to the Tor, then to each other, and then broke into a run.

Everyone within the Tor was silent and hurried. None seemed to acknowledge the two young strays, save for the odd warning glance markedly never followed by instruction to leave.

They climbed the tower to the upper levels, where Enyart had his quarters alongside those of the Empress and her family. Attendants passed them, carrying medicinal bowls and towels, faces cold like stone. Edging further around a corner, they saw a lone figure standing in the hallway ahead. He looked smaller, somehow, with his shoulders low and his head arched back in sadness. A sigh drifted to them through the desolate corridor.

"You were told not to come," he said quietly. They jumped, then crept shyly towards him.

"Sorry, Commander," Kier mumbled. "We got worried."

"You have good instincts." Enyart muttered, not turning to face them. He paused for what seemed a long time, then spoke quietly. "I will shortly be leaving Xayall."

"What?" Bayer cried. "Why?"

Enyart's voice was dark, but soft. "Do not question me, Bayer," he chided. "My duties here are done. The Empress is dead, and so is my duty of protecting her."

Kier and Bayer fell silent. Kier swallowed hard and pulled his fingers, his head hanging low. Bayer stared, wide-eyed, at the senior cat.

Enyart let out a sharp, dismissive breath and strode away, pushing between them. The students watched him leave, standing wordlessly in the corridor. A few seconds later, one of the Empress' nurses emerged from the other end of the hallway, carrying the young Princess Faria. She was three, and clung apprehensively to the nurse's robes. Bayer and Kier both stood dazed as she was carried to the large central doorway and through the softly flowing veil. They kept their gaze on the threshold for long afterwards, hearing muffled words and muted cries within.

"What should we do?" Kier whispered. "We never finished our training."

Bayer balled his fists. "If Enyart's gone, we're their guards now. So let's guard them."

The two saluted each other and walked to either side of the doorway, standing immediately to attention. For hours they diligently protected the door, as attendants, scholars, officials, and physicians came and left, until darkness sank through the building and their legs gave way, and they fell asleep on the floor, heads against the cold wall.

Quiet footfalls in the darkness woke Bayer. He scrambled to attention again, swaying dizzily, then nudged Kier awake, who sat up, bleary-eyed, and groaned.

Commander Enyart stood before them. "You shouldn't fall asleep at your post," he said quietly.

Bayer rubbed his eyes. "Sorry, sir."

The curtain swept open. From inside came a male fox, looking more tired than all of them together. He was dressed in robes of green, crumpled from being sat in all day. His blue eyes were alight in the dark, glistening with tears.

"Mai," he started. "I'm sorry, I meant to find you—"

Enyart held up a silencing hand. "It's fine, Aidan." He looked away for a second, and gave a silent sigh. "Thank you for… for looking after her. I just… didn't want to pay my respects with all those busybodies around."

Aidan nodded. "I'll get Faria."

The snow leopard looked between the two volunteer sentries by the door. "You need to do more than just stand by a door to be a bodyguard. Did you check anyone who was entering or leaving?"

"They looked busy," Kier mumbled.

"We'd learn more if you stayed to teach us," Bayer muttered, kicking the floor.

The curtain opened once again and Aidan appeared, cradling his young daughter. "They've been here the whole time, Mai. Didn't even leave to eat." He smiled weakly. "You've trained them well."

For a second, Bayer felt sure he saw the commander's expression soften, but it was quickly overridden. "Not well enough, apparently. If this sovereign is going to be worth anything after I've left, I'll have to ensure their training is complete."

Kier started, glancing excitedly at Bayer. "Do you mean you'll stay, sir?"

"I mean that I have one more task before I return to Pthiris," Enyart rumbled. "To fulfil my promise to Empress Kaya and ensure Faria is protected. I will train you two to be her guards, and personal protectors of her family. It's the least I can do to honour her."

They froze. "Are... Are you serious?" Kier stammered.

"You're questioning me?" Enyart quipped, although not harshly. "I would trust nobody else." He looked to Aidan, who nodded appreciatively.

The Commander saluted to the cubs. "Stand down for now; get some food and sleep. But be at the arena at sunrise. You will have two training sessions for missing today's."

He passed through the curtain.

Aidan faced the young guardians, regarding them kindly even through his sadness. "Thank you for staying. Faria will need friends."

"But *you* will, too!" Kier blurted. "We'll protect *you* as well!"

The old fox smiled. "I know you can. But right now Faria's

more important than I am. Come on, there are some spare bedrooms on this level. You can sleep up here tonight."

They gave him a smart salute, and followed him into the torchlight.

Chapter Nine

F ive years later.

Crunch.

The hot, bitter sand dried his mouth instantly. Bayer pushed himself up from the arena floor and wiped his face. No blood – at least, not yet. Commander Enyart whirled his long wooden stave behind his back and brought it clashing against the training sword of Kier, who had advanced for the attack. The stave's back-end swung to follow the arc of the first, smacking the fox in the forearm. He recoiled, almost dropping his sword. As Bayer lunged forwards, he found Enyart's weapon aiming straight for his face; he dodged right, moving inside the weapon's range. In an instant, Enyart shortened his grip, brought the staff over and in front of him and jabbed Bayer in the shoulder, unbalancing him and forcing him to the floor again, this time with the staff pinning him to the ground. Kier gripped his sword tightly, left arm poised in front of his chest, ready to defend or parry.

"Time's running out, Lugos," Enyart bellowed. "If this were a spear it would already have punctured Kanjita's shoulder. Act quickly and you might get to utter a few words of friendship before he dies."

Kier aimed his sword at Enyart's left forearm. Mid-swing, Enyart released his grip from the staff and brought his arm around the back edge of Kier's sword, brought his fist underneath it, then braced the blade against his underarm and wrenched it sideways, pulling it from the fox's grasp, all while still holding Bayer down with the spear in his right hand. Kier balled his fists, and a ringing hit the air. Suddenly, Enyart released his hold on Bayer and whipped his weapon to smack Kier straight in the forehead.

"No resonance. Your ability is a great asset, but without learning technique you'll never unleash its true potential. Or yours."

Kier stumbled back, hands pressed to the bridge of his nose. Bayer pulled himself up, rubbing and rolling his shoulder. Kier's eyes were watering. The fox shook his head and went to pick up his sword.

"So how do I achieve my potential if I'm holding myself back?" he growled.

Enyart cast him a sideways glance. "This is not about holding yourself back; this is about patience and practice. What would happen if you were to lose your resonance abilities? How do you protect someone when everything you've relied on is taken away?" He jabbed his staff into the ground. "This is not my favourite weapon. I could beat you more soundly with twin swords. But if I fail to practice with everything, there will always be a gap in my armour through which a blade will slip and destroy me. Am I clear?"

Kier shook his head, trying to rid himself of the swelling between his eyes. "Why can't I practice both?"

Enyart's jaw tightened. "I cannot teach you both. I can teach you with a weapon. Would you complain to a blacksmith that they couldn't teach you archery? Believe me, the way you learn martial arts through me will be a far better foundation for your skills."

"Sorry, Commander," Kier murmured, gently rubbing his nose.

Enyart turned to Bayer. "Anything you wish to add, Kanjita?"

Bayer shook his head.

"Good. That's enough for today," Enyart barked. "You have studies to attend to in the library." He spun on his heel and marched away. The two students watched him leave, then dragged their weapons back to the storage rooms in the barracks.

Bayer watched as Kier threw his sword into the rack, his ears flat and his tail swinging stiffly as he moved.

"How's your face?" Bayer chanced, leaning his sword carefully against the wall.

"Fine. Hurts." Kier muttered.

Bayer nodded, pulling his shirt collar down to try and see the back of his shoulder. There was a small tear in the fabric.

"Hey, can you check see if he cut me?"

Kier walked over and pried his claws into the collar, pulling the front into Bayer's neck. "I can't see far enough down, you'll have to take it off."

Bayer slipped out of the shirt and held it in front of him, while Kier gently ran his fingers through Bayer's short, coarse fur. "I can't see any blood," he said quietly. "Can you feel anything?"

"Just pain. And humiliation," he scoffed. "Sorry about your face."

Kier patted Bayer's shoulder. "I'm used to it. Pretty sure he'd prefer if I wasn't a resonator, or a fox. Aidan says he's always been like that with him too."

Bayer shrugged. "Yeah, but he's not exactly friendly with me, either. My thigh still hurts from that bruise he gave me last week."

"True," Kier sighed. "I just… he wants us to be strong, but he makes us feel like we're not good enough. If he doesn't believe in us, how is he supposed to give us the best lessons?"

Bayer released a sharp sigh of exasperation as he pulled on another shirt, folding up his damaged one to repair later. "Maybe he believes in what we can already do and wants us to be better? If he went easy on us, we wouldn't be pushing ourselves."

The fox rubbed his pawpads on his thigh, trying to brush the sand from the abrasions suffered during the sparring session. "All I'm learning is the kind of person I *don't* want to be. Sure, I'm fighting well. Or, at least, I'm standing my ground. But as a teacher, or parent, or whatever, I want to be different to *him*."

They paced through the barrack doors and into the hallway, past guards returning from patrol, or resupplying from the armoury. The orange of early evening sunset pierced the narrow windows, illuminating the stone in columns of fiery glow. They gave cursory waves, nods, and salutes to those they knew; despite their relative isolation from the rest of the guards they seemed to be fairly well-regarded, likely due to Aidan's praise, or times that they'd taken part in standard drills and helped with event construction. It was still surreal for him to wander the halls of soldiers who bore such similarity to those he came to fear in Andarn, but in such a different space. Despite his closeness to their duties he knew he would never be one of them. His ideals were different, and his awareness too great.

"Maybe that's what Enyart wants, too, to avoid people

becoming like him," Bayer said eventually as they passed into a crowded, echoing hallway between the barracks and the Tor, the quickest way to access the library.

Kier's ears flattened in incredulity. "So… he's trying to be strict so we're better than him?"

The ocelot shrugged. "Kind of. Like… he hits us when we let our guard down during drills, right? I wonder if he's kind of doing the same with our emotions so we can be strong and not hurt people with ours. Or we make sure people around us are treated with kindness, so *we* don't become cowardly or nasty," he muttered, face falling a little darkly.

Kier frowned. "You don't need to attack someone to make them kind. I think fighting is all he knows and doesn't care about us outside that."

Bayer sighed. "He's not our carer. It's not his job."

"It's nobody's 'job' to be a good person," Kier retorted bitterly. "You're all right with Enyart because you're an ocelot. It's like he respects you more."

"Yeah, really felt that way when he pinned me to the floor," Bayer scoffed. "I don't want to be his friend, I just want to be better. Every time he hurts us, it's a place where we need to learn more."

"Well, *I* don't want to be *his* friend either. I want to be a hero."

"Heroes get hurt too."

"He doesn't seem to think so!" Kier blurted. "He's just angry, bitter – it's a wonder he has any reason to like anything at all."

"Look," Bayer huffed, jabbing his companion in the shoulder with a paw, "Do you want to *be* good, or just have people *tell* you you're good? Because everyone praising you isn't going to change how well you *do* whatever it is you want to be good at. But, this way, if you do something good it'll actually be worth something when someone says it."

Kier scowled.

Bayer rolled his eyes. "We're still just learning. You have powers I won't ever get, so don't complain."

"I can't use them!" Kier protested.

"You're using them right now, to see and hear me! You've *been using* them this whole time, working harder than I do just to… be here!"

"I already know you're better than me!" Kier yelled. "I know what I have to do to fit in, and it stinks! I want to see properly! I don't want to worry if I'm hallucinating all the time and have my eyes burn after being awake all day! Or worry if I sleep too hard I won't hear muster or a fire bell! I don't want to stop hearing if I lose concentration, or trip over stupid things! I want…" He twisted his claws against his pawpads. "I want to be like you."

Bayer paused, glancing around. "What?"

Kier threw his arms up in frustration. "You don't even know how easily you do things. I watch you move, pick up a sword, listen, do *everything* so well. That's why he keeps throwing you to the ground, because he already knows the second you get up again, you'll be better. He knows I'm behind, so he keeps challenging me to break his guard and rescue you. And…" He clenched his jaw. "I can't yet. It makes me feel stupid. Because I w-want to save you."

"It wasn't real, though," Bayer said, a little timidly.

Kier threw his arms to the side. "That's not the point! What if it had been?"

"The Commander's the best fighter in Xayall. We're always going to be behind him, but that's already ahead of a thousand others. Most soldiers aren't even as young as we are."

Kier scrunched his face. "Well, actually—"

A light shove from Bayer interrupted him. "Don't give me that rubbish, I know about pages and polearm training, blah blah blah. They're just troops. They all get the same drills. Not one-on-one sword technique training like this."

"Mnn, I guess so." Kier pouted.

By now they had reached the library's door. They strode through, collected their assigned books, and took their aged stacks to one of the private rooms upstairs. They studied for some time, answering questions left for them by a collection of scholars, with special written assignments from Aidan and Enyart. After a while, Bayer noticed Kier had stopped scratching with his quill and was staring at the ceiling. Bayer kept writing for a while, and as he was about to ask his friend what was on his mind, the fox stood up and marched through the door.

Bayer spent another minute silently scribbling down his train of thought, then laid down his quill. He drummed his paws on the table, staring at the crack in the door. With a flick of his tail, he set off.

The library was quietest in the darkening evenings, with a few librarians stacking and organising the shelves, or supervising the lone students who sprawled great research projects over the tables or nested quietly in a corner for hours with a favoured tome or six. Bayer stuck his head around each shelf corner to catch sight of Kier.

"Are you hiding again?" he muttered, stalking the shelves.

Something grabbed his wrist and yanked him back in the direction of the room; he turned to see a hefty book hanging in the air. "I found it," Kier whispered. The book floated bouncily down the aisle, matching what Bayer recognised as the fox's stride.

Back at their sequestered table, the book thumped onto the flat surface and opened, the pages turning at Kier's transparent handiwork. Bayer closed the door and shook his head, watching the animated tome.

"So what did you get, Ghost of Kier?"

The fox rematerialised, one eye closed, with his hand to his head, and jabbed at the subtitle on the top of his current page. It was a records book denoting the population of Xayall.

"Is that really secret?"

Kier shook his head. "You're not supposed to take these without the custodian's permission because they're official records and they don't want people doctoring or losing them. I didn't want to ask, because it's none of their business what I need to know, and I don't want it recorded that I was looking around."

He flipped through the pages, tracking his claw down the list of births. After a while, he paused, then overturned the book and opened a section near the back; in hard calligraphic text it read 'Admissions: Sanctuary, Incarceration, Migration, Abandonment'. A puff of determination escaped Kier's nose as he scanned the hand-ruled grids.

His claw scraped to a stop in the 'Abandonment' section.

"Lugos, Kier. Fox. Red fur. Born in military custody. Sensory recognition issues. Parents relinquished authority. Admitted to Leafhaven Orphanage, name assigned on entry."

Bayer glanced at the fox, who stared blankly at the pages. "I guess you were right, they weren't good people."

"Military custody doesn't mean bad," he replied quietly, his voice a little tight. "Laws aren't always fair."

Kier stroked the ink over his name for a few seconds. "Aidan told me they were resonators too, each of a different kind. Sometimes two types together can cause…" He whipped the book shut. "I guess I was too much of a problem if they were running from something, or… whatever they were doing. I would… I may have… been a noisy weight."

Bayer pulled at his arm. "Well, I mean… maybe they just didn't—"

"It's fine," Kier sniffed. "They left me. Better here than throwing me aside in the forest. At least I know a little of what nobody else would tell me."

He scooped the book into his arms and strode towards the exit, stopping as he reached the handle. "I hope… they were safe."

He pulled open the door.

Bayer shifted in his chair. "You're… you're coming back, right?"

"…Yeah."

The next day brought with it punishing sunlight that baked their fur as they trained. Kier's sword swings were sharp, precise, and quick. His eyes glinted, tracking the motion of the tip in his stances.

"Focus on your target, not your sword," Enyart drilled. "When you face your opponent completely, your blade will go where it's needed. You'll know if your movements are wrong when you get hit."

He brandished his sword to the fox, settling into a guard as easily and effortlessly as breathing. "Defend, six moves."

No sooner had he finished the words, he set upon Kier in a volley of strikes, to the head, then head to leg, leg to arm, to the opposite arm, then two more strikes to the head. Kier defended each with a beat of his wooden sword, backing away.

"Now, attack. Six moves. Random pattern."

Kier returned Enyart's moves, spiralling his sword over

and across his body to match his targets, fixing the Commander with a steely glare.

"Defend, again. Twelve moves."

Enyart advanced, more quickly this time, each of his strides a little wider than the last. Kier backed away, but not at the same pace, so the snow leopard loomed further over him with each movement. He raised his wrist to brace against the back of his sword as Enyart rapped the wood with a heavy strike. They held for a second, staring each other down. Bayer watched, distracted from his own drills.

"Attack."

Kier punched Enyart's sword away and lunged forwards, striking again and again, meeting the Commander's sword every time. He pushed, further and further, taking wider and wider steps, a snarl cracking his lips. He took a final, enormous lunge, his blade aimed for a thrust at his master's stomach.

Enyart parried the sword down and away. Kier's momentum carried him past the snow leopard's right flank. As he passed, he saw Enyart's sword whirl round for a smack to his legs. He landed on his left foot and wrenched himself round in a flash, sweeping his sword down. The two blades met with a clash, then Kier flashed his weapon upwards to land on Enyart's ribcage, under his arm. They stopped in place. Slowly, Kier slid the sword from his master and backed away, lowering his head to a bow.

"Sorry, Commander. I broke rank."

Enyart paused, and let out a quiet breath. "I broke rank first. The strike was yours to make, and you did. You found your spirit."

Kier swallowed and nodded. "Sir, can… I can be a hero, right? If I fight hard enough? Get past… all these things."

The Commander turned, and slid the sword into his belt.

He stared at the ground for a time, then gave a long, deep exhale. "A hero is someone who fights at the right time, for the right reason, for the right person. The fight may not even be a call to arms – it could be as little as standing tall, making your voice heard, raising someone else's, or not giving up, whether on yourself or on another. But yes, whenever you do fight, always fight hard, with your whole body. Clarity, focus, and steadfastness are the keys to knowing your place as a warrior, and then further as a hero. Remember these are two distinct paths, though they may deeply entwine. A warrior fights for himself, a hero fights for all."

The world around you will be vast, and move quickly, like a wide river. You need to be the stone at the centre of the water. Solid, parting the events and energies around you; being both of them, and separate. To know your place in the world, see what is rushing ahead to meet you, and to effortlessly break through it, is the path you should aim for. You are both in this world for a reason. It may be the same reason, or completely different ones. You will discover them in time. You must be ready for when that happens."

He looked to his students, who both nodded. Kier gripped his sword with determination, and Bayer straightened his back to stand as tall as he could before the Commander.

"Now, both of you, you're to work on your overhead strikes…"

Chapter Ten

The first siege of Xayall burned in the city below. The Dhraka had arrived so swiftly in the night, Bayer had been walking with Faria bare minutes before they had attacked. The ocelot lay against the hard marble floor, breath rasping from him, as the stirrup of a primed and loaded crossbow forced against his chestplate. The grinning hyena hybrid commander, Vionaika, grinned and tightened her clawgrip on the weapon. His body ached; he could feel blood oozing from his wounds, and the heat and noise of the attack swirl into one sensation in his mind.

But Faria had escaped at least. The rest was up to her, and Bayer could no longer follow.

Vionaika stroked the trigger hungrily.

"Fool."

This was it, his death.

Faria was safe. Bayer let himself relax, and a strange silence descended upon him. He saw the hyena lick her teeth as she prepared to send her bolt through his heart. His armour would be no match for the force of a crossbow.

Confusion flickered across her face. She shook her head, as if trying to loosen something from her ear.

Too late, she realised what was happening.

A dull impact, more like an intense pressure, filled the room. The Dhrakans behind her were flung forwards. Vionaika just managed to stay on her feet, crushing Bayer with the weight of her foot, but as she turned, an invisible force stopped her crossbow mid-swing, and her elbow buckled and twisted, forcing her to drop the weapon. Something connected with her jaw, sending her reeling back against the huge oak table in the room's centre.

Bayer felt an arm haul him upright. He gripped it tightly and, seconds later, his transparent rescuer took them both over the balcony's edge.

Their descent was fast: two armoured creatures laden with weapons were not aerodynamic. Watching the streets approaching fast, Bayer's head swelled and throbbed with the rush of blood. His vision started to turn red. He clenched his eyes tightly shut.

A cascade of rippling force rushed up around his legs; a series of repeated, heavy blasts that rocked the air around him. His friend pulled him into a tight, protective embrace. Chancing a look, Bayer was now facing the sky. One final, heavier impact channelled through his back, and then everything was still.

Towers of grey-orange smoke rose into the sky, obliterating the night. His head pounded. He closed his eyes again, trying to gain the strength to sit upright. He rolled to his side and fell off the body of his companion. Still weak from his injuries, he mustered strength to jostle the fox.

"Don't you dare be dead," he rasped.

Kier groaned in reply. "You're heavy. Where's Faria?"

Pain swept across Bayer's body; he twisted round to nurse his shoulder.

"She took the same exit we did. I don't know where she landed."

The fox pulled himself to his feet, eyes wide and teeth bared.

"It's not your fault," Bayer hissed.

He didn't reply, and Bayer knew that was the end of the conversation. It would be pointless to argue right now anyway; they had to find refuge, either in the city or outside it.

"We have to go."

Xayall guards stormed along the roads either side of them, guiding citizens to safety. Kier watched more dark shadows fly across the night sky; winged Dhrakan hunters. "She'll be making an escape. We have to trust her," he said eventually. "With luck, we can get to Andarn and meet her there." He held his hand out to Bayer.

He took it gladly. Kier lifted the ocelot's arm over his shoulders, bolstering himself to aid Bayer's movement, and they stumbled urgently towards the open eastern gates, which were being defended from the siege by Xayall's soldiers and defensive block of archers.

Kier's abilities made escaping a straightforward but terrifying affair; a slow trek past burning debris, around blockades, and ducking away from opportunistic Dhrakan raiders trying to pick off individuals. Most of Xayall's civilians were being marshalled through the gates they were headed towards, but some sections of the city in the south had been barricaded off, and were putting up intense resistance to keep attention away from the evacuees. Strong as Kier could be, he was no match for an entire army. Their best hope was to follow the trail of escapees and hope there were enough soldiers to protect the line from Dhrakan marauders in the forest.

Kier was projecting a shield, of sorts, that refracted the

light around them, making them all but invisible. They would be too easy a target if spotted, and both knew the soldiers had enough on their hands to dedicate time to them, especially when the pair of bodyguards were already precious minutes behind Faria, wherever she may have escaped to, if at all. While Kier's shield made their escape easier, not being seen had its disadvantages, as rampaging Dhrakan troops or fleeing civilians would see no obstacle, and hence make no effort to avoid them. Several times they had to twist against walls at the last second to avoid an accident that would give them away.

It was also difficult for Kier to maintain. The amount of energy it took to obscure himself and Bayer, as well as be able to keep his visual acuity as strong as possible, was incredible, on top of the exertion he'd spent racing back to Xayall and scaling the Tor to save Bayer. His body shook with each step; he was in danger of losing his grip if they didn't pause often enough, and waves of heat from fires or explosions distorted the air, illuminating the rippling camouflage they were enveloped in. Any tracker with an acute sense of smell would eventually break their cover, but amongst the smoke and fury of the siege, that was unlikely for now.

When they finally reached the edge of the forest, following behind the last of the evacuees, Bayer could see the fox's silver eyes were bloodshot and twitching erratically. They struggled on for almost a mile in a wide arc, then collapsed in a ditch by a tree. Kier lay on his back with his palms in his eyes for several minutes, breathing deeply, his knees and elbows quivering. Bayer had seen his friend this way a few rare times after extensive use of his abilities, but tonight was different. The fox's pained expression was more than a reaction to his physical condition. The battle was an insurmountable presence of loss, destruction, and injury, and Bayer knew he would take it as his own responsibility.

"Don't blame yourself for this," Bayer murmured, leaning against a high root. Pain and exhaustion swept over his body.

Kier inhaled to speak, but something caught in his throat and he erupted into a hacking cough, violent enough that he rolled to his hands and knees to force himself to breathe again.

"So dramatic," Bayer said quietly, with a smile.

Kier threw him a look askance. "Fine talk coming from you, mister cosmetic injury."

"These aren't cosmetic," Bayer grumbled, demonstrating the blood caking his paw.

"No, but once you heal, you'll have stories to tell. I'll just look like an old fox in a young fox's pelt."

Bayer shook his head and closed his eyes. They sat in silence for a while.

"I'm glad you found me," he said eventually.

"Knew you'd be with Faria. Glad I got to you in time, at least."

"Me too," Bayer replied, croakily. "Listen—"

"Don't tell me not to feel guilty," Kier warned. "You were in the middle of throwing your life away for her survival."

Bayer let out a weak, whispered laugh. "I know that, Kier. I'm just… thank you."

The tree's rough bark was strangely comfortable. Bayer tried to pull his torn sleeve tighter over his wound, but the blooded fabric kept slipping from his claws. Kier shifted round to inspect his bleeding arm.

"This looks pretty bad," he said quietly.

Bayer shrugged with his good shoulder. "I have another one."

He felt Kier's glare even in the dark. The fox unwrapped the long, ornate sash from his waist and slit it in half along its length, then eased Bayer's shoulder forwards. He removed the ocelot's breastplate carefully, then wrapped one half of the sash neatly over the wound, binding it tightly.

"Your leg, too," he said.

Bayer winced. "I was hoping you wouldn't notice that one."

"There's not much you can hide from me, Bayer," Kier replied quietly, unbuckling his friend's greaves. Bayer's trousers were tacky with blood.

"Are you all right?" the ocelot asked quietly, feeling Kier's paws shake as he tied the rest of his sash around Bayer's thigh. The fox shook his head.

"All these injuries and you're asking me if *I'm* all right," he said, with a slight laugh. "Arrogant sod. You've saved me every day since you came here, Bayer. It's my turn now."

The ocelot felt himself turning hot. "It's not like you haven't—"

Bayer jolted as a spasm of pain hit his leg. Kier flinched for a second, before further tightening the makeshift bandage. Bayer looked into the forest canopy above them.

"I just know this was one of your worst fears," he said softly.

Kier nodded. "Yeah, well, it's my turn to live them. You already had yours. I'm not going to pretend I'll come close to what you've been through, or what Faria's going through right now. I just... I want to protect the ones I love."

His eyes glistened in the dark; he glanced briefly up at Bayer, then looked back to the wound.

Bayer nodded, a tired smile on his face. "Yeah, I know."

The fox sat back on his knees for a second. He rubbed his eyes briefly, then looked around. "Did Aidan get away?"

Bayer nodded, stifling a groan as he shifted against the tree.

"Left around sunset. Hopefully ahead of a pursuit."

Kier fell silent and wrung his paws, then looked back over towards the city. "Get some sleep. I'll keep watch for you. We should head straight to Andarn in the morning. I just met one of Aidan's friends there; he could help us protect Faria, if we can find him again."

Bayer closed his eyes. "And if we don't?"

"We'll raise the alarm, and bring back an army."

Their night was uneasy. Twice Kier had to shield them from nearby Dhrakan pursuers, and project noises into the opposite directions to draw them away. In the smoky blue haze of the next morning, Bayer struggled to wake, but mustered enough strength to hold onto Kier as they began a slow, laboured trek north.

Some way into their journey, Kier's hearing piqued. His ears flicked, and he and Bayer crouched in the ferns.

"What?" Bayer hissed, reaching for his sword. Kier immediately swatted his paw away.

"Dhrakan campsite up ahead. Keep low. I'll see if I can take some provisions."

Bayer grabbed at his arm as he stood to leave, and shimmered briefly. Kier's camouflage rippled and faded as he crouched back down again.

"What is it?" he asked softly.

Bayer froze, a frown slowly forming on his face. "I... I can't help you."

Kier nodded. "I know. That's okay. Sometimes that's how it is."

"I'm—" Bayer began, his paw tightening on Kier's arm.

Kier gave him a warm smile, gently lifting his paw away. "Don't worry, you won't be down long enough to get comfortable with it. Just stay safe for me."

He stood, and vanished. Bayer watched a ripple of ferns trail away, darting behind trees, circling in a wide arc towards the campsite, which he could see if he knelt further down, and crawled forwards a little.

One of the Dhraka was poking last night's fire with a stick, its smouldering ashes producing a weak, skeletal column of smoke. Suddenly he looked to his right; two other Dhrakan heads popped up and their accompanying bodies marched into the overgrowth to investigate. The fireside Dhrakan kept his stick clutched in one hand while the other reached for a dagger. On the other side of the campsite, Bayer watched a satchel slowly, tentatively, lift from a tree branch and begin gliding back around towards him. It disappeared behind a tree, and for a few seconds no amount of squinting or listening could detect it.

Suddenly, a soft paw pressed at his shoulder. He flinched a little, and Kier's smiling face appeared next to him.

"That never gets old," Kier replied, affording himself a laugh at the ocelot's expense.

Bayer frowned, and jostled him slightly with his good hand. "What's that, a tactical joke?" He scowled, looking away, the fur in his cheeks flushing slightly.

Kier was already rooting through the satchel. "Look, last night was a lot; forgive me for trying to find some humour." He pulled out some dried meat, a waterskin, and some bandages and personal medical tools. His face lit up with relief.

"Okay, sit with me for a second and eat, then I'll change your bandages again."

The food was a huge bolster to their energy, and despite his non-verbal protests, Bayer was relieved for the fresh bandages. It didn't stop the pain, but not smelling crusty blood whilst having a degree of cleanliness was a relief he had not anticipated. They weren't safe yet; he was shaky, and sometimes deliriously tired, but gritted his teeth through all of their awkward movements to keep a steady, if slow, pace. They rested for another two nights before even reaching Midia, a free town about halfway between Xayall and Andarn. By the second day, Bayer was able to walk under his own support, albeit for short bursts. He took advantage of his energy when he could, eager not to overburden Kier.

When they reached the outskirts, they saw that some tents had been set up, and there were long lines leading into the city of folks waiting for food. Kier and Bayer approached from the forest line, anticipating Dhrakans, but so far couldn't see any.

A gruff voice barked to them from the nearby wall, underneath an awning that had been lashed to the wooden stayposts.

"Lugos! Kanjita!"

A wolf, the one whom Bayer knew well as the first Xayall guard he had ever spoken to, marched towards them. He was taller than them both, with a powerful frame and piercing yellow eyes. His name was Henryk, and his usually lustrous white fur was dashed with dirt, grass stains, and some dried blood. He had a nick in his right ear and his cloak had been torn.

"Henryk!" Kier replied. "How many Xayall folk are here?"

The wolf grimaced. "Not as many as there should be. We've been trying to coordinate everyone to get back, but nobody's reached Andarn yet." He leant in grimly. "They're looking for Faria and Aidan."

Kier's eyes widened; Bayer let out a distasteful grunt.

"But Aidan left, he should be almost at Skyria by now. Did… Faria escape? Have you seen anything of her?"

Henryk shook his head. "There was a battle here involving

someone escaping from Xayall."

Bayer and Kier exchanged worried looks. "We need to head to Andarn," Kier murmured.

Henryk nodded to Bayer. "Not with that wound, you won't. I'll take Kanjita off your paws, you can—"

The ocelot all but snarled at him, pulling himself a little away from Kier's support. "I can make it."

The wolf didn't even flinch. "You know your capability, then. But their forces are strong and they're controlling the roads; anyone they can identify as from Xayall gets either turned back or taken in. If you can get word up there, I'll keep everyone safe here till I hear from you again."

Kier nodded. "We'll bring back support, I promise."

Henryk whirled round and grabbed some supplies from the table under the awning, along with another bag which he carefully placed over Kier's shoulder. "Take this. If anyone can get there, it'll be you."

Kier nodded thankfully; Bayer gave him a curt, tired salute. They turned away, moving back into the treeline as quickly as Bayer's step would allow.

The ocelot gave Kier a chiding whisper. "So you can break the checkpoints and convince the Andarn army to support us, can you?"

Kier kept his focus ahead. "Aidan had a friend. He could help."

"So who is this 'friend' and what is his miracle power?" the ocelot asked in a low voice, with a healthy dose of scepticism.

Kier's voice rang in his ears even though his mouth hardly moved; pin-point voice projection being another of his skills. "You have to promise to believe me."

Bayer's tail flicked inquisitively.

"He's a gryphon," came the grave response.

Bayer let out a gruff sigh. "Of course he is."

"You *don't* believe me."

Bayer let out a dry snort. "Oh no, I believe *you*. I just don't believe Aidan. Of anyone to be hiding a friend of a presumed-extinct race, it'd be him. He has too many secrets, some of which I'm sure would have helped us if he hadn't kept them all this time."

"It's not like Empress Kaya didn't," Kier retorted. "We don't even know which of their secrets are his and which are hers."

"You've heard stories of how they met, right? You don't just appear in the desert. Nobody knows why he was out there."

Kier shrugged. "Maybe the same reason The Empress was in the desert herself? Studying? He could have been a fugitive, or a nomad."

Bayer held out his hands. "So *that's* the kind of person an Empress decides to marry, a potential criminal or nameless wanderer? This just doesn't ring true. There's something else behind it. We wouldn't be here right now if there wasn't something worth ransacking the city for."

Kier sighed. "Channelling Enyart fairly heavily there, Bayer."

Bayer flicked a tired, dismissive claw. "Someone should. He wouldn't have let the defences become so run down. Aidan got complacent. Once Kaya died he withdrew everything. He isn't a fighter, he doesn't know what a city needs to defend itself. I think he believes it just… happens."

Kier stopped; Bayer froze for a second as he heard a terse breath whistle from the fox's nose.

"It's not wrong to believe in better. Sometimes you have to set the example."

Bayer kicked a stone roughly into the trees, and immediately winced at the exertion of his ire. It bounced through a veil of leaves and hit a trunk with a satisfying 'crack'. "But if you do, especially if you're the first, you have to be ready to receive the brunt of what the world already throws at itself. It's not unexpected. Enyart would have known that."

Kier shot him an incredulous look. "Enyart left, Bayer. Over a year ago. Without a word. If he knew what Xayall was expecting to face then he should have stayed to protect Faria."

Bayer threw his paws out. "How can he be expected to submit to a duty he knows nothing about? His service was to Kaya. She died, his duty ended."

"So that's it?" Kier retorted. "She died, so her daughter is just a reluctant afterthought? Did he hate Aidan that much that he'd forsake Kaya's half of her?"

"Enyart wasn't a parent. He trained us to protect them."

"You don't have to be a parent to care," Kier scoffed. "He taught us to fight but didn't touch on the logistics of city protection aside from telling us 'soldiers often don't look past their commander. Be better'. He knew the city; faults, flaws, people, more than Aidan could. He should have guided him."

"So you're saying it's Enyart's fault we weren't prepared?" Bayer gave Kier a bitter look.

"How were we supposed to do that without him?" Kier snapped. "Aidan didn't want to put the city in danger, so he prioritised evacuation over military power and combat drills. He wasn't a strategist. You saw the civilians being defended, and look how many there are alive in Midia. You don't only protect someone by the point of a sword. You trust your heart when you're left to fend for yourself!"

Bayer rounded on him. "Is *his* heart the only one that matters? Do you know what it is to linger in a place that doesn't belong to you, and have your only tie to it disappear before your eyes, forever? You can't force anyone to stay if their heart has already left."

The fox sighed, and his shoulders shrank forwards a little. He fidgeted with his claws as if to construct a conversation between them, but then slid his right hand to his shoulder to pull at his coat. "I know he was sad. And there are plenty of reasons he could go, and many more why we lost the city. It's not as if he could have stopped the siege by himself, although he damn well would have tried. But he didn't have to disappear in the middle of the night. How is that supposed to instil confidence in anyone? How do you know whether you're doing enough to protect people when those around you keep vanishing? I mean… if you left… you'd at least want to know we were safe, right?"

Bayer grimaced as his thigh twisted. He grabbed it, digging his claws into the muscle to try and dispel the intensity on the crossbow wound. Kier paused and turned to tend to him, but Bayer waved him away.

"We could have been safe," the ocelot hissed through gritted teeth. "He believed in us, and we should have been better."

Kier's stare hardened. "We haven't failed yet. Even Enyart knew some battles were better flown from. We're alive, and we need to keep going."

Kier stopped, and knelt forwards, gesturing for Bayer to climb onto his back.

"Let me take you. I'm feeling up to a few bursts, if you are."

Bayer shook his head. "I can walk. I'm getting quicker."

"We're already behind. And we can't use the roads, according to Henryk."

"I know! I can do this."

Kier's ears flattened. "Don't hinder yourself with pride, Bayer. We need to move. If Faria's been captured, we have to rescue her. If not, we still need to get her safely to Aidan. Ignoring your wounds will only make them worse."

Bayer pulsed his fist.

"Don't lecture me, Kier." The ocelot closed his eyes and let out a curt sigh. "I don't need to be fixed."

"I'm just… trying to give you some rest."

"I don't want to rest!" he hissed. "I want to fight, to not be carried by you, to use my wretched arm again! I don't want to be beaten by something that I could have been prepared for if we had the truth about what we could face!"

"Yell at Aidan about it later. Right now, we have to move. If we raise the alarm in Andarn then maybe we can lift the siege. We might be the only ones on Eeres who can make it to save him and Faria."

Bayer winced. "I could… I could stay here, make my own way after you."

The fox shook his head. "You're coming with me. I'm not letting you deny yourself medical attention just to avoid Andarn."

Bayer stopped in his tracks, gnarling his claws. His tail swept stiffly back and forth. "I'd sooner limp back to Xayall and let the Dhraka take me. Besides, you can move faster, you know that."

They stood in silence for a few seconds, away from each other, faces marked with frustration.

"Do you really believe in yourself so little that being helped would destroy you?" Kier bristled. "You're not a lost kit anymore, Bayer."

The ocelot's hackles raised and his eyes flared. He clenched his good fist so hard that it shook. "Then stop *treating me like one!*"

The fox's head snapped round, met by the ferocious glare of his companion who had wheeled to confront him.

Bayer continued. "You think I'm not aware of what you or this city has done for me? Do you not think I live in debt to that every damn day? I could have done more! I *should* have done more! Now it *and* the place I most despise are being thrown in my face by someone who could have had the decency to tell me how dangerous it could be. Xayall did not deserve a war, but Aidan sure as hell threw us into one!"

His chest heaved. His teeth, wet with his fury, glinted in the light. Blood trickled from his shoulder. He smeared it roughly into his fur with a snort of derision.

Kier looked away. "I'm sorry, Bayer." He shifted nervously, pulling his jacket over his shoulders. "None of this is right. I know you're strong. You always have been. But… sometimes… we need more than strength. We need others. And… I need you."

Bayer let out a deep, reticent sigh.

"Fine." He clambered unsteadily onto Kier's back, wrapping his arms around his neck. "Just… go easy, all right?"

Kier nodded. He leaned forwards, and in a split second, they both vanished. The trees shook, and a soft, echoing boom rippled through the forest.

Chapter Eleven

The orrery's gentle rumble and occasional metallic groan echoed in the library. Kier gave a long, wistful sigh, looking over to the ocelot in his Kyrryk robes, wresting himself away from his memories.

"How long will you be staying in Xayall?"

Bayer flinched at the broken quiet. He shook the fog from his head. "Not long. Raede has some ex-Shadow's Claw comrades that she'll be rallying to our side, ones who knew and were trusted by the Kyrryk locals, and Jed has given us a detachment of Sinédrion soldiers to help get Andarn clear and make actual reparations to the sovereign."

Kier frowned. "That… won't be easy."

"Not with the few warlords still kicking around who'll want their lands back. One of the problems the sovereign had in the first place was lack of unification. It's why they were never able to properly secure a Senate seat. I'm hoping to change that, so we can properly help find a place in the world."

"Will you fight them?"

Bayer steeled his eyes. "Hopefully not. I'm not making bargains with despots, but they have as much right to reclaim independence as any other citizen. If they are at least in agreement with that, they may be able to help bring more people together."

Kier folded his arms, and leant on his knees. "And what about you? Once it's rebuilt, will you stay as Representative?"

Bayer fell quiet for a second. "It'll depend. I'm not expecting it to be easy. I may find someone much more suited to it than I am, and hand it to them. So I don't know. I'll have to see what the future looks like when I get there."

Kier shot him a wry smile. "There's your stone in the water for you. Of the events around you, and separate from them."

Bayer returned him with a blank look.

"I don't know whether I'm impressed or annoyed."

Kier laughed. "I guess we take after him in different ways, then." He stood up, and offered his paw to Bayer. "Come on, the fishery opened up a few weeks back; I've missed eating there with you."

Bayer raised his remaining left arm, and felt the comforting squeeze of his fox's paw. He hauled himself up, and together they marched towards the exit.

"Sounds perfect."

RUIN'S WAKE

Chapter One

The sky was gone.

Columns of dust billowed up to a darkening, spreading ceiling of rolling grey that entombed the stars. Streaks of blue lightning shattered the air, climbed the choking pillars from the ground and forked out with screams of light, lashing at the golden ship that desperately rode the storm. Rocks crashed into the deck, thrown from Nazreal's fissure. Dust spattered the Coriolis' bridge's windows in a thick, deadly film that slowly trapped them in even closer, more ominous darkness.

Osiris grasped the helm rigidly, fighting against the impacts that rocked and pulled at it. "Dhalen!" he yelled into the communications funnel to his right. "Dhalen, up here now!"

Within seconds the grey wolf appeared, steadying himself against the wall.

"The windows!"

Dhalen looked around for a second, and seeing no means of protecting the panes from encroaching dust, slammed his fist through them in turn. Glass and debris exploded mostly inwards as a suffocating wind flooded the room from the force of the maelstrom. Osiris rocked at the pressure change, bracing himself over the wheel as it shuddered in his claws. His wings were spread and his tail flared, keeping his balance as the entire ship shuddered from the colossal buffeting from all around them.

He could barely breathe, but he could see. That would be enough for now. The glowing, undulating pillars of debris were clearer, as was the front of the ship.

Someone was on the deck.

A figure pulled their way along the railing.

Elysser had their arm locked around the Coriolis' guardrail. They gripped it tightly until the ship steadied, flinching, ducking where they could under the stones and flecks of metal thrown by the vicious, explosive air currents. Debris thundered onto the deck around them, and ricocheted off the hull. One grazed their left paw; they winced through gritted teeth and chanced a quick look as they felt blood seep into their gloves. A gash beneath the fabric, but not terrible.

They could barely hear through the relentless thrashing of the resonance squall, fur caked with dust and flecked with blood from flying stone. They tucked their muzzle down into their chest, breathing through any available break in the vortices to keep themself alive. Blue sparks fizzed and danced from their axe, their claws, their ear tips. The resonance blasts illuminated the dust-bombed sky through their eyelids, and every flash brought renewed scale to the disaster they were riding. If they looked down, they saw through the ship to the fractured land below, and the juddering waves of resonance that rippled in violent aurorae; a terrifying, infinite whirlpool of light and blue fire. At times they sounded like deafening explosions; others, like screams.

They opened their eyes briefly to gain a sense of direction. Over the edge of the deck was nothing but rumbling dust climbing higher, threatening to engulf them all. Ahead was the same. This would end everything.

Bracing themself against the wind, they kept edging towards the bowsprit, a trail of bloody, glowing paw marks in their wake.

They had to get there.

They had to stop the ship from dying.

For all they knew, the Coriolis was all that would be left of the world.

Osiris watched in desperation as Elysser reached the bow, knowing a single impact from a boulder could annihilate them or bring the ship down… if the growing crust of resonance debris didn't stall the engines first, which roared intensely beneath the lowest deck. By the miracle of their design and construction they were steady so far, but every impact sent cold waves down Osiris' dorsal feathers, and every now and again they hit a surge of energy that he had to ride the Coriolis through or over.

Dhalen plunged down the bridge's steps in a rush to support Elysser. The door to the deck creaked and rattled, bowing inwards, pressing against the metal bars that held it in place. The handle was all but immovable. With a burst of strength he wrenched the gilded hatch open; immediately the wind threw the full weight of it against his right shoulder and knocked him into the wall.

He lay for a few seconds, the roar of the wind swirling through the room, flooding his ears. Shakily, he picked himself up and ran his paw over where he'd been hit.

A few cracked bones perhaps. Maybe a muscle tear. Nothing permanent.

With a growl he sheltered beside the door, slipping his paw under his armour. His eyes flashed purple and the bones snapped and knitted back into place, his arm took more of its usual shape.

Good enough for now. Fine tuning would wait.

Elysser was behind the Coriolis' prow. They drew the crystal blade of their axe along the deck in front of them and a metal frame spun around their legs, back and waist, locking them in place like a figurehead. The ship rumbled and swayed, crushing the metal into their sides and stomach, but now their hands were free. The blue gem mounted at the centre of their buckler shimmered and spat like embers as the charged air blew over it. With a deliberate, hard tap to the metal, Elysser cast a bolt of blue energy along the bowsprit, wrapping it in a web of crystal with a spiralling shard at the tip. As the Coriolis continued its shuddering flight, sparks of blue danced over the crystal spire at its head; slowly at first, then quickly, building to a pulsing, blinding mass of blue.

Punching their buckler to the metal a second time, Elysser swept their axe to the right and the gyrating crystal cone launched from the bowsprit, curving through the air to one of the dust columns by the starboard of the ship. It pierced the veil, fingers of resonance energy drawing it inwards like prehensile vines. A split second later, a flash of blue burst at its centre and the dust collapsed inwards, sucked from all sides, condensing the pillar to a rapidly-growing rock that plunged to the cloud below. As it fell it collected even more; a rumbling, swelling vortex of debris.

Elysser turned their attention back to the bowsprit again.

More crystal had gathered, making the next charge quicker. They launched another missile to the left and eliminated an eruption of ash and rock, leaving an ionising, receding whirlpool in its wake below them. Again and again bolts of blue shrieked into the clouds as they tried desperately to find clearer sky once more, and free it from such brutal, electric suffocation.

Dhalen paced behind Elysser, watching above for debris and slamming them away with his swords or shielding the fennec from ones they couldn't duck underneath. His steel chipped against the hot, dense stone from deep under Eeres' surface. If all he had to replace after this were two blades, it would be a grateful sacrifice.

After an exhausting, interminable salvo that lasted hours, or longer perhaps, the resonance energy had mostly dissipated, leaving them drifting in a smog of sand and dust. They could no longer see the energy spikes nor hear the explosions; in their place was a steady rumble and quiet crackle of ambient static. Once Elysser could no longer draw enough crystal residue to form their ionising missiles, they forged a new formation at the tip of the bowsprit that channelled the air around it like a blade through water, cutting space for the Coriolis to sail through. It was a paltry accent to their terrible visibility, but it filtered particles away from the engines and guaranteed them an extra degree of stability.

The swamping, grey darkness made it impossible to tell if it was night or day; the combined exhaustion of each passenger muddied any estimations. All were fatigued, from fear and exertion, and the growing apprehension at what would be left when they returned to Eeres' surface.

Elysser released themself from the brace, paws shaking and twitching so much that they lost grip on their buckler and it clattered away. Dhalen picked it up and lent out his arm for them to balance on. They took it gratefully, jaw tight, treading with stiff, aching steps. Their fur stood on end, their nose trickled blood.

"It's okay. You can rest." Dhalen said softly.

"I can do more," they scorned themself. "I blocked the worst of the eruptions, but I don't know where we are, and the sun…"

Dhalen's ears flicked. "The sun will still be there. It's up to us to find it," he replied, possibly as much to himself as to them. "You aren't doing that alone. We can breathe, and that's enough for now."

The gaze in their eyes, through their tiredness, suggested to Dhalen that nothing would be enough at any point until they discovered what happened to Nazreal, and Aidan. He took them up to Osiris, who looked just as haggard, still clutching the wheel.

"Thank you, Elysser," he said flatly. The fennec raised a tired arm in appreciation, then sank to the floor of the bridge. The wind whistled through the broken windows, and the stony skies rolled overhead.

Even with the prow-blade dispelling the currents of debris ahead of the ship, the air was thick and had a sharp, metallic scent. Dust collected everywhere, forcing many to breathe into their clothing. The three-to-four-hundred huddled Nazreal refugees below worked together to nurse injuries from the hurried launch and battered flight. Virvel, Nidhimes, and Elysser inspected the hull and engines as best they could with guidance from Teratai, and managed to free the important sections from a solid coating of dust. The rest would need to wait until the Coriolis could land. And they would need to land soon, whether there was light or not. Supplies began low from the outset, having not anticipated the desperate flight they'd had to maintain.

About a day later soft glows were spotted above the drifting mass. Osiris was loath to ascend further in case the ship or its passengers weren't able to withstand the change in pressure, but it gave them hope that there was an end to the thick haze somewhere.

After another day, they broke through. Light returned to the world, and the Coriolis, beaten and tarnished, soared high over the murky ocean's surface. A collective wave of relief washed over all aboard. Almost immediately Osiris ordered a descent, taking them down urgently, without disintegrating the Coriolis on the waves. Teratai was among the mechanism on the lowest deck, constantly patrolling her way from one end to the other for any signs of failure.

She eased power to the engines, allowing them to descend slowly, aiding Osiris in his control. Just before hitting the water he cut the engines directly and angled the ship upwards to land the keel almost square in the water. It created a violent shudder that sent everyone reeling backwards, but the ship righted quickly. Immediately Teratai set about turning off any and all systems possible to let them rest. Once all had settled, those few passengers with nautical ability gathered on deck to assist with preparing the ship for seafaring. The first concern was the integrity of the hull. Dust had to be cleared, and impacts checked for cracks and leaks. Osiris, and a trio of otters, dove under the water to make assessments; Teratai and Elysser gave advice on what needed fixing.

The ship groaned and creaked as it drifted in the waves, at the mercy of the horizon's infinite expanse. With the engines sealed and secured, the arduous task of rigging began. A hazy sun and pockets of overhead dust made it even more exhausting, but after a time the ship was ready, and when the next sun broke away a grudging night of rest, Osiris set the ship into motion towards Skyria.

Or, where it should have been.

The longer the journey went, the more tense Osiris became. Night fell, day broke, and still no sign of the island. The gryphon strode back and forth between the deck and the navigation room atop the sterncastle, growling wildly, compass swinging from his wrist.

"This is *not* where we are supposed to *be*," he cursed, slamming the dial onto the control console, glaring vengefully at the maps strewn across the table.

Elysser ran their paws over the compass' casing, a flash of blue restoring its fractured glass and dented metal. They gently studied the quivering needle. "Did our instruments break?"

Osiris exhaled sharply through his nose. "They've been checked. Repeatedly." He darted from the wheel and jabbed a claw into the waters northwest of Skyria. "At our speed and bearing, we should be here. We should have been *past* here. Something is very wrong."

Elysser looked warily out over the deck. Nothing but infinite ocean and a hoarse, cold wind.

Osiris handed control of the Coriolis to Teratai and stormed to his cabin. With a furious clatter he cast his armour away and swept himself into a robe of leather and cloth. When he punched open his door again his wings were already arching, ready to take flight. Elysser followed, but he pierced them with a stern look before they even got to speak.

"It will be quicker if I go alone."

"No, Osiris. Look." They cradled the compass in their

paw. The needle tilted and shimmered, veering eccentrically.

"Hold it steady," he muttered.

They gave him a derisive glare. "I *am*. Look."

They rested it on the floor. When it lay still, nothing changed, but the slightest movement of their paw, by nudging a corner or sliding it laterally, caused the compass to pivot to the right, and every movement changed its course in a relative direction.

"It's no longer attracted to a single direction, but to its own movement," Elysser observed. "If everything on the ship has been self-magnetised, if we thought we were going in the right direction, nothing would have appeared wrong."

His beak gnarled to a frown. "I at least have a memory for how far we should be. There has been no land nor any sign of it. We cannot continue with this regardless."

He threw open his wings. "I will return." A second later he launched into the sky, the downburst from his ascent billowing dust from the deck. Elysser watched Osiris leave, then immediately returned to Dhalen and Teratai.

"Do we have nets?"

Teratai flicked her claw. "There's sailcloth, some rigging rope. We can make something."

Elysser nodded. "That'll do. Dhalen, we're going fishing."

Between them, and with the help of Virvel and a number of Nazreal's escapees, they fashioned a net large enough to trawl under the ship, and began preparing the kitchen to feed those who could do without the diminishing herbivorous supplies in the hold. Over time they refined the net to catch more, and while it wasn't a feast, it sustained them, just.

There were still losses. A few passengers died – one of heart failure, more from sickness and lung congestion. Many had lasting, hacking coughs from dust inhalation. There were physicians enough to help, but few resources to do so effectively. The resonance crystals and tinctures many had grabbed on their panicked evacuation were often part of bigger systems and needed apparatus to work; by themselves they were largely ineffective. Dhalen had learnt most of Oakhe's abilities to heal others before he passed, but lacked his delicate depth of knowledge, but any Kitaia resonators using too much of their energy exhausted their bodies and risked further hunger. All on board were operating on what little would keep them alive, and trying to save the rest for the uncertain journey ahead.

A week later, Osiris returned. He landed on the deck with a deafening crash and marched up the sterncastle steps. Teratai looked to him gravely, as his face was ashen.

"Skyria still stands," he said. "But…" He unfurled a crumpled parchment, on which two large shapes had been hurriedly inked, and handed it to her.

She glared at it, her feathers flaring in alarm. "I… what is this?"

"This," he rumbled, "is our world now. Two continents, and a vast ocean at their centre."

Elysser strode to the parchment, their gaze darting from one side to the other trying to ascertain the orientation of the split. Osiris tapped his claw to the ocean west and slightly south from the crest of the right-hand continent. "We are here." He dragged his claw across the top of the continent to a series of splotches to its north-east. "Skyria is here."

Teratai's crest rose. "And Arete is here, correct?" she intoned as she pointed to the east central coastline where the gryphons' city used to stand, a gravity in her voice.

Osiris' beak tightened.

"It is… not."

From a leather satchel across his waist he pulled a small, golden finial, in the shape of a wing, formerly mounted on the roof corners above the central tower's beacon.

"Nothing stands. No-one remains. Not claw nor feather."

Teratai stared solemnly at the page for a while, then let Elysser take it into their paws. They twisted the two continents together, trying to ascertain it as a whole again.

It didn't fit. No matter how they tried to align them, a massive section between them was missing.

"Osiris," they said quietly. "Where… where would Nazreal have been?"

They held the folded sheet before him, and he, with a quiet sigh, pointed at the void between the two, now the centre of the deep, vast ocean. The fennec's fur bristled, tail stiff and quivering, their eyes deep and wide with a distal, consuming coldness.

They stared for a few seconds, then looked out to the horizon again. "What's our bearing?"

Osiris gently placed the finial away, and began assessing the chart.

Chapter Two

Skyria, the island of megalithic trees, was waiting for them. Joyous solemnity welcomed them; a heartbreaking reunion of normality in a world of infinite uncertainty. The relief was intense, the anticipation alone enough to bring weary passengers to tears, some of whom were now finally returning home and anxious to anchor themselves in familiar spaces.

But the world was still forever changed.

As soon as the giant trees were visible on the horizon, Osiris spurred the Coriolis into action, having everyone prepare the injured for an immediate transfer to land. Weaving the golden ship through rippling shallows was an arduous process, a newly-created obstacle by the seismic upheaval making what should have been a simple route painfully circuitous. Once they finally reached the dock, teams of creatures were on the quayside ready to shift everyone into hospitals, beds, and residences – wherever they needed to be. Between dehydration, exposure, malnourishment, inhalation and other injuries, everyone had an affliction of some sort and the few Kitaian resonators were exhausted, or too hurt themselves to do more. In all about thirty died between Nazreal and Skyria, most of whom had to be buried at sea to prevent further infection to the remaining survivors.

The city of trees was in a disorientated, confused state, but seemed to be pulling out of its shock to tend to the needy and make emergency repairs. The focal point of their own distress, and many of the domestic injuries, were the city's towering central trees, some a couple of hundred feet thick, and thousands of feet tall. These sentinel arbours were the pride and heart of the island city, yet now looked to have been torn through by a massive whirlwind. They were missing boughs, stripped of bark, and, most dangerously, some were no longer as directly skyward as they should be, instead listing precariously, threatening to dash themselves across the ground in a devastating fall.

Virvel leapt onto the dock, bypassing the busy gangway, and craned her head back to see the disjointed, ruptured skyline of her city. The gilder's ears flattened immediately and her fur stood on end.

"Oh, my sad, beautiful logs. Look at the state of you."

She chewed on one of her claws while Elysser led Nidhimes next to her. "I don't know if we can save them, Nid."

The slothbear bashed his knuckles together. "W… well, maybe we could… there has… there should be something… if there is time…"

"You are a treasure, Nid," Virvel sighed, "but this is… beyond anything that should have ever happened."

He shrugged, performatively optimistic. "W-we've only just arrived, so we… we need to know what's damaged for sure."

She sucked through her teeth. "Okay. Let's get this done."

She immediately strode into the crowd, hunting for those overseeing the recovery. Elysser dragged Nidhimes in pursuit, trying to keep up but distracted with any flash of orange fur that caught their eye.

They knew he wouldn't be here.

He *couldn't* be here.

But yet…

They slipped to a halt just behind Virvel, who'd stopped at a line of soldiers about halfway down the quay. Nidhimes bumped Elysser, and between them they stumbled past the Skyrian Councillor to stand awkwardly beside her. Nidhimes immediately shied away behind the resonator fennec.

A red panda was addressing Virvel. "…but the roots are strong for now and the arborists have stabilised the upper areas. Flooding is our major concern – it'll continue to erode the foundations. We are trying to get everyone safely away to set things right before the trunk completely snaps."

"Where are you sending them?"

"We have a line of lifeboats on the north quay, and have surveyed the archipelago for a temporary camp. Our supplies should hold; we rescued what we could before they were flooded too."

Virvel raked her claws through her muzzle fur. "How much of our resonance systems are in place?"

"The chamber's flooded, possibly collapsed. We can't tell what nutrient channels are still viable, nor the lifeline to the archipelago. All we can tell is where the surface splits are, for some indication of the damage underneath."

She held a low, growling sigh in her throat. "Do we have anything to counterbalance the trees?"

The panda scratched his ears. "We've lashed the roots and have tethers running to the other boughs so for now we're stable. We can't wait, though – if this decides to fall, now or later, nothing will stop it and we can't risk bringing others down. We need to get this standing, stable, and set as soon as possible."

Virvel winced. "This is a nightmare." She glanced to Elysser, who was analysing the trees, and glancing down to the stone floor. They flexed their paws, as if trying to rid themself of paresthesia. They let out a long, controlled exhalation through their nose, and steeled their gaze on the unsteady, enormous forest.

"I can help."

Virvel was often brusque and blunt with anyone but Nidhimes, but her ears flattened with concern at the fox's volition. "You can rest first, Elysser. The trees will stand for a day yet."

"No." They were steadfast. Their paw trembled against the stone. "It has to be now."

Nidhimes tugged on their sleeve. "Th-the chamber may help, if-if it's accessible, that is…"

Their tail flicked apprehensively. "Then I'll fix that first."

They set ahead towards the tree, whose leaves were still gently shedding in the high breeze.

Picking through the displaced residents and upheaved root networks was an athletic process. The massive subterranean weave of wood had kept things from shifting previously, but when the trees began moving, ripples and distortions undulated through the ground and pushed the stone into treacherous ridges and troughs. Uplifted roots and fallen branches created traps yearning for unsteady paws to disappear into and bring their owners crashing to the ground. The biggest movements had caused channels of seawater to flow into the city which had to be traversed or skirted around. Elysser, Virvel and Nidhimes were forced into a harried lateral clamber to avoid the chaotic flow of soldiers and citizens to reach the resonance chamber's entrance.

Dhalen deposited his final injured passenger into the care of Skyria's waiting physician team and sped after them. Physical prowess boosted by a resonance ability to hone his body at immediate necessity meant he could bound over uneven ridges like a stone skipping over water; he caught up to them as they arrived at the base of one the enormous central trees at the heart of the city. Water rippled around their paws, a thin sheen covering the street's broken stone. The gigantic conifer teemed with creatures clambering to counterweight it, secure it, remove vital supplies and injured occupants. Steady, cautious groups navigated the twisted bridges to other trees, and deft climbers surveyed the best areas to secure ropes that, for the sheer size of the tree, would do nothing more than snap like a hair around a brick.

Virvel scanned the tree up and down. Most of the boughs were intact, but there were splits and tears in the bark where the great tree had contorted and the ground twisted in different directions. Several large chambers within the wood were visible through the fissures. She let out a low, rising groan as she saw exposed roots rising with the swell of waves breaching the previously-impermeable barrier around the city's central landmass, and tried to ignore the frequent snaps and creaks from the canopy above them.

Its progression downward had been slowed by the entwining of its base with root networks from neighbouring towers, and by the quick emergency work of the resonator teams who had prepared for certain amounts of movement. With the sheer strength of the seismic upheaval, however, they had untangled and loosened their support. Its weight was pushing upwards against its almost-as-gargantuan neighbours, and threatened to unsteady them if it tilted further. This single tree could destroy the security of two or three more. Even moving only a few degrees was enough to threaten the whole thing with collapse.

Dhalen's ears pinned back. "That's… a big tree."

"Yep," Virvel muttered. "And a big problem."

The fennec glanced around. "So… where's the chamber?"

Nidhimes' claw-bashing had reached audibly discomforting levels. He gave a brief, nervous motion towards an arch-shaped root, underneath which was a pool rippling with the tree's vibrations.

They blinked. "I don't see."

Virvel picked up a small rock and threw it into the murk. It disappeared with a dull 'plop', immediately demonstrating that the water pool was once, in fact, something far deeper.

"That's the stairway."

Elysser grimaced, but slowly unravelled their axe and buckler and strode towards the water. As soon as their paws touched the wet stone their blades glowed, and the water ahead began to part, revealing the crumpled stairway. They ducked down to ascertain the height of the tunnel, and continued, pushing the water ahead of them. Dhalen, Virvel and Nidhimes followed gingerly behind.

The stairway had survived, in a way. What had once been a neatly hewn, wide spiral around its circumference was contorted and strangled – several sections required weaving between in single file, sometimes flat against the sides, they had warped so badly. Elysser only spent energy on the water right now, to make sure nothing would collapse and drown them all.

Soon they were met by a wall of debris-darkened water. The fox paused for a second while holding their axe blade still, then pushed their buckler tip to it in syncope. A soft blue hue rose in the darkness, and with a further push forward, the water oscillated back, vanishing into the cracks in the walls and ceiling, which Elysser quickly sealed with a deft flash of their axe blade.

Virvel cursed under her breath as the state of the chamber came into full view. Its once high, domed ceiling was almost obscured by one of the walls, bulging and fissured, and the crystal array once serenely above them was not only displaced but half broken on the floor. It also looked to have been intensely depleted, its once-sharp edges and needle-like points melted like candle wax close to where they had been faceted into their base.

She gave one a tap with her hindpaw. It teetered slightly, glistening with watery residue. "Without them Skyria would have been completely lost. They did what they needed, but… there's not much left."

Elysser stifled a rush of breath to their chest, trying not to think about what that meant for Aidan.

They studied what remained of the walls, the vibrations of the sea rumbling just past its darkened scars. The entire chamber had been crushed in several directions. The floor looked like it had been sucked up in some kind of energy vacuum created by the crystals trying to rebuff the massive seismic waves thundering through the island.

"Can we save anything?" the glider asked, not harshly, but with pointed urgency. "Or is this a lost cause?"

Elysser touched their paw to the wall. Underneath the slime and sand, they felt the faint glow of resonance in its surface. Perhaps even annealed slightly, by the power that coursed through them.

"Nothing's lost till we give it up," they said quietly, gripping their axe. They turned, with a soft determination. "I can remake the chamber. As I do, I'll try to push the tree back into position. Make sure the arborists and ready to set it, as I'll seal the rock. I'll need you to tell me when it's correct so I can solidify the rock around it."

Virvel nodded, and clicked her claws to Nidhimes, who had been scribbling notes into a small parchment pad by the entrance since they got down there.

"Know what you're doing?"

The slothbear gave a vague twitch of affirmation, still scribbling. "I see where the displacement occurred, s-so that should help Elysser. The nutrient veins and support struts will be easy once everything is back as it should be. After that, the tree's health can be better ascertained for trauma care, but I-I already have a base assessment for that."

Dhalen blinked at Nidhime's efficiency. "Impressive."

Virvel stroked a claw over the uneven chamber wall. "Nid is an incredible asset to us, a compassionate genius. You'll get to see all of it now we're back home and away from Dhrakan conflict."

The wolf smiled. "I have no doubt." He glanced to Elysser as Virvel and Nidhimes began bashfully ascending. "So you can focus on everything up there, I'll act as an ear for your command. Let us know when you're ready."

The glider raced up the steps, Nidhimes close behind. "Listen up!" she cried, the sound of her voice trailing off as she strode. "Nid has—"

Dhalen turned to Elysser, who was standing next to the shattered column of fallen crystal. Aside from the low sensation of waves, more a feeling than a sound, the room lay in a cold stillness, a silence pregnant with unspoken litanies of grief and exhaustion.

"You can stop if you need to," he said softly. "The world can wait a few moments."

In response, Elysser strode to a wall and held their shield

up to meld a crack that needed strengthening. "To do what?"

"Nothing," He responded. "To let the weight of the event fall from your shoulders so you know who you are beneath it."

"I know who I am, Dhalen. I have to finish this."

The wolf frowned. "If the world is truly to be saved, there is no *finish*. You know that's not how this works. That's why you need to give yourself time. It is not a weakness to be tired, or mourning."

For a second, their teeth flashed. "So you've left behind Oakhe's death already?"

He flinched slightly, touching his partner's headband that hung around his neck. "It's not about that. Have you even slept?"

They looked away.

"You are vital." Dhalen continued, looking to the dark and misshapen ceiling. "It's because of our need for you that you have to pace your burdens. You are not alone."

They paused, their resonance tool tightly in their grasp. Their tail was rigid, fur rippling. "I *am* alone, Dhalen. For a time I wasn't, and it… it was wonderful. But now…" They thrashed the air with their axe ruefully, gesturing wildly to the empty space. "Look at all this. There's so much to fix. Every second wasted is another second closer to everything disappearing again."

The walls pushed out and flattened to their original curvature, stretching and connecting at the ceiling with a powerful quake as a cascade of geometric channels snaked up and across them. Dhalen made a nimble jump to a slab of rubble and perched there, watching Elysser with gentle concern.

"You are finite. Our future doesn't have to be, and much of that will depend on how you treat yourself now."

Their ears flicked irritably. "You're different. You get to heal whenever you want."

The wolf stepped forwards, his voice a warning growl. "Don't tell me I don't still ache. Don't tell me I'm less damaged because I don't have physical injury. Don't tell me for one second I wouldn't change the world to bring him back to me."

They looked away, arms shaking. Dhalen rubbed his muzzle and sighed. "A body is not a soul. A heart is more than blood and muscle. If you consider yourself nothing more than a utility then you will consume yourself quicker than you realise."

"I'm sorry, Dhalen," they said quietly. "That was unfair of me. You and Oakhe deserved far better, and I... I'm sorry I can't bring us all back."

He nodded. "There's no end to what I would do if I had the ability. The world was ours for a long time, and we kept finding more of it. But... even I am finding my limits in this."

Elysser regarded him for a moment, the sheen and dents in his armour, the metallic spines in his coat, and the headband of his soulmate at his chest. "Does your resonance hurt, even to heal yourself?"

Dhalen scrunched their muzzle. "To a degree. It takes a different toll, perhaps, an exchange or dissipation of pain. That's why I can tell you from experience that the best conduct you can give to yourself on a long journey is a slow, nurturing change. Trying to do it all at once will destroy you. When you do that..." He held his hand tenderly to his chest. "...you can change an entire body."

Elysser saw rare, tender honesty that was reserved for few in the first place, and often now hidden under solemnity at his loss, and gave him a warm smile. "That sounds like a great transformation."

Dhalen smiled back. "It was, and still is. I hope we may all find ourselves, and each other in likeness, in due course."

They stood in silence for a time, Dhalen's claw drifting back up to the headband around his neck, and Elysser playing the axe grip over in their paws.

"Do you think he's still alive?" the wolf asked quietly.

Elysser's whiskers sagged, and they barely managed a shrug. The cold dread of defeat seemed to suck the energy from them in moments. "I don't know," they whispered. "We don't know where Nazreal went. We don't know if he went with it, if he's waiting for us to find him…" They cast Dhalen back a tired, glistening stare. "Until I find out, I can't let go."

Dhalen bowed his head quietly, and sat back down. "Whatever you need, Elysser, in any time you seek. I'll be here."

They nodded thankfully, then moved to the centre of the chamber and whirled their axe into the ground before them. Shimmering blue spiralled along the floor and up into the misshapen walls, wrapping over the stone and roots. They raised their arms and the room shuddered and stretched. Rocks unravelled and lifted under the enormous roots overhead, pushing upwards. At the same time, they saw the roots flex and straighten, as the plant resonators above took their chance to wind the roots back into place and realign the tree's body. The whole room shifted, tilted, and above them rumbled and shook.

Dhalen pricked his ears, hearing cries of amazement outside even from this far beneath. The resonance chamber swelled, its ceiling domed, walls sprouting buttresses that crept from the edges and pushed to the apex, each surface gleaming with crystal filigree. As the room hit its original size, Elysser's eyes flashed brightly.

A wave of blue cascaded from their axe and glided across the floor, sweeping into the resonance veins. The strange, structural roars and cracks of fusing rocks flooded the room, growing more distant as Elysser's control spread to the further reaches of the island, eventually fading into the distal hum of the room's ambience in harmony against the waves.

The fennec exhaled shakily and tucked their axe into their sash once more.

"Is it done?"

Dhalen leapt up the first few steps; Nidhimes was already descending, with congratulatory glee alight in his step.

"Safe! Safe safe safe!" he chimed.

Elysser breathed a tired smile, stroking back their ears. "Good. What next?"

Chapter Three

Nazreal's evacuees remained in Skyria for some time, strengthening the trees and sea defences, creating underwater buffers and high sea walls that would prevent strong waves from flooding the island. Elysser was not the only resonator, but was one of the few with completely honed powers, and with such an affinity that large-scale tasks could be completed quickly. They were an invaluable resource, which they took great, almost obsessive focus to. They were eager to help, but held just as much anticipation to see if their lands still existed in any familiar way on the other side of the now-divided continents.

Most weren't hopeful. Arete's destruction was a sobering fog over the future, even if their abstention from the world aside from anything resonance-related had painted them as a somewhat predatory benefactor.

"A fitting hubris for Arete's old guard," Osiris said bitterly, standing on the bridge of the Coriolis. "That their first venture into global 'reconciliation' was only a means to perpetuate their own traditions and cloak it in the guise of generosity. We refused to learn, change, or listen, and sequestered ourselves into haughty destruction at the mildest inconvenience."

Elysser rolled a small golden bead over in their paw. "I don't believe anyone deserves such a fate."

The golden gryphon flicked a claw over the map. "I had hoped there would be time to overcome our arrogance. The world… or at least, our eternal grudges and the mistakes we harboured for generations, decided otherwise."

The gold bead came to a rest at the centre of Elysser's pawpad. They stared at the reflections shimmering on its smooth surface. "You sound like you're resigned to die in the same way."

A rustle of feathers indicated Osiris' turn to the map, and he said nothing further. Elysser waited by the console for some time, but the captain had thrown himself into the detailing of new maps, and a plan for a voyage back across the new expanse of ocean, to the continent they had seemingly escaped from.

They quietly left him to his embittered silence and crawled to their cabin to sleep. It was the first time in almost two days they had allowed themself rest, struck with a similar sense of fervid hollow-with-anger duty that Osiris was in the throes of. Elysser still held an ache of kindness, and a need to see and enkindle hope in the world despite their pain, but they wondered if Osiris was too embattled to see anything but loss, and now view the world as an obstacle to pass and not a place to nurture.

Dreams of lightning lashed their thoughts. Burning electric pulses cast into infinite darkness, each bursting with a scream that bored through their head. They were drifting, searching at the heart of a dark, crying world for another soul in the void.

Something came to rest under their feet. A dark, dusty

surface which shifted with unbalanced energy and roiled at the touch of their paw like a snake rearing back for a fearful defence.

They focused on the surface beneath the dust, a disorientating swirl of everlasting black and dancing blue sparks. Beneath was a familiar yet tarnished stone. As they drew their eyes across it to the horizon ahead, it fell into view.

Nazreal. Ahead, the Tor rumbled in a storm of resonance fog, its stone tines surging with a violent blue glow. Its sharp edges disintegrated slowly, flaking off and ascending to the dark like charcoal from burning timber.

At the tower's base lay the heart of the storm, still beating strong, throwing the space around it into a constant scream of violent energy.

They had to find it.

As they stepped forwards, the ground beneath their paw opened to a deep chasm, and they fell.

Elysser woke with a sharp breath but their eyes refused to match their sudden wake. Their body ached, raw and hollow, trying to rouse from its deep well of empty rest. They sat up unsteadily with a shiver as the chill shadow of their dream echoed into their waking torpor. Slowly their eyes acquiesced to permit sight of the room around them, and light and stability pierced their vision, eventually banishing the dizzy fog.

Keeping as much focus as they could on the floor, they swivelled their legs round to slip from the bed and stretched out a few knots in their shoulders. A wide yawn from a voice that wasn't theirs resounded, and eventually they came to see another presence in the room.

Teratai flipped idly through a journal. She gave a quick, bright glance to Elysser and kept scanning the pages.

Elysser pulled the sheets over them and reached for their robe, furling it under the covers like a snail eating a leaf.

"Morning, Teratai," they said, in a cautious murmur.

"Mmm, hello," she replied. "Sleep well?"

"I don't know yet. I don't think so. It's… weird."

"That's fair, it has been over three days."

Elysser blinked. "What?"

Teratai couldn't resist a smile. "You were asleep for three days."

Elysser looked around hurriedly for a second, then stopped, their eyes fixed on a pillow next to them.

Before Teratai could respond, her world became dark and padded as the pillow landed squarely on her beak. After it dropped, Elysser was staring vengefully at her, fur bristling.

"Look, you gilded chicken, you can't do that to me right now."

The gryphon's smile broke into a laugh. "Listen, nothing will have fallen apart even if you did. Nobody would blame you." She flipped another page. "But fair enough."

There was a long pause as she stroked the edges of the journal with her claw to flick the pages forward.

"It was two days."

Elysser gave a low grumble and disappeared under the sheets to wrestle into their robe, rolling around like a tumbleweed into nearby furniture in an effort to remain concealed from Teratai. A few minutes of muffled grunting and yelps of pain after colliding with the wall several times, they freed themself of their puffy veil by rolling into an unsteady stand, fur ragged and rustled, trying to untuck their tail from the leg of their robes.

Teratai shook her head. "You are hilarious."

Elysser pulled their belt tight with a snap of the fabric, then reached for their arm sleeves, which appeared to have been laid neatly over the back of a chair by Teratai during their indeterminate period of slumber. "No, you are. What are you searching for, by the way? Can I help?"

Teratai clicked her beak thoughtfully. "I am looking for Aidan's metallurgy work. Before leaving Arete he wrote about lightly magnetising a surface or joint to counteract wear that was really interesting, but I cannot find it..."

Elysser tensed a little, but tenderly reached for their own journal, which had almost toppled off the edge of the nearby shelf in their struggle to get dressed unseen. "It's... here. We combined them when we were working on the Coriolis' ailerons."

They walked the journal over to Teratai, who took it with a grateful smile, and immediately began poring over it. "Thank you, this is a huge benefit."

Elysser stood anxiously next to her, pressing their pawpads into their palms. "What do you need it for?" they asked quietly.

"Teratai scratched her crest without lifting her beak from the pages. "I am working with Skyria's surgeons to finish the prostheses I designed in Nazreal. I want to ensure the metal used is both light enough for flight but strong enough to take my weight and not crush itself in working joints. Anything good enough for me will absolutely be of the strength for creatures of normal stature."

Elysser was silent, and it was not unnoticed by the gryphon.

"You are concerned."

They nodded. "You... are remarkably brave."

"I do not consider it brave to offer myself as vanguard for

this. It is a natural part of my desire to function in a world that does not accommodate the permanently injured. To offer someone else in my place before it has been refined, where it may cause great pain until such skills are developed, would be an undue torture. It is a baseline decency to do the minimum required of us in times like this. It should not be considered brave just to exist as myself."

"What will the procedure be?"

Teratai gave a small shrug. "They will remove my legs, adjust my organs, spine and body as it needs, and see to the connections that they work."

"Sure, that sounds simple, completely painless, and not at all invasive," Elysser intoned bluntly. They paused, watching Teratai leaf over the parchment, and their ears fell. "When you say 'adjust'…"

Teratai's disposition shadowed. "I will lose my womb, if that is what you are inferring. The damage was already done, I cannot hold onto a shattered vessel of a future no longer in my reach."

"I'm sorry."

"I am, and am not. There was much I had hoped for, but now there is more I hope for still, on this new path. It is one we have been forced into, but no matter how small a corner I am backed into, to lose myself is to lose the world that was given to me. I will not forcibly eliminate hope for anyone I can help."

Elysser had their hand at their neck, trying to quell the emotions that were threatening to explode. "I don't think you understand what 'brave' means to someone watching you," they whispered.

"And what of you?" Teratai quipped, glancing round. "You cannot tell me you are without credit in that regard. We are here in many ways because of your work, your compassion and fortitude. I know that you are suffering, as many of us are. Do not think for a second that your achievements, nor our gratitude, are undermined by pain, no matter how encompassing."

Two arms wrapped around Teratai's neck, as Elysser buried their muzzle in her feathers and hugged her tightly.

Skyria became a hub for the land's restoration over the next weeks. The Coriolis, as well as supply trains travelling along newly-forged bridges down the archipelago and the new half-continent, distributed pure water and gigantic ionisation towers that helped pull dust and resonance particulate from the air, alongside plants that would help do the same. The Skyrian botanists worked tirelessly to preserve and cultivate crops, working out how the soil composition had changed and what would survive in which areas. The start was slow, gruelling, and relentless. Shattered cities brought new refugees, fleeing ghostly remains in ruined deserts. Very few places escaped damage as well as Skyria had.

Progress was helped in places by the formation of crystal fissures weaving underground, forged by surging energy from Nazreal's destruction. Elysser was able to dowse for them with reasonable accuracy, but trying to find their origin was a frustrating and elusive task, as their roots passed too deep for her to detect. They had no idea whether they had a common origin or were spontaneous manifestations like those erupting in the skies as they'd escaped in the Coriolis. But being able to draw from their power as they found them meant accelerating development around new settlements, and restoring safety and stability to older ones.

Thankfully not all of the land had been laid barren – some of it was just displaced and warped, or under a layer of dust that could be cleaned away. The climate change of specific areas was the biggest threat to plant life, and Skyria had teams moving from place to place restoring, cultivating, and retraining anything they could.

The other continent, where Dhraka had lain, would be the greater challenge, given its distance from Skyria and the difficulty of transporting resources so far. Elysser hoped that their village, and perhaps Mahrae, had survived, or even that somehow Aidan was already working to restore them himself. But as ever-present as that fantasy was, until they knew either way, it was just a fantasy, and they needed to prepare as much as they could to establish a new base across the ocean rift.

Several ships had appeared at the dock, some of which had been travelling since very soon after the cataclysm. Survivors, once rested, were happy to provide their vessels and selves to any kind of useful cause, and had some detail of surviving areas that needed attention.

Elysser had just returned to Skyria from relief efforts towards the south. They dismounted the wagon as it ground to a halt past the city's bridge to the mainland. Up ahead was a steady stream of supplies being funnelled to the west dock, where the Coriolis was due to leave from. The fennec had been away for almost two months, and had expected Teratai to visit them in order to collaborate on a windmill, but she hadn't voyaged down. Between projects, Elysser had been alight with anxiety that something had gone wrong in her prosthesis, and had been completing their tasks as swiftly as possible to return and check she was all right.

They strode along the pavement, dodging past carts of relief supplies and soldiers ferrying crates to and fro, coming to the ship's gleaming hull at the dockside. They looked around fervidly for sign of their friend; but a gryphon should have been easy to spot among so many other, smaller creatures. Just as they began a line for the gangway, a hefty claw clapped them on the shoulder. They spun round, to be greeted by the breastplate of a tall figure, beneath which were ornate mechanical legs, gleaming with grey polish, and above which was a broad smile on a high, friendly beak.

"You made it!" Teratai chirped.

Elysser flung their arms around her waist. "*I* made it? You were supposed to have been down to see me! I'm so glad you're okay." They scanned her up and down, almost drooling at the shine on her prosthetics. "They came out amazingly!"

Teratai beamed. "They were a pain in the tail!" she sang. "And the hips. And the back. But I can walk again, and that is something."

Elysser circled her, ears pricked and forward, tail flicking excitedly, and occasionally running a claw over a piston or armoured sweep. Their teeth gleamed when they smiled, and before long they realised they were almost bent double admiring the detail work on Teratai's new claws.

"So… your old legs…?"

"Donated for Skyria's study. The damage was not only crushing injury, but strange resonance distortions to my form that could not be undone. It is taking some getting used to even now. The pain remains, in strange waves. But I am hoping in the future it will be easier, and mayhaps we shall find ways of making it adhere more naturally to bone and body. For now this is a good test of skill, will, and craft." She leant forwards, with a glint in her eye. "I have already made extensive notes for the next set."

Elysser stood back with their paws on their hips, taking in the new Teratai. "Well let me know when you get them, because we need to give you some extra flair."

"It will be an honour," Teratai responded, her neck feathers puffing proudly outwards like a blooming flower. "As will this next favour I must ask of you," she continued, putting her arm over the fennec's shoulder to lead them up the gangway, metal claws thudding resonantly up its length. "I was called to examine the Coriolis' battery and make improvements to its longevity. I do not have your skill, but I think I understand what should be done, if you would not mind the indulgence."

Together they descended into the Coriolis' lower hull, and their eyes quickly adjusted to its dim blue lighting that helped eliminate glare from the metal but provided just enough ambience to see what was where. Separated by the girders comprising the keel were two large cylindrical structures, with pipes, thick cables, and axles sprouting from them. They each had a sliding metal cover on their top section, and were connected in the middle by a smaller set of parallel tubes, a rescue system for in case one of the batteries failed.

Teratai rolled the lid open from the first battery, and a crystal glow enkindled the room. A series of spindles within a canister full of resonance crystal dust suspended in liquid shone before them, staunchly secured within its base to power the ship. For now the crystal dust was mostly settled at the bottom. When the battery was coaxed into life to provide power, it would rotate and the dust would disperse, allowing the spindles to collect energy and pass it to the engines. Elysser looked to Teratai, who then produced a scrap of parchment from her satchel, on which was daubed in charcoal a smudgy central diagram, surrounded by hurriedly-scrawled notes. Elysser frowned at its condition.

"Did you draw this on the way to meet me?"

The gryphon cleared her throat authoritatively. "It has been a busy and exhausting few weeks. Having your legs removed, adjusting your nervous system to new ones, and learning to walk again is not normally condensed into a matter of weeks, but both my process and this are essential, so I had no choice. You can still read it, correct?"

Elysser smiled. "I can, yes."

Teratai pulled a large lever on the side of the battery mount and the axis within shifted, lifting it free of its mounting. The lights flickered slightly as the mechanics switched to the second battery.

Elysser gently peered around the battery to ensure its condition. Attempting to modify it with any kind of fault could be disastrous. Holding the parchment in one hand, turning it over to make sure they matched the poles of the battery, and studying the notes carefully, they ran the blade of their axe along the edge of the metal case. The spindles split, rotated and extended, increasing their surface area.

On one of the metal battery caps was a small valve used to disperse more crystal dust into the cell. Refilling it needed them to be disconnected completely from the Coriolis to avoid a potential power surge, and they didn't have time for something so delicate, especially where the gentle sway of the boat could spill resonance dust onto running mechanisms with a high explosive capacity. What would be a pressing issue in future, was the location of crystals with enough potential to be refined into dust, and without the volatility that would make them explode outright. Elysser was reticent to explore them as a direct fuel source, given the repercussions of such concentrated energy bursts.

Once the two of them had realigned the second battery and slotted it back into place, the lights steadied and strengthened, and a low hum bloomed through the ship. They gave one final check to the cell array to ensure it was safe and stable, then ascended the sterncastle to the bridge. Osiris was drawing lines across his map, scribbling bearings and altitudes to plot the course ahead.

"Are we ready?" he grunted.

"Of course," Teratai responded, sounding a little clipped.

He nodded, then after a few seconds swept the map onto the angled plinth next to him. "Good. We're leaving as soon as everything is in the hold."

Elysser sat on the deck outside as the ship was prepared. What few possessions they had were already on the Coriolis, so they hadn't needed to gather anything from the city of trees before heading out again. It was… a surreal, busy transience, but a welcome one that kept them distracted and occupied. The more they could get done, the closer they were to investigating what they had been most concerned about since the cataclysm: the fate of Nazreal, and Aidan within it.

Dhalen had made himself available for the journey, being somewhat of an interloper currently. Duty to his friends was as much a priority to him as the care of the world. To him, a world existed both within and without the body, and both required sustenance. That came from love, and compassion, and protection, all of which he had tried to pour himself into since leaving Nazreal. It left him somewhat divided, however, with the splitting up of the Kitaia between southward settlements and some remaining in Skyria to develop their skills and aid in prosthesis adaptation for the injured. He was no longer a leader as such, but a coordinator and giver of blessings to leave. As his pack diminished and drew their own focuses, he had been seeing to Teratai's care. He, along with the other doctors and prosthetic engineers (under her guidance) seemed pleased with her progress, but he wanted to ensure all of their efforts continued to her safety and health, at least insofar as the legs were concerned. Everything else was up to her.

As the preparations were being finalised and the cargo secured, Dhalen leapt onto the deck, scanning the ship with a piercing urgency.

Something was wrong.

"Dhalen?" Elysser called. He gave them a brief acknowledgement but skirted quickly into the ship. Their claws began an unconscious tap on the ship's metal railing as their apprehension grew; just as they were about to follow him, he emerged again, concern now exchanged with a grim despondency.

"Lhian's taken herself away," he murmured.

Elysser's ears flicked towards him, upright and alert. They hadn't known Oakhe's first assault victim personally, but she had been one of the very few to survive his vicious onslaughts around Nazreal after his transformation at Raikali's hand. "She's not well enough for that."

"I know." He looked out to the sea and its cold, grey waves. "Nobody's seen her since yesterday."

"Did something happen?"

He shrugged, letting his fist fall with an exasperated thud on the rail. "She was getting restless, sometimes combative. She clawed a physician when they tried to replace the gauze on her mouth. They think she ran some time after that."

Elysser swayed from one hindpaw to another, looking out over the crowds at the pier for some vague sign of Dhalen's injured companion. "Could she really have left for the mainland? Do… do you think Nazreal, and Oakhe, was too much?"

He let out a low growl and rubbed his paws into his forehead. "Maybe not that alone. I don't know. Lhian and Oakhe… they had known each other before, closely. Maybe that was why he found her first. Perhaps it was random. Whatever it was, she was affected by it more deeply than any of us anticipated." A stiff sigh flared from his nostrils. "I've asked everyone to keep an eye out for her, but if she doesn't want to be found, it'll be a dangerous discovery for anyone who does."

"I just hope she's safe," Elysser said quietly.

Dhalen nodded, gripping his claws together tightly. "If this was not her place to be, may she find peace."

In the uneasy silence that followed, the ship's load was completed and all crew had boarded. The Coriolis' sails unfurled, and it sailed cautiously towards the wider sea, navigating the coral-rich shallows beneath the waves. Dhalen and Elysser watched the island of trees quietly drift away, the dock sounds and rustling of leaves fading into the rolling push of wind over water. The further they went, the colder the wind became, and the harder the silence pressed as thoughts of Lhian burned into their mind.

Once the ship was above the open deep, the sails were rolled tightly shut and folded away, and its wings and ailerons rumbled into place; a sign to disappear below deck or risk being thrown away on ascent. After a minute of its engines escalating their roar, the ship burst forwards and took to the sky.

Their flight took a few days at a steady pace; Osiris was meticulous with their bearings. This ocean, which some were already calling The Great Rift, hadn't existed before, and this was the first time Osiris had consciously navigated it. The waters below were a mottled mix of mud silt and debris, with many dead creatures lying bloated on the waves. They were high enough not to smell any decay, but it painted a grim picture of the ocean life with such a tumultuous seismic upheaval. Elysser worried if the ocean could be restored, even before any sign of Nazreal could be hunted for.

The further they went, the darker the sky became, and the more particulate hung in the air. It wasn't anywhere near the choking storm at the cataclysm's advent, but it was noticeable enough to leave a film on the deck, and many of the crew tied masks around their muzzles to act as filters.

Elysser tried to use the bowsprit as a blade to slice through the air again but it gave them little advantage, save for keeping Osiris' window clear at the helm. Although Elysser could feel the buzz of resonance energy in the cloud, it wasn't enough to disperse or attract with great strength, and couldn't be collected in the same way as in Nazreal's aftermath.

After a few despondent attempts at clearing a path, Elysser stood by Osiris at the bridge. The Coriolis was forced into a descent through the thickening smog while they still knew water was below them; at their current speed, the sight of land may come too quickly to evade it, and they had no guarantee of any new mountain formations.

Osiris skimmed the ship over the top of the waves, then slowed it to an almost complete stop, resting it gently on the water's surface. The sails unfurled once more and they continued towards the slow, uncertain conclusion to their oceanic journey.

Almost a day later, they sighted a coastline. By the time they saw it, they realised they were in the mouth of a massive gulf that was spearheading them towards a round, crater-like bay.

Elysser felt their fur tingling; they tried to push away the nauseous anticipation that crept up their body, but an inexorable energy persisted, and they kept having to stamp their paw to dispel it. Their ears felt red and itchy, and a strange fizzing noise buried into them, one that nobody else seemed to notice. They flexed their claws as they peered into the settling murk of the sky, the water's choppy surface coated in a layer of grey, ash-like silt.

There was something more. The cliffs around the bay seemed… they couldn't quite tell, but it didn't look like a natural formation. The scent of burnt earth hung past the stale dust.

Once moored within the circular bay and ashore with the landing party, they were able to get a closer look at the land. Elysser stroked their paw through the ash and scorched earth. A strange, electric heat swept along their arm as shreds of desiccated grass shook from under the surface debris.

In the dried, grassy leaves were black flashmarks where veins of crystal had once run through them, extinguished so fast by the dust to not even give the blades time to ignite.

"This…"

They ran up the side of the craterous ridge, almost slipping on areas that had been turned to a glass-like rock beneath the sand. The damage was haphazard, almost panicked. A legacy of an adirectional yet infinite fury. Reaching the apex, they stopped, holding their scarf tightly to their muzzle to catch their breath. Through the swirling grey sand, buffeted into vortices by twisting winds, a familiar landscape faded in and out of view.

The broken mountain range that had once encircled the Zenith, and Nazreal.

They stood in silence, legs threatening to give way, and

scanned the distance. No buildings. No shelters. No walls. Nothing.

They trod forwards, and within a few steps the sand tilted like a loose floorboard under their paw. Elysser bent down to inspect what they'd stepped on.

The dulled, flat side of a sword greeted them.

Circling their axeblade, they created a whirlwind before them that rocketed forwards, clearing a channel in the sand ahead.

A grave of bone and blades. Dhrakans, Gauros – all creatures who surrounded Nazreal at the apex of the explosion, buried in decay. Elysser's glance kept darting between visible skulls as if tricked by each that Aidan may have been among them, but… he had been inside the walls. So maybe…

They turned back out to look over the Coriolis. Beyond it lay the vast, clouded sea, veiled in fog and thunder.

This bay was once the epicentre. Nazreal had been here.

Now, empty.

Elysser tightly gripped the collar of their robe to ease the rising, quiet panic, and shakily descended the crater's slope to help the landing party.

Chapter Four

Teratai and Elysser's designs for a siphon to clear the air around the landing site were inconsistent. The Coriolis hadn't been able to transport one of the full-sized ionisers, but the air here was even thicker. It needed to be tall enough to draw from upper air currents, which meant stretching out the available materials to their furthest limits, and hurriedly searching for more in an already barren wasteland. Nothing of Nazreal remained, not even a basement, and where the huge crystal that had once lain beneath its heart was now a sinister, cold absence.

The first ioniser they refined worked well until choking to a halt, having accumulated so much dust that opening its drive shaft caused an avalanche of detritus, and its mechanics groaned under the weight. The second they erected worked its way loose in a burst of high wind, wrecking its shaft and splitting the crystal array used to attract the particles from the air. It was several days of fraught, painstaking repair work. But after more shipments from the Coriolis with resources, and repeatedly solidifying the dust into stones numerous enough to build a rough quay for the ship to dock at, the air was comfortable and clear enough to breathe for some miles inland from the bay.

Skyrian botanists had been studying the sand for nutrients to extract and seed within the land to grow plant life again. Using the once shimmering, now dead, resonance grass as a sort of additive seemed to help; filtering sea water into fresh irrigation channels was the major project that Elysser had to attend to direction from Skyria's botanists, as the fennec had little experience with such specific cultivation needs.

Nidhimes arrived on the Coriolis' third voyage and immediately knew where to centre their efforts to make the land sustainable. For his timidity, and for looking like he regularly got dressed running away from something terrifying, his knowledge was insurmountable. Within a week of his appearance they had a soil mix into which new grass had rooted, and the irrigation lines had been perfected. Most of the botanists, and the rest of the crew when not fishing, were now enlisted to create a huge payload of seed pods to throw from the Coriolis as it flew across the land, with the hope that it would create new plant life for the changed continent. It was impossible to tell whether the continent itself had shifted, whether both halves had moved, or if this had stayed stationary and the split containing Skyria had been the one to move away; regardless, the climate had changed, and it was important to take advantage of its conditions before any hope of regaining a population was lost.

They introduced light electrical fields to stabilise and uncloud the water, allowing sections specifically for fish and aquatic fauna to flourish under protection, and set up breeding programs to ensure the sea creatures could be kept in a natural equilibrium. It was complex work that sometimes came to frustrating debates about haste or priority, but most knew that Nidhimes' work was vital, even if he was not a bold enough leader to assert himself over its necessity. His ideas were always protected by Elysser and Teratai, and stern orders from Virvel came with Skyrian ships that helped enforce the need for his respect.

With the landing area now stable, the stage had been set for wider exploration of the continent, something Elysser had been itching for since the yawing emptiness of the land had stretched out before them.

They waited impatiently in front of the helm as the Coriolis was prepared for its voyage, with barrels of seed pods lined up along its railings set to be ejected at Nidhime's approval whenever a suitable patch of land drew below them. The amazing, hopeful display was only a tenuous reprieve from the desperation and urgency under which it needed to be finished. This was the first time they had ventured far enough outside of the already desolate mountain range to see how the other settlements on this half of the landmass had fared. Elysser thought of their own village, and whether it would be standing. They thought of the lands to the South, and hoped, somewhere, they may find a clue as to Nazreal's disappearance, and not feed the solidifying dread that it had sunk beneath the enormous ocean rift or been completely vaporised.

Dhalen had been with them, but had disappeared below deck to sleep. Despite how many times he had flown on the Coriolis now, flight still disquieted him, and he preferred to sleep the journey away instead of wander the ship or grow nauseous from anxiety with every unsteady movement.

Outside, Osiris rapped his hindpaw on the deck as the seed barrels were fastened into place. His gaze was disapproving enough that the crew all scurried out of sight as soon as they were able. Ultimately he knew it was necessary to lash the dispersal pods to the ship's elegant frame, but hated that it needed to be. He began a slow march around the ship. Every barrel he passed he gave a hefty kick or rattle with his claws to ensure they were secured. Any that showed even marginal swaying prompted a sharp command for someone to return and secure it more thoroughly.

It happened six times on his circuit.

He would not have his ship dented nor dashed by an errant barrage of pre-plant.

Nidhimes had followed slightly behind the gryphon, hooking his claws together while rocking up and down slightly, occasionally risking a glance at Osiris to see where his attention was fixed, and making apologetic murmurs to those who had to come back and adjust the pods he'd designed. Overall they were working fine, but every fault or flaw seemed to make him shrink, such that he was more like a wandering shadow by the time Osiris returned to his supervisory position by the sterncastle entrance and folded his arms.

A claw gripped the slothbear's shoulder from behind; he froze and gave a sharp squeak, a noise which made Osiris' crest twitch.

Teratai leaned over Nidhimes' shoulder. "Do not feel anxious," she said calmly. "You have engineered a brilliant solution. He is ingrained in a duty of old appearances compounded by new responsibility, one which he tries hard to shake. But it is not a reflection of you."

Nidhimes laced his paws together and wrung them, allowing his body a little freedom to move under her powerful claw that felt as heavy as his anxiety. "W-well, I know it's somewhat an imposition regardless, but it is the best way to deliver these quickly and study the land patterns…"

"You are doing well," she reassured. He caught her smile

as she stood to her full height and strode next to Osiris, standing almost with her wingtip to his, but not close enough to brush against him.

"You mirror the state of the world instead of reflecting what you hope it to be," she murmured. "A softer countenance may help move those around you to inspiration."

He let out a low, long breath through his nostrils. "I will find time for levity when I find levity itself. Right now, all I have in mind is restoration."

"Your mettle is admirable," she said, with a stern patience that belied perhaps a little of her own doubt that his severity was enkindling. "Remember that to protect a world you have to show that it is worth living in. Do not scorn all others to fear and duty alone."

He turned slightly towards her, his focus on the skies above them. "This world has suffered catastrophic loss, as have we as part of it. I cannot begin to process that until what remains is safeguarded. We may always be living in deficit and I will not turn away from it as long as I have breath to change it."

Teratai sighed. "I am of the same mind, Osiris. But... remember, compassion is a duty to yourself as much as to others. It is as far from unnecessary as breathing, and as strong within us as the bones that hold us upright. You would owe it to Aidan, if nobody else, to embody that as well."

As she turned back to the sterncastle, a quiet statement stopped her. Osiris was still looking to the sky.

"It... is easier said than done... when so many of my hopes have fallen already."

"It is a measure of our strength, to persist."

"To rest now would feel like a nightmare," he muttered.

Her eyes sliced towards him. "For the injured, it is not

always a choice."

As the final barrel was re-secured into place, the gangway was lifted free and stowed into its split under the deckboards. From the bridge, Elysser watched Teratai, then Osiris, followed meekly by Nidhimes, enter the sterncastle.

Osiris must have flown up the decks, because it felt like mere seconds before his wings sent a fierce bluster throughout the bridge and rushed through their fur and ears. Elysser allowed themself a shiver at the shock and sudden chill, then looked cautiously back at him.

He was unfazed, already moving the ship away from the quay. Elysser couldn't tell from his gaze whether he had already started the journey in his mind, or on some other destination altogether. They leant on the wall, grasping a handrail to brace themself for the irate takeoff.

The lands were a distorted contraction of the areas Elysser had seen before. Deserts shifted under their own currents anyway, but the topography of the mountains was completely new. Where they had formerly radiated out in huge, silent circles from the impact the Zenith shard had wrought upon its landing, the undulating, jagged peaks now lay in strange zigzags, their tips leaning outward from where Nazreal stood like trees in a storm.

Osiris' keen eyes picked at the land, seeming to recognise a few rare areas of stillness and making course changes appropriately. The further out the Coriolis flew, the more familiar things appeared to be, and the less the surface had shifted. It gave Elysser some hope that somehow the energy had been controlled enough to not destroy all but the outermost reaches of the land. But Eeres was an unpredictable world, moreso now, and Arete had been levelled despite its distance from Nazreal. Until they were able to see any signs of life, scanning the whole world for changes and survivors, it would be impossible to know what happened.

The Coriolis decreased altitude as the world became more distinct, crossing out of the desert sands to a richer, temperate floor of sharp-leafed trees and billowy grass. Some of the palms were at odd angles, clinging to pieces of vertical land that had been pinched up like stiff dough. The ground was shaken into a standing wave, with sharp ripples and wide divots that stretched in regular intervals for miles. A few small birds flitted across the deck as they slowed, and some of the crew leant over the deck rails to peer into the vegetation, hoping to catch further signs of life.

Osiris' eyes narrowed. Ahead lay a forbidding set of char-topped mountains, their slopes dotted with black and grey rocks. Around their bases was a ring of thick, verdant foliage, but among that lay toppled ruins of dark-brick buildings. One tower stood, listing, surrounded by a small circle of decimated village houses, their walls partially swallowed by the surging, pulsing ground.

Osiris wheeled the Coriolis around in a wide circle, eyeing the buildings with an intense, hunting glare, every so often glancing back up at the mountains.

"We've found Dhraka."

It was as much a command as a statement, as almost immediately all who heard him checked their weapons and equipment. Even those who hadn't, but were just on deck scouting the land, had been wary of how long they were in proximity of the desolate tower, and were nervously readying bows or blades.

"Should we descend?" Teratai ventured.

Elysser pressed their claws into their pawpads. "We had been close to cooperation when patrolling Nazreal. This may be an even more desperate event for unity."

The ship rattled slightly, hitting a patch of warmer air venting from a fissure below them, as if in response to Elysser's statement, or perhaps Osiris' consternation.

They remained in a terse silence for a few seconds, before Dhalen spoke, his paw against the window.

"Oakhe would probably have reached out. But he was an eternal optimist."

"Dhraka has demonstrated what they do to optimists."

Teratai's wings bristled. "Not Dhraka. Fulkore and Sarr Crawn are despots and tyrants. That does not mean all dragons are as such. If any have escaped, or the Crawns have perished, they may be as wayward as we are. We will not know if their baleful reign may continue if their lands are devastated."

Dhalen turned to Osiris. "Even if we aren't optimistic, being prepared is no frivolity."

The gryphon kept his claws steady on the wheel but seemed in some way to hunch forward and stiffen without losing any of his height, as if his feathers bristled out in defiance.

"First we surveil. We remain cautious and with plans for a quick escape. I will not endanger the ship."

After almost an hour of circling and grim surveyance, Osiris pulled the Coriolis to a wide bay mouth some way behind the mountains – the Dhraka's previous coastline. More crumbled, sunken, collapsed buildings lay before them, along with a few ships that lay broken in the water, consumed by shifting sands and dashed against the rocks. That anything had survived at all would be a miracle.

As they passed the longer crescent of the bay to circle back for a landing, a huge cascade of black rock spilling into the sea yawed open before them. Broken swells of volcanic flow spread from the back of the broken mountain summit all the way down to the sea. Below the water's surface the spill continued further, a wide swath of lava that had broken from under its own surface and spread deeper along the sandy bed.; a dark, grim shadow that reeked of sulphur and char.

"This may have been it, between the eruption and the gases," Teratai murmured, her vision as acute as Osiris' but still uncovering nothing.

Osiris shook his head. "I do not trust them to be killed by something so mundane."

The Coriolis touched down in the waters, sending a gentle ripple over the calm beach and broken, drifting dockyard. Dhraka would have looked almost tropical, were it not for the high, solemn clouds and ashen film that covered everything. Plants drooped under the layers of dust, buildings were abandoned piles of rubble or ghostly shadows of the former life that filled them. It was a far picture from a society either thriving or militaristic.

Elysser had only known a few Dhrakans aside from the General himself, and many of those had been Nazreal's guards, and often silent in his presence. Those that the fennec had gotten the chance to speak to seemed as indifferent to hate as any other, but followed Crawn because of his authority. It was not, they felt, representative, but it was a hard line of communication to break with such tight control exerted over them. The rest of Elysser's idea of the dragons had been built from Osiris' resentment, and Aidan's caution. They had heard tales of the struggle under Sarr Crawn and his son, the iron claw and brutal wing he used to extort servitude and fealty; this land seemed a far cry from the images conjured by fearful warning.

Osiris and Teratai stood on the deck, staring out over the

Dhrakan wharf. The murky blue-green waves lapped quietly at the shoreline and the gnarled, twisted quays of metal and cracked brick.

"They cannot be dead." His voice was cold as the broken stones.

"Will you kill them, if they are not?" she replied.

"I did not come here for a slaughter."

She shook her head, adjusting the javelins in the holster at her back. "Your words are a poor mask for the hate behind your eyes. You had often wished them the same fate that since befell Arete."

"Would you have blamed me, even now?"

"I will not waste time on hypotheticals – nor should you. Your resentment builds with fantasies of histories you could not change and futures that have not happened. Be here, Osiris. Now. We survive, or we die. Those outcomes will exist whether the war rages within us or not. All that will change is how soon they arrive."

He tightly gripped his sword hilt, the leather creaking in his claws, and the feathers of his brow furrowed. He could bore his eyes into the ground to find them if he could, to know one way or another where his future lay. Elysser was nearby them both, and Dhalen close behind. Osiris shot them both a glance, which made Elysser flinch slightly, then he gestured to the land.

"We are flying over. Small scout party. I want those familiar with Dhrakans to be with us, and wary."

"And for diplomatic balance, perhaps?" Dhalen said somewhat pointedly, as he latched onto Osiris. The gryphon stiffened, and some kind of low noise rumbled in his throat.

Teratai motioned for Elysser to take a place on her back, which they did, and within moments the gryphons and their passengers took to the sky to begin their closer survey of the scorched nation.

They circled around the quayside and then swept further inland, before coming to a rest in the centre of a wide square, near the leaning spire. The flagstones were cracked and buckled, some completely thrown out of place. Layers of grey-black dust drifted in the breeze, sometimes falling from rooftops and high leaves in disintegrating clumps.

With cautious claws resting on weapon hilts, they patrolled the twisted, broken streets. From buildings where doors had been snapped from their hinges or trapped open by the disturbed walls they once fit perfectly into, long trails lead towards the mountains, signs of things being dragged onto a large vehicle rolling down the centre of the streets. The tracks did not look recent, however. The houses were abandoned, or perhaps plundered, and the only sounds that rang out other than the echoes of the wind through the peaks were the sparse sounds of local wildlife.

They surveyed the eerie disturbed townscape for hours, ducking into burnt houses and navigating carefully over the smouldering rivers of crusted lava that cut through the paths. There were remnants of bodies, victims of pyroclastic flow or sundered rock, and buildings that, although completely disintegrated, held grim energy of those who may yet remain entombed within its crushed carapace of brick.

They were looping back to the tower to track through a different section of the city when Dhalen's ears flicked, and he looked urgently to the top of the spire. Atop it was a purple dragon in a mix of plate armour and sheepskin, her poleaxe held across her chest in a defensive warning.

Osiris reached for his rapier; Teratai's wings instinctively flexed but she didn't advance. Elysser immediately stepped in front of them with a wide, open stance, keeping their gaze fixed on the dragon above them.

"We're surveying the land for survivors. Do you need help?" they called.

The dragon fixed them in a wary glance. "No."

"We're not scavengers or opportunists, we just came to search and assist, if necessary."

"Then why are the Aretians here?"

Elysser didn't look round, although she could feel Osiris' movement to respond. "They brought us on their ship. We were all from Nazreal, and are trying to rebuild a safe place on this continent for us."

The dragon looked around, scanning for more potential movement. She spread her wings and twisted her poleaxe threateningly. "There's more than me here," she called down. "If you try to eat me, we'll attack."

"We definitely don't do that," Dhalen interjected.

"Well now you make us sound suspicious," Teratai chuckled. Elysser frantically waved a claw at them both, while Osiris remained transfixed on the dragon's polearm, his intense eyesight catching every tiny movement of its point as she stood cautiously at the tower's peaked roof.

"Do you need aid?" Elysser called.

The dragon glanced furtively to the treeline to her left, behind where the group was standing. "If you have rations, it would keep us from crawling into the mountains."

"We'll bring some."

Elysser glanced at Teratai, who immediately nodded and took flight towards the Coriolis. The dragon flinched at her burst of action, but eventually swept down to the cracked flagstones a good distance away from them, losing some of her wariness but not giving up any grip on her weapon. She had bronze eyes, a broken upper right horn and a series of teeth mark scars on her neck.

Teratai reappeared some while later with a large sack of supplies, which she laid out onto the ground and spread wide on the cloth so the dragon could take in what they were offering. The gryphon took to her knee and bowed her head reverently.

"Please take all that you need for your group. I am sorry for the catastrophe that has befallen you, much as it has for us. You would be welcome to join us at our new safe harbour."

The dragon glanced at the food, then behind her, then to Osiris.

"We will not go to Arete. We've heard that you flay dragons alive."

Osiris' beak tightened and his feathers rippled slightly. "We do not. And in any case, you would not be taken to Arete. It has been destroyed."

"We are all that remain," Teratai said softly. "That we know of."

Elysser offered the dragon a piece of firebread, a sort of emergency, easy-made sustenance that they'd stockpiled for the journey. The dragon stepped forward and took it gently, before breaking a piece and holding it out towards the trees.

Three more dragons came forth, all of them slightly smaller than her. One deep blue-green, one dark brown, and one white. They were all adorned in scraps of armour and carrying various weapons, looking to have been scavenged from Dhrakan soldiers. The white one lifted their helmet up – it was too big to fit properly and kept tapping their muzzle as they walked – and looked tenuously at the bread. The purple dragon opened her palm and the white one took it, giving a thankful glance to them both.

"My partners," the purple one said, wistfully. "My name is Cove."

"Cove," Elysser repeated, kindly, and held out their claw. Cove took it, and shook it gently. "Mine is Elysser; these are Dhalen, Teratai, and Osiris." The others all nodded or bowed respectfully. Osiris was still sceptical, but seeing the timidity of Cove's partners seemed to quieten his severity a little.

"Where is everyone else?" Elysser asked, watching some of the black soot move in the wind by their paw. "Are you all that's left?"

Cove stuck her poleaxe blade into the charred ground and leant it against a decapitated statue. "Well, you live in this world, I doubt there's a single part that wasn't touched by what happened." She gave a resentful glare to the mountains beyond. "But no, we're not all that's left. Most of Crawn's fascistic Dhraka brigade retreated to the mountains, and many others were granted sanctuary in return for fealty. Those of us who would rather risk the end of the world than confine ourselves to an eternal tomb with him decided to take our chances outdoors. Crawn's machines have been a destructive legacy for us already; following would have been no guarantee of safety. I had collected breathing bags from the soldiers for my partners anyway; we had enough to give to others."

"Breathing bags?" Dhalen furrowed his brow.

From her back, Cove whipped a strange, pointed cloth-and-leather sack with glass eyeholes riveted into it, and held it in front of her. "For the volcanic fumes. The soldiers take them because they spend so much time underground, but we take them for when their machines go wrong and cause eruptions or gas leaks."

She looked to the slanted tower. "Despite Crawn's military might, his success is built on the backs of our engineers. Our city was built to withstand reasonable geological forces, but this... was too much. Most of our towers fell in the quakes, and more sank under the flow. We managed to escape to higher ground and weathered out the storm, then searched for survivors."

She dug her claws into her fist. "We did not find many."

Teratai looked to the mountains, her gaze distant and calculating. "Where are the machines? Are Crawn and his soldiers in there now?"

"Only Fulkore's sect. Sarr and his machine never returned. Fulkore's soldiers are less disciplined but still voracious. They're a blight on dragonkind and have been setting us on a path to isolative ruin for centuries. The rest of us have tried to survive as best we can outside them, but it has been tense at best." She whirled her poleaxe and pointed the tip towards a broken, partially-collapsed peak to the northwest. "With luck they'll stay buried and give the rest of us a chance in the light, but if you've made it out here then it won't be long before they venture back into the wider world too."

Osiris looked to the peak, his claw tightening around his baldrick, while Teratai and Elysser exchanged wary glances.

Chapter Five

The mountains were already harsh for those unaccustomed to their razor crags and knife-like slate outcrops. The unnaturally hot stones stoked an unnerving atmosphere akin to being near a rotting corpse, an invisible presence of death and danger that never relented in its intense discomfort and need for constant vigilance. Cove led them along the safest paths she could but some outcrops still came dangerously close to slicing through fur, snagging on clothes and clipping at claws. Osiris and Teratai kept their wings in as close as they could whenever they didn't need them for balance.

"What are you going to do if we find them?" the dragon asked, deftly curling round a shard of slate.

Osiris' feathers flared. "That depends on how we are received. If it were me I would leave them under the ground to rot. I may yet."

Teratai looked to her counterpart with stern regard.

The dragon was more cautiously affirmative. "Crawn's brood are indoctrinated by his ideals." She quickly gestured to her purple-hued scales. "You can tell we're not the same. We'll more than survive without them, let's put it that way."

They crested the ridge ahead. In a flattened trough below

them was a cavern entranceway, dug into the side of a tall, forbidding pair of mountains. The further of the twin summits bore a large crack down one side, which gently billowed steam. The nearer peak stood sentinel over a wide circle that appeared at one point to have been paved flat, but was now distended and covered in rubble. Pillars, formerly eminent decorations standing tall along the roadway, were shattered and strewn in pieces. The braziers that used to lie atop them to mark the winding pathway through the mountains had been tossed to the ground like wicker baskets, iron frames crushed and twisted to ribbons of scrap.

Leading into the mountainside sat a warped doorway surrounded by rubble, the gaping entranceway bolstered by metal beams and hastily-hammered wooden stays. Parts of the broken stone around the slopes still held some kind of structure, and split timbers jutted out like bone fractures. It had been a gatehouse.

Standing guard were three red-scaled Dhrakans wielding spears and shields, occasionally breaking from their station to march around the circle or sit on a nearby smooth outcrop that looked at one point to have held the foundations of the demolished towers.

Cove kept behind the rocks. "This is as close as I go. I've no intent of letting them know I exist outside of a distant threat."

The force of Osiris' boiling breaths produced a cloud of ash from the rock he was kneeling behind, swirling around his face as an embodiment to his ire. "This is not an advance I make lightly. I would prefer to have no need of it. But…" he chewed the words in thought, trying to make them palatable. "We should at least know their mentality if we are to prepare defences."

Teratai watched the entrance warily. "Fulkore was, for a time, less of an avaricious presence than his father. But who knows if that has now changed."

Elysser was behind Osiris' wing, and cautiously reached out to touch it. "This isn't a surrender. We're not looking to forgive anything that happened. If they survived they'll find us sooner or later; better that it be on our terms," they said severely, not optimistic at the prospect thanks to their own experience with Crawn's militant faction alongside Osiris' unpredictable mood.

"Hardly what I would consider favourable for 'our' terms," he muttered.

Cove remained behind the jagged formations, keeping her polearm in hand. "I'll be here if you emerge, and will guide you back."

Osiris nodded. He stood upright and marched around the rocks, followed by Teratai, who gave a thankful bow and salute, then Dhalen and Elysser, trying to flank the gryphons as best they could to look like they led as an equal front and not a militant deputation.

The dragons spied them immediately and brandished their spears, standing tightly together.

"Hold yourselves!" The first called from under his helmet. The others locked their shields together, and as a unit they began a slow, guarded retreat to the entrance.

Osiris raised his arms wide, claws open, to signify he was not arming himself, even though his rapiers hung tightly at his side. Teratai did the same; Dhalen and Elysser acted as a sort of emissary duo for them both, walking ahead and slightly to the side of each. The Dhrakan soldiers backed to the door. One glanced over his shoulder and then bolted into the torchlit darkness, leaving the other two to station themselves to block as much of the entrance as they could.

As the four approached, the Dhrakan spears extended towards them.

"No further!" the leader snapped eventually, when they were within lunging distance. "What's your business?"

Osiris fixed his steely glare on them. Elysser stepped forwards. "We're just making contact. We… know there's been disruption. We had previously been on a council with Fulkore Crawn in Nazreal."

The dragons side-eyed each other. "Is this all of you?"

"Yes," Teratai replied.

They gave each other another warning glance, then split, flanking the entranceway and gesturing with their spears to enter. "You first, we'll follow. Any suspicious movements and you'll be run through. The rest of our battalion is inside."

"Why inside?" Osiris asked darkly.

The lead dragon hissed. "That's not your information to seek, Aretian."

After keeping in tensely diplomatic silence during the walk through the tunnels, they came to a yawing, partially-collapsed cavern. Metal beams braced against sloping, cracked walls which sprinkled dust from dark fissures. The cave rose to a twisted apex above them and had the semblance of four triangular walls but the space within was not what it once used to be. Whatever it once housed was gone and the walls now bulged inwards. Massive tree trunks, split and shattered, made up the rubble on one side, along with ropes and colossal hinges that once anchored them in place. Teratai caught sight of crushed vents, smashed pipes and walkways that used to exist around the upper levels, all of them in the distinctive black metal of Crawn's Dhrakan sect.

The Leviathan once stood here, before making its last

journey towards Nazreal.

There was a deafening sense of anticipation in the cave, like the air before a thunderclap. While the collapse had subsided for now, its structure and survival looked to be hanging by the thinnest, most fragile thread.

Instead of the titanic siege engine that had loomed here, at the centre of the tomb-like expanse was a machine that Osiris and Teratai knew well from its destructive ambitions prior to Nazreal. Sarr Crawn's uncontrollable, disastrous device that he'd used to try and threaten the world into submission decades ago. The machine for seismic assault, known as Quakebringer. The dormant monster lay at the heart of its cavern, covered in dust and partially obscured with rubble, looking barely damaged by the upheavals it twice survived. Osiris glowered at its presence and Teratai kept a firm claw on her javelins.

As the dragons led them through the chamber, other teams of Dhraka watched the strangers' approach. Some tensed, some growled and chattered in heightened voices, some began echoing insults around the chamber. They had been ferrying supply carts of raw materials, salvaged weapons and debris in various directions, including two large tunnels leading into other antechambers, with 'Colossus' and 'Gargantua' embossed in metal signs above each.

Dhalen kept an eye over his shoulder as several Dhrakans began to follow and close distance. The ones leading them seemed to give no mind, acknowledging each of the dragons they passed with a nod or tip of a spearpoint. The confused whispers and indignant growls increased in volume as they were marched past the fallen rocks shielding the earthquake machine, into the arched tunnel heading towards Colossus.

The Dhrakan traffic was heavier inside. Noises of

construction and collection grew loud, with reverberation bringing it to a constant drone punctuated by crashes of metal, the roar of a furnace, or piercing warning yells to the shuffling supply trains and harried rebuild teams. More eyes turned, more teeth bared, more hostile bemusement, and more than a few claws being flexed. Elysser tried to keep their focus ahead as the archway opened into another huge cavern, but they couldn't help tightening a paw over their buckler handle, and checking that the handaxe was still in position for quick access at their waist.

As they broached the tunnel's exit they came under the rim of another war machine, lit with bright yellow crystals that channelled energy from outside. Even with so much vivid light, the tip of the pyramid was shrouded in shadow. Dragons dipped in and out of view under the Colossus' peeling carapace where rocks had crushed it, and on the far side it appeared that the entire mountainside had collapsed onto it. Teratai couldn't tell if they were deconstructing the machine or repairing it, as indistinct machinery travelled both toward and away from it, through side tunnels leading towards the Gargantua's lair.

"Of all things to survive, it would be these abhorrent behemoths," Osiris growled, sneering up the machine's dizzying slope. Above the building-sized caterpillar tracks was a fortified walkway made for troop deployment over city walls. One of the guards that had escorted them inside took flight to it, veering to the right before disappearing behind the deployable pavises.

The Dhrakans that followed them kept their distance. Everyone was on edge, and the silent apprehension of the Leviathan chamber had been erased by the palpable tension of knives under the table, a massacre about to be sprung from any, or all, sides.

"This may have been a mistake," Dhalen murmured to Elysser. His eyes flashed with his purple resonance, priming his body for an exit fast or fierce.

They furtively held him back but kept their eyes on Osiris, whose wings flexed and bristled. "We'll find out soon," they whispered back.

After a few seconds, the dragon reappeared above the metal palisades, and with a flick of his wing teams of dragons clambered to winches and ground them into action. The shielding groaned and split, sliding aside to reveal the armoured bulk of Fulkore Crawn, serrated axe in hand, crashing its butt on the walkway with an authoritative ring.

"Here to finish us, or simply to gloat once more?" Fulkore seethed. The Dhrakans around him fell to silence, watching the encircled delegation.

"Neither," Elysser called back sternly. "What happened to you happened to the entire world. We came to make contact, and offer help and resources, should you need it."

Fulkore gave a scornful toss of his head, the webbed frills either side of his jawline flexing irately. "We have never needed you. We did not need your vehement prejudice, nor your destructive attempts to equalise an unequal world, and we do not need your arrogant, pithy outreach." He thrust a bulky, sharpened claw at them all. "This was your disaster, your convenient genocide for which you should be torn to pieces."

Osiris wrested past Elysser. "You besieged, undermined, sabotaged, caused untold death, and allied with Raikali's twisted ambitions!" he roared. "We did nothing but build and give, yet both you and your filthy ancestor tried to take all of it for yourselves, leaving everyone with nothing but fire and dust!"

Fulkore swung his axe into his second hand, straightening, broadening his wings. "We took what you forced us to, after years of subjugation—"

"You escalated this conflict of false martyrdom through your own greedy volition and bared your teeth whenever anyone gained ground near you. The world had to defend itself from your petty malevolence and you still dare to cry persecution." He raised his wings. "You should have been left to decay in the rubble."

The dragons gnarled, growled, and began yelling back. Fulkore stood impassive, but a fire in his eyes relished the conflict.

He needed an excuse.

Now he had it.

Teratai began to slide a javelin free.

He cast his axe over them, demonstrating to the baying crowd. "Consorting with traitorous denigrates to murder us in our sleep – we see how the noble Arete truly conducts itself, at the end of all things."

His eyes narrowed and his teeth glinted behind a grimace.

"I saw the battleground where Nazreal fell," he snarled. "I saw the devastation your aspirations wrought." He threw his arms wide and called to his audience of loyalists. "Everything destroyed! Not a single Dhrakan left standing but for bone and metal, and not a shred of Nazreal itself. The greatest shame of your experiment's ignominious demise was that it did not pull its own creators into the abyss with it."

"We don't *know* what happened!" Elysser stepped forwards suddenly, casting their paw over Osiris' to prevent him drawing his rapier. "Your father had us surrounded! He was prepared to sacrifice thousands of soldiers to gain control of the city – it had to be defended."

He sniffed dismissively. "Using bilious accusations to excuse your partner's genocidal devotion. A loyal tool of the

Aretians to the very end. Your city shall be next to fall, I can guarantee it."

"Arete is already dead." Dhalen's voice, although soft, still seemed to carry up to Fulkore's dais with a halting gravity. The dragon, who had ignored him completely until that point, turned his head slightly, to focus one eye solely on the wolf with the purple smoke markings.

"Your war is done."

Fulkore shook his head slowly.

"Not yet. Not while they stand."

Dhalen gestured to the dragons. "You have an empire still. A family, if one could call it that. What power do the two last Aretians hold over you that makes you so fanatical about their death?"

Osiris and Teratai's claws flexed on the handles of their weapons again. Elysser was still a barrier between them and the circle of dragons, which was closing around their flanks amid the jostling for view and quiet unsheathing of blades.

Fulkore paused, staring at the gryphons. His tongue flicked with intemperate hunger, then he broke into a slow grin while a deep laugh rumbled in his throat, echoing through the metal and stone. "So you truly are the last. Two – no, one and a half – creatures of renown, bane of the free-willed, missionaries of subjugation for all lesser species. And yet you walked so blithely into the fiery maw of your enemy. It would almost be honourable, if you weren't so loathsome."

His eyes narrowed hungrily. "But as I have so longed to see your head upon my wall, rest assured that the joy of doing so will not be diminished."

Elysser took their axe in their hand and readied their buckler. Behind them, Dhalen exhaled and readied his claws.

"Fulkore, don't."

The Dhrakan general bashed his axe on the walkway once more.

"Kill the gryphons, trap the resonators."

The circle of dragons exploded inwards. Teratai launched her javelin directly at Fulkore. The piercing metal shot through the air like an arrow. He barely had time to dodge – it pierced the elbow of his wing, splitting the joint. He let out a deafening roar and staggered behind the palisades, which began winching closed.

Osiris' twin blades clashed against the incoming mob; Elysser whirled their axe and sank it into the floor. Two walls of rock erupted either side of them, sending Dhrakans into the air, giving them an alley that led back to the tunnel. Several Dhrakans still stood in the way. Dhalen ran to meet them, throwing two over the wall and into a third that was climbing over. Osiris rounded on them alongside, while Teratai protected Elysser. Teratai raised her javelin defensively, just as something glanced off its shaft and plunged into the ground beside them.

Above, crossbow-wielders amassed on the upper platform and had begun shooting. A large Dhrakan swooped in the air above them. She threw her readied javelin, landing it square in his chest. The weight of it pulled in him into a spiralling freefall to the stone barrier, where he landed atop other Dhrakans with a gargling screech.

A crossbow bolt hit the wall over Elysser's shoulder. Another by their flank. They turned to close the walls over their head as a blur of wood and metal flashed above them. They raised their shield just in time for the spear to clash with the crystal at its centre. The weight of the thrown polearm struck the buckler against their head and dropped them to the stone. Teratai punched an approaching Dhrakan square in the snout, then rounded on the fennec and scooped them into her arms. Osiris and Dhalen had cleared some of the troops ahead, so Teratai began a run. Elysser rubbed their bloody forehead.

"Don't, I can stand, I can stand."

The gryphon ignored them. Elysser scrabbled to free themself. Their arm wouldn't move.

They looked up, and dozens of shadows fell.

"Teratai!"

Elysser felt the ground hit their back as Teratai dropped to her knees and shielded them with her wings. A thunderous hail of bolts struck the ground, some skittering into their side. They looked up, terrified, as Teratai bore the impacts of the Dhrakan rage.

"T-Teratai?"

The gryphon opened her eyes shakily. Blood trickled from her beak.

"Can you stand?" she said.

"Yes."

"Good. Run."

"Not without you."

"RUN!"

Elysser rolled to their knees, then clambered up and screamed for Dhalen. The wolf turned, and immediately bolted for Teratai, his fur cascading with glowing purple flecks as he pulled her onto his shoulder.

With the buckler crystal split and their arm disabled, Elysser could only throw the axeblade into the wall, closing it over the top of them. Where Osiris was still fighting the Dhraka ahead, the fox sent a ripple of stone careening past him, sweeping the dragons away in a tsunami of rolling rock that carried well into the next chamber and sent them flying into the distance.

They ran, and were met by the earthquake machine. Teratai dug her claws into Dhalen's bicep.

"Drop me here."

As he lowered Teratai to the rocks by Quakebringer, Elysser could see the number of bolts in her back and wings. Some had pierced down to their fletchings, dripping blood from between the lames on her heavy backplate.

"Leave," she breathed, leaning against the rock. Her mechanical legs, strong enough to withstand all but three bolts, kept her upright as she hauled herself into the control module of the machine. "I'll stop them."

"Can... can you operate that?" Elysser asked, while Dhalen quickly attended to their shoulder as best he could.

She gave a wry, bloody smile. "Whose plans do you think they butchered to make this? A fitting end to have me destroy it."

"I can carry you," Dhalen said softly. "Or heal you."

He was met with a dismissively stern, yet exhausted, glare.

"You would not outrun them were you to heal me enough to continue, nor will I outlive the journey without you. Let me give you this measure of protection."

Elysser clutched her arm desperately.

"Can we remove your legs, make you lighter?"

Teratai gave them an admonishing, fiery look. "My legs are fine. Removing me of my self-made freedom would be a poor way to make my death feel even worse."

The fennec buried their face in Teratai's neck, and clung desperately to her feathers. "I'm sorry, Teratai. I'm sorry."

She ran a claw over their ears. "You have all that you need, Elysser. Go with strength, for a future that those we have lost would be proud of."

The gryphon looked to her partner, who had sheathed his

swords and was looking distrait. "Protect them, Osiris. Protect them all."

He opened his beak as if to protest, or offer some hope, but instead stood back and clenched his claws. "I… it will be done, Teratai."

"Good."

Soft booms and crashes echoed from the sealed archway, as the Dhrakans attempted to use small explosives to break through. Yells and shrieks rang from the tunnel's throat.

"Go. Leave, and live."

Elysser stifled the cries in their throat and bolted. Dhalen gave a sombre bow and followed. Osiris gave her a lingering look. She said nothing, but closed her eyes and hammered a lever into action, sending the whirring motor into crunching, grinding drive. Beyond her, Fulkore appeared at the head of the troops that had broken through, axe raised.

She guided herself round the machine and leant over the controls, giving a few exploratory cranks to levers and switches. The machine groaned and creaked, then the buried engine rumbled further into life at its core.

A tremor spread through the mountain. Teratai watched as Elysser waited at the tunnel's dark entrance for Osiris to pass through, then with one, final, tearful glance, sealed it with their axe.

In the tunnel, Elysser held their axe above them, forming a blue barrier which spun the falling rocks to each side as they sprinted. They burst across the threshold and kept running. The clearing shook, tipped, and split. Cove and her partners were circling in the air above — as soon as Dhalen, Elysser and Osiris broke into the open the purple dragon made a sweeping dive for the path ahead of them, wings tilting around a vent of hot gas that burst from the stone. Dhalen leapt onto Osiris' back and Elysser grabbed hold of Cove's claws – together they leapt into the sky, feeling the thudding vibrations of the ground below warp the air. They banked directly towards the Coriolis, which was already moving further to sea as the waves began to shake, and landed heavily on its deck.

Dhalen chanced a look over his shoulder, back to the mountain peak. The stone peak cracked, then erupted into boulders and dust. A fiery boom split the sky and the top of the mountain began to crumble away, revealing a spewing froth of molten red in its wake.

As the Coriolis began its unsteady sail away from the Dhrakan shore, avoiding the chunks of debris that were beginning to rain down, Osiris trod the stairs to the helm. He took the wheel from the otter first mate, who quickly saluted and disappeared below.

Elysser followed behind, still holding their wounded left arm.

"Osiris…" they whispered, voice cracking.

He looked back at them, barely.

"I'll take us back," he replied quietly.

They shut the door, and leant heavily against the closest wall, before slumping to the floor. They sat there for a long time in silence, listening to the cracks and rumbles of the breaking Dhrakan peaks split the sky behind them.

"We could have let them sleep," they said quietly, mostly to themself. "We lost her, and killed them just as they said we had tried to."

Osiris gripped the wheel, his beak tightening. "We cannot change it."

They turned to him fully, eyes full of dejection and disbelief. "Is that it? Teratai's loss relegated to bitter experience? Is your prejudice so deep that you'd forget her so quickly?"

He finally broke from the wheel and swirled round, his wings nearly hitting Elysser as they opened in ire. His armour rattled and his feathers bristled. "Do not accuse me of such callousness!"

They fell silent as his rage boiled over.

"She was better than me! She was everything we *deserved* to be! Resilient, compassionate, hopeful! Everything I could not be!"

He turned and slammed his claws onto the navigation table, swept the maps aside and tore them to shreds in his claws with a pained, grieving roar. "I do not take pride in this! I am not standing upon a pillar of victory gloating about my position as the sole survivor of a pathetic, endless war!"

"I am not proud! Not now, nor of anything I have done," he continued bitterly, turning away again and letting his wings fall.

Elysser looked away. "Not even of finding Aidan?"

He fell quiet for a second, staring into the middle distance.

"Not when it led to his destruction, and this. He deserved better, even if the world that fought him did not. I have… I have a bigger hand in destroying the world than any of us."

They crossed in front of him, where he couldn't look away. Their ears flattened, and they clenched their jaw to quell the pain bursting in their chest and throat. "I have lost as much as you. I have no idea how much time I have left. But, I promise, I will make the most of it. If Aidan and Teratai were worth anything to you then they would want you to do the same."

He fell silent, breathing heavily. His eyes glistened. They rested their paw gently on his wrist. "I need you, Osiris. Don't martyr yourself for a world we haven't yet lost."

Osiris wiped his eyes as Elysser quietly turned to the window and gazed forlornly at their solemn, quiet return.

"I am sorry, Elysser."

Chapter Six

Teratai's absence was felt heavily throughout the recovery, and in Skyria also. Engineering skills aside, she had been a bastion of support and comfort to many beyond Elysser and Osiris, to whom she had been inseparable. The two had thrown themselves into duty as much as possible, often without sleep and as little communication as they could manage, save for each other and Dhalen, whose concern for their emotional health made him almost a shadowy bodyguard to the two. Each had lost someone immensely close and they had a shared grief, but each had their own hue of mourning.

They continued surveys and outreaches to as many stranded and struggling populations as they could, installing air and water purifiers where resources allowed. It was still a battle, as some extant towns and camps were doubly wary of any help from Nazreal's association, revoking it as a cursed, destructive void that would bring further death to anyone within its radius.

Nevertheless, the Coriolis continued its journey re-mapping the world after the rift, and where possible Elysser tried to garner trust of resonators and bring them into some semblance of safety and communication. The results were mixed, and they took the impression that many resonators had been scared into hiding after stories of Nazreal's destruction. Given how few knew the truth, they could only imagine what could be invented to explain such worldwide devastation.

While the golden ship flew over yet more uncharted desert territory and Osiris, with the help of Nidhimes as cartographer, inked out new maps, Elysser's ears began to ring. They shook their head, thinking it may be a burgeoning cold from too many long nights, or a change in pressure.

It persisted, and grew stronger. A familiar, strangely erratic feeling crept up their paws and through their fur; a soft electricity that crawled and pulsed with soft, irregular beats.

They moved to the windows and paced around the helm while scanning the land below. The Coriolis was flying under the clouds to make landscape contours easier to chart and travellers and settlements easier to locate.

A stone mesa loomed some distance away over the port. The way the massive stone stretched from the sand, with sharp straight crags and an area like a distorted oval, made it seem as if it had been extruded directly upwards.

They focused on it intently as they swept gently by.

"Osiris, can you turn us back round to that mountain?"

He dutifully tipped the wheel and the ship began a wide, gentle arc around the mesa. "See something?"

They pressed their muzzle to the glass and slid their pawpads along the clear surface. Tiny snaps of energy buzzed from the imperfections in the glass and into their paws. Their eyes lit up, and their tail straightened like a dart.

"Osiris, take me down."

"What is it?"

"Now, Osiris."

The gryphon gestured to Dhalen, who swiftly took control of the helm. Elysser and Osiris thundered down the stairway, barely touching the boards, and broke onto the deck. Elysser had scarce lifted their arms before Osiris grabbed them and they both took flight, swooping directly towards the mesa's rocky surface.

The gryphon flared his wings and braced them for a landing that Elysser still tensed at the speed of, dropping to their knees. Osiris hurried to pick them up, but they waved him away and kept their paws to the red-hued stone. Their eyes glowed. The sand atop the mesa was drifting, but not with any kind of wind. Instead it vibrated softly in a wide circle as if on the skin of a drum, or softly rippling water.

They jumped forward a few feet, stroking the stone with their paws, sweeping them from side to side like dowsing for water. Eventually, they stopped towards the centre of the mesa. They raised their arms, and the sand around them glowed in a soft blue light.

They turned to Osiris, shaking.

"It's here."

They whirled their axe from their belt and plunged the blade into the mesa. They spiralled open a hole large enough for Osiris to fit through and gazed into the space below.

The twin tines of Nazreal's central tower loomed in the darkness several dozen feet beneath them. The bulky, blue-grey shadows of the surrounding buildings were barely visible beyond. A burning scent laced with the sharp bite of resonance energy rose from the void, and in the sunlight small flecks of blue dust glistened as they drifted into the open.

Elysser peered over the edge, leaning on their knees as far as they were comfortable.

"A-Aidan?" they called.

Chilling silence.

Not merely the absence of sound, but the seeming

absorption of it. It didn't feel like their call had even passed the threshold.

"Do you see anything?" they urged Osiris.

"No, the darkness is too thick."

They called for Aidan again.

Nothing.

They climbed onto Osiris' back, and together they dove into the broken city.

Elysser held their shield aloft and sent a flare of energy into the crystal, casting a soft blue light over the areas they passed. Drifting particles of resonance energy swirled in their wake, attracted to the gentle glow. It sparked and fizzed like rain on hot metal as they flew and swept through the streets, seeking any remnant clue of survival.

The city's outer edges had almost been melted and drawn upwards. Buildings stuck out from the walls, half-consumed, hanging sideways over the streets they once neighboured. Others had shattered or crumbled, and many of the streets that remained untwisted were torn to pieces with fissures or bursts of crystal. The once pristine, immaculately engineered streets that cast comforting light onto its pavements were now a silent wreck, a decaying exoskeleton of the life and promise it used to hold.

They circled the perimeter first, calling out for Aidan, or anyone who may have been left trapped within the city. There were no signs of bodies, no tracks, no gaps in the wall. The life had been stripped from it and left behind somewhere else.

Osiris swept to a halt at the base of the tower. It was slightly distorted, and bore hefty scars of a strange battle, with undulations and warping that could only be explained by those who had witnessed resonance in combat.

Elysser followed the twisted scars of distortion as best they could. Everything bore a burning, electric cold and their footfalls left glowing pawprints. It would be beautiful if it weren't so desolate.

They came to the strange, partially-caved in tunnel towards the base of the spire. Crystal protrusions threatened to block the way for any creature not lithely built. They looked to Osiris urgently. His beak tightened, and even though his grief had been exhausted many times over, on his face fell yet new apprehension of a probable loss confirmed.

"Go. I'll wait here."

Elysser steadied themself with a long breath, then ducked into the narrow crag. Even without natural light above, the crystals' hue pressed into their eyes; they had to shield them whenever they came close or it threatened to give them a blinding headache. The air stung their nostrils, and pricked the fur at their ears. Eventually they broke through to the chamber at the base of the tower. It looked completely alien, with twisted, burnt metal and uneven resonance spires piercing the space. At the centre of the room was a black engine, mostly destroyed, sitting atop a glassy surface of crystal that, when they gazed into it, seemed infinitely deep. They touched the surface gently.

It burnt. They snapped their paw away and rubbed it. It was more like anger, or fearful reaction, than heat. They rocked back against the device's broken frame and sighed into the lonely blue hollow.

"I don't… I don't know if you should be here. This wasn't the world you wanted."

They closed their eyes, and let their head fall against the metal plate. "But a world without you isn't the one *I* wanted." They traced a claw through the resonance dust, creating a line of tiny sparks along it. "Can I be selfish, and ask you to return, somehow? Maybe… even if not for me, then for you? To a world that can continue with some light, and love? And if it won't be for me, then… may it be for one who brings you even greater happiness."

They placed their paw against the sheer, glass crystal beneath them again, and for a second let the burning persist. They closed their eyes as the heat circled and spread through the room, lighting the crystals all around them, then out further. Osiris jumped as soft blue light coursed through the city like a ripple, settling the stones, easing the earth's chill and the air's burning. The gentle blue cascade rose up the walls and met at the ceiling's apex, where it burst at the centre and dissipated into soft crystal rain.

Osiris watched it fall, and felt his heart sink. A few seconds later Elysser emerged from the tunnel and sat at its entrance, raising their head to the dark above them.

"Everything is empty."

Osiris looked to the rough, shaken floor and the debris that littered it. "Such as it will be for a time. This is what I had come to expect."

Elysser closed their eyes in exasperation. "There are no Dhrakans here to blame, Osiris."

He spoke in a low, rueful voice, claws scratching against his breastplate. "For every single one of them, Teratai and Aidan alone are the greater loss."

Elysser balled their paws tightly and stood up, baring their teeth. "She didn't hate them, Osiris, neither of them did." They stepped forwards, pointing a shaky claw. "And Teratai *knew*, warned you outright that your hate would hurt you one day. So congratulations, your self-fulfilling prophecy forced her into death."

Osiris' eyes flared with anger and his claws jerked as if to move, or bite back, but in a second he caught himself and gripped them even more tightly into themselves.

"You see what your faith gave you?" he rumbled, gesturing to the emptiness of Nazreal that bore into them both. "You see who it took from us? Did you not heed any of my doubts or warnings when we foresaw this cyclical violence coming to bear once again?"

His tail flicked with anger. "Kindness is a privilege for the protected."

"Don't you dare tell me my beliefs caused this!" Elysser yelled back. Their voice seemed to rumble in the streets and buildings; a hollow, infinite echo that shook Osiris' feathers. "Don't you dare say my compassion is the weakness at the crux of it all." They stood and walked towards him. "Is Arete boiling inside you still? Is it your way of guardianship to blame the world's pain on those who suffer it? You sound more like Crawn with every passing moment you let this hate take control."

They kicked up a rock covered in resonance dust; it skittered and bounced, casting blue sparks as it flew through the darkness.

Elysser turned to face him once more, glaring through angry tears. "Did Teratai deserve that? Do you think she'd be the person we loved if she guided herself with the same selfishness?"

Osiris looked away. "She should have been here," he said quietly.

They gripped their axe and shield, and held both in front of them. "Look at this. I should never have needed to make my power, my strength and my gift to others, a weapon. But against a contagious darkness fed by greed and fear, this is what I have to be, and will be until that darkness is gone."

They looked at the shield, its scratches and dents casting shadows against its surface. They could have remedied it easily, but had not devoted time, bearing each impact as memories. "Nobody is born hateful. It's seeded by hateful people, inherited from their fears. And we, the ones who give, have to give twice as much to keep it from engulfing us all, rejecting it from ourselves in the process. That's where you have to be, Osiris. If you want to change this world, that's where it has to start. I'm… I'm not forgetting any loss, and I will work hard to make sure neither of us has to suffer it again. But we are the ones who are left behind. We have to be the first to try."

They looked to the ceiling above, and its silent, cold glint in the dark. "I will miss them both, forever. But I will not betray their loss by betraying what I loved, nor what they loved in me."

Osiris saw tears, glowing in the light of the resonance, flowing down Elysser's cheeks. They closed their eyes and the tears flowed faster, leaving luminescent streaks that faded when they left their fur. The gryphon gently stepped forward and took them by the shoulder, then softly pulled them into an embrace.

They gripped him tightly.

Chapter Seven

Years passed, and the work escalated. Cities were growing – some quickly, some at a more measured pace. Elysser stood at the balcony overlooking a city they had designed in an image similar to Nazreal's but in silver-white stone, in a low valley set amongst several copses of trees. Xayall. With Skyria's help, it would be able to seed a whole forest, and maybe spread even further. The shadows cast by the older trees, and the patches of saplings that were slowly being planted between them, were a welcome comfort in the early evening as the sun drifted silently to the horizon in the clear orange sky.

It had been a long day of meetings and delegations on where to grow, how to expand, and thankful tributes from areas now beginning to flourish under the resources provided to them by Elysser as a proxy for Skyria. They hadn't wanted to be alone, but Dhalen was in Ohé and Osiris was keeping away from public meetings to eliminate lingering resentment or accusations of portended disaster. But they had gone well, despite how tiring the process was and how many more steps were revealed as soon as one was completed. They let in a deep breath that cooled the heat in their muzzle and soothed their chest, then walked back inside.

On the large round table in the centre of their room were three large leather-and-metal-bound journals, their covers brimming with parchments both loose and fixed, with hefty lockable clasps on each side. Next to them lay a sketching frame, a set of maps, drawings of ships and mechanical legs, and some artworks of sigils and familiar faces, stylised in shapes akin to water and leaves; Aidan, Teratai, Oakhe, and Dhalen.

Their ears flicked as they heard a movement behind them, and the familiar shape of Osiris swept through their room.

"Elysser," he greeted, bowing his head. "Or Emprex, I suppose now."

They waved their paw. "They're only calling me that because of the city design. Apparently giving aid makes some think they're vassals. I've told them they don't need to do that. I don't want an empire and nobody deserves that inherited servitude."

He shrugged impassively. "It seems to be a better reputation than that of Nazreal's, at least so far."

They scrunched their muzzle. "Having to keep quiet about yourself because of fear and misinformation is hardly sensible, but for now it helps build goodwill. I just... don't want this to become another pillar of expectations again. I'll do all in my power to lift each of us up."

Osiris nodded. "A noble goal. For my part I will dissuade those who would see that as an opportunity for exploitation." He tucked his thumb-claws under the belt that hugged his breastplate. "We have just recovered the last of the ionisation towers, and will take it to our deep mountain cache to be dismantled."

The fennec nodded softly. "That's good to hear. I'm sure the taste of Nazreal will remain in some areas, but hopefully the air will stay clean enough to keep everyone healthy."

"There have been some… odd side effects reported," Osiris said quietly.

They sighed. "I had no doubt. Resonator children?"

The gryphon tapped his tassets with his claws. "You may not be as isolated as you think in your power… in ways both good and bad."

Elysser nodded, looking tired. "Is Nazreal still safe, though?"

"I promise there were no signs of entry or exploration. I take it you will cordon the land?"

They sighed. "It's… mortally selfish to restrict land from people who may need it. Nobody has ownership of it, but I find myself a reluctant protector. Nobody can be trusted with it yet. Nor would it be trusted, I think. Silence and distance are best for now." They rapped their paw on the table. "But, I'll create further safeguards to deter unwanted visitors."

He gave a soft grunt of agreement as he moved to the balcony railing alongside them, looking over their city from above. "It looks like a kind place," he said quietly.

They laughed softly. "I hope so. I don't know if Xayall will ever feel the way that Nazreal did when we were most passionate, and unguarded. But… I will do my best to make it grow to that, in time."

He turned and looked up at the Tor's pinnacle, its wings reaching up into the sky. "They were a nice touch."

Elysser smiled wistfully, looking at their paws. "Another tribute to Teratai. The wings that saved me. And… maybe ones that will yet carry us on."

The gryphon closed his eyes for a few seconds, and took in a deep, long breath that he exhaled as a forlorn sigh. When he opened his eyes, they reflected a deep sadness, and a sense of finality in accepting what he had long resisted.

"Will you carry on his work?" he asked quietly.

They shrugged and flicked their tail as the trailing emotions of Aidan's loss flowed back to the fore once again. "Maybe not all of it. Experiments are to be in secret, mostly in Skyria, as is my training. I'll try to reach out to more resonators, find the scattered remains of my village, maybe, and bring some network through which we can learn and protect each other. One thing I'll always carry with me is his vision of peace and stability. I don't... I don't know if I can trust as much as Aidan did, but I have to try."

"That sounds... admirable." He turned to the room, looking at the map that hung on the tabletop's slanted canvas. "Regarding this: upon my last talks with Virvel, Skyria has agreed to act as an advisor to discovery and experimentation, but there is no wish to plan the governance of the world and they choose to remain mostly self-guided. You will always have an ally in them, but the rest of the world is too unknown right now. All named efforts will be done under your sovereign instead. Do you accede to this?"

They shrugged. "I don't have a choice. As long as they're willing to help, I see no difference. If Xayall acts as a proxy for Skyria's safe and measured discoveries then so be it; we'll be a diplomatic buffer to protect it. And actually..."

They turned away from the balcony and walked inside, then gestured to the three leather-bound journals of themself, Aidan, and Teratai.

"These should be in Skyria too. I know you'll be sleeping soon, so... please, keep them safe. They'll pass our knowledge along. If you find anything on your travels, please keep them safe somewhere until we find time to research them again."

The gryphon nodded, and handed them a small parchment on which was scrawled a list in black ink, with some untidy graphite sketches besides it. "Our latest collection run found these debris pieces and crystal remnants strewn along mountain settlements. Is there anything to worry about?"

Elysser looked up and down the list, studying each sketch carefully.

"This looks like a spoon."

"It is a lot bigger than that."

"A big spoon, then."

"It is not."

"Ah," they responded, with a wry grin that was only amplified by the flustered rippling of Osiris' facial feathers. "I'm not sure, maybe some kind of Skyrian cultivation bowl. I'd give it back, just in case. I don't see anything potentially volatile among the rest."

He bowed his head, the feathers on his crest rippling gently in the breeze through the open balcony. "I trust your judgement." He paused, rolling his claws over the wire-and-leather grip of his rapier in consideration. "It is a shame… all of this must be so guarded."

Elysser's ears folded back. Every time Osiris admitted his truer feelings, they knew it was from a vulnerable place he rarely liked to reveal. They traced a claw over the table, pausing to dig it into the surface and leave a dent, another permanent scar on a plane already covered in similar indelible marks. "We'll do what we can."

He nodded. For one who spoke little, Elysser knew that for Osiris, to give words freely was a gravity they were still learning to balance against their own feelings. Despite how much the two shared, the loss both spoken and unspoken was sometimes an energy that kept them from being too close for too long. But they needed each other, and they knew few others would understand their struggle, their shared loves, and their sadness.

"Do the Coriolis' batteries need restoring?" they asked quietly, after a time.

Osiris shook his head. "Not for now. I will ask for your help when we circle around, however. It is trickier to choreograph when having to keep so far from the city's view."

Elysser nodded. "I appreciate the discretion, though. As much as I hate it, your ship is the most distinct in the world, and carries Nazreal's legacy in its silhouette. Certainly so in its flight."

"Are they really so afraid of what we could do?" he asked ruefully.

They shrugged. "Most who knew the ship understand what Nazreal was meant to be. To others it was a cataclysm of great, unnatural hubris. I hate ignorance, but people trust too little, and…" they sighed. "I'm tired. There are times I just want to shut myself off and sail the world alone. I envy you of that opportunity, sometimes."

He stepped back a little and held his arms out demonstratively. "We are both relics, in our own ways. Not that it is a justification, nor does it become any more comfortable." He gave a small, reluctant smile. "We are now even more scrutinised for how much smaller the world is. I have no desire to begin another conflict with my presence."

"May that be a goal for all of us," they replied, beginning to tidy some of the drawing supplies at their desk, and sealing the journals to pile them together for transport.

Osiris gently ran a claw under the edge of Teratai's journal, and to the artwork Elysser had drawn.

"You captured them well."

"So did my heart," they said softly. "You can take hers, if you like."

He returned her portrait to the table. "I have many mementos of her in the Coriolis, not least of which is the ship itself. It will be the greatest tribute to keep it alive as long as I am able. She would be more disappointed in me for failing at that, than anything else."

Elysser smiled. "Yeah," they whispered, before looking at the other two paintings. "I had meant to give Dhalen's to him before he left. I'll have to remember it next time."

"Of course. Thank you, Elysser. I'll wake, and return, as soon as I'm able, and will help however you need me to."

He picked up the journals and gave them a long, deep bow, then swept round and strode through the door. It drifted quietly shut, and Elysser was left alone as the wind blew from the Eastern deserts.

They gazed over the darkening purple sky at the distal shadow of Nazreal's mesa as the stars, one by one, broke through the veil above.

LAST CALL AT CAULDRON'S REST

C rash, clatter.

The metal tray hit the slab flooring and rolled a few feet, sending fruit rolling in all directions, save for the ones that hit the ground a little too hard and exploded into a paste of seeds and pulp that pebble-dashed the floor.

Djo the pangolin adjusted their protective metal visor and got to picking up the debris, slowly but meticulously wandering around to brush the fruity carrion into their pitch-lined bucket.

Some shocked exclamations and bashful apologetic whispers carried down to them, but they were well past minding that they didn't come directly. That's why Djo worked at Cauldron's Rest, after all: to clean up, and it was a long way from the floor to the ceiling where the residents ate. Few others were confident or physically resistant enough to last.

Djo had been here for a few years now, and their curved back and general quietness often led to accusations of them being old. The opposite was true; they just quiet, and typically content to wander in daydreams, occasionally breaking to slip their tongue into the elongated leather flask full of bugs that they carried to snack on. Outside their cleaning and service tasks, Djo painted, and sculpted wood and clay models of creatures they imagined, or met, and would sometimes sell them at the tavern's entrance, occasionally taking commissions when they had the energy. It was pleasant. But in a city of trade and war, contentedness was often seen as an anomaly for anyone without extravagance to pay for it, and the idea of idle relaxation was something one did only when all other possibilities or resources had been exhausted.

There was nothing wrong with just being happy, Djo thought. But you had to BE happy. And Djo was.

Few pangolins lived in Andarn, so those who didn't fancy the attention of being such a rare creature tended to enjoy smaller, more modest positions or work under their own agency, save for a Captain that Djo had the pleasure of meeting a few times.

Cauldron's Rest, unlike most taverns, was almost entirely devoted to accommodations for travellers who needed to sleep hanging from the ceiling – mainly bats, but some opossums too. Any inclusive place worth their salt that admired diversity among their patrons could be found furnished with a sturdy rail bolted a room's wall, or one that could be hung up or swung into place to allow for proper rest. But as far as places to congregate, Cauldron's Rest was one of the few dedicated solely to their community. While bats weren't a majority species around Andarn a dedicated group of locals and travellers made it a point that each journey up and down the continent would include at least one visit to the tavern.

It was founded by a circle of bats who relied on Andarn, as thousands did, for trade and social enrichment; they wanted a place to be themselves but not be confined to the inverted resting landscape of the pedestrian species. As such, Cauldron's

Rest was born as a place for their extended polycule to meet, and it quickly became a community hub. But not all tasks were made for all creatures, so Djo had been a custodian of the cafe for many years, starting when, as the bats joked, 'they had just grown into their scales' and slowly became the only one patrolling the floors to clear up debris. Their thick scales protected them from most of the objects that descended during lively conversations or party groups, and where scales didn't reach, such as their head, they had been given an ornate visor to protect their eyes and snout. Thankfully direct impacts didn't happen often, but when they did, Djo was given adequate apology and thanks by the owners, Vune, Rephuen, and Lumo.

The cafe itself was a large, tall building with a ground floor that was open to about three storeys high. Around the edge of the room were tables and benches with colourful canvas awnings above them, angled towards the centre of the space to deflect falling debris (or, very rarely, drunken creatures).

For the building being a few generations old, and one of the most consistently travelled taverns in the city, the wooden staircase that circled the outer walls and rose to the dining areas above were still in good condition, mainly because they were barely used – those who dined above typically entered through the welcome balconies on the roof or upper floors, and those who dined below rarely ventured upstairs.

Above the empty space were the gantries that crossed between tables and hanging areas attached to the ceiling. Below these, under the shade of the wooden slatted walkways, were hoops that descended when the aerobatic games were being held. Peering upwards, Djo could see the staunch bronze ladders that allowed visitors to latch onto the ceiling bars, and glinting in the light of the covered glass torches were the railings that covered the upper side walls to allow for lateral movement or more casual congregation.

The topmost stories of the tavern housed the bedrooms, which Djo seldom ventured up to. There was a duo of younger bats who took care of the living areas; Djo didn't mind, as the space was better catered to bats, who often appreciated familiarity rather than the very different form of a pangolin. Djo spent a lot of their time sweeping around the dim floor, picking up debris and dropped cutlery or tankards, and occasionally herding confused transients who expected to find a more traditional tavern, and having to explain its intricacies.

Thankfully tonight's crowd were regulars, even if their energy felt a little disrupted. There was a guest of particular note arriving tonight, but one for whom absolute secrecy had to be kept, so only the owners knew who or what they were. All other rooms had been closed off. Djo hadn't been told anything about them except their calibre of secrecy, so they diligently kept quiet.

A rain of tree nuts rattled down their scales, their previous safety of a wooden bowl landing a few feet ahead, having been upended by an excitable patron. It didn't hurt, but it was always an odd shock when something actually hit them, even as a hail of snacks. Djo glanced up to see the bat clutching their muzzle apologetically, and they gave a brief salute back to signal they were okay. Maybe it would lead to a nice tip later, but it didn't matter much. They were made to withstand far greater, not that they ever held the desire to test it. Circling their broom over the cobbles, they pondered the teardrop-shaped, woody precipitant, thinking each nut could be carved into little tree pangolins curling under a branch.

A few more projectiles ended their edibility on the stones that evening, creating radii of variable viscosities. Djo had to break out the mop and bucket, which was less amenable in the dim light. Not many animals were made for smooth stone and they were one of them; water made the experience more unpleasant and tricky to navigate.

As the patrons dispersed it became easier to clean, and the rain of wine, juices, nuts, and anything else slowed to a drizzle, then to rogue drips, and Djo's rounds were soon more or less complete. Most of the guests respectfully took flight before the allotted time, yet some remained till the last vestiges of spilt dregs had been wiped clean from the surfaces or lapped from the rims of tankards, and reluctantly made their return flight home.

Since there was only one guest tonight, the two bat stewards had been dismissed for the evening, leaving Djo to quietly make their way around the floor, humming soft bars of the music from the market fare. Eventually, with all pieces of debris banished to their sack, and subsequently to the purgatory of the dustcart in the back alley, they began their last scan of the cobbles and planning what they would prepare at home before sleeping. They mapped the journey home as it meandered through the torchlit streets, and places to dodge around if things were loud or unruly.

Andarn was often called the 'city of a million possibilities' by the ones who needed to extort its riches, so it was not unreasonable to have expectations of weird or alarming events. The city had been casting rumours and grandiose hypotheses about the Senate meeting that happened today, about what it might mean for continuing armaments against Kyrryk, or the beleaguered fantasies about some mythical lost city. When everyone spoke about the same thing, it was hard not to feel a connection to it, but Djo tried to put assumptions out of their head and focus instead on their task: to clean, to help, and to be kind.

As they circled the floor, a metal curve glinted in the shadow. A tankard had rolled behind a crate. A little beaten now with its fall, as many of the drinking vessels were characteristically misshapen by their many tumbles to the stones far below the drinking ceiling. It added an extra sense of otherworldliness to the place truly generated by unique, very *this*-worldly circumstances. They turned it over in their claws and began their climb to return it to the stores above.

As they crossed the gantry to the suspended bar, they heard something large impact on the landing deck above, an external platform that visitors could use to enter the building from above. Flying within the city walls usually required a licence, and was heavily restricted at night. This must have been the guest they were expecting.

Djo looked around for a few seconds, tracking between the bar they hadn't yet reached and the stairs, wondering if they should just pocket the dented drinkware and return it at a less conspicuous time, or hurriedly plant it on the bar and escape before potentially breaking the contract set by the guest.

As heavy footfalls tramped along the bedroom floor above, Djo quickly, shakily, clutched the tankard to their chest and began a line for the stairs. A voice with a quiet, rumbling depth mixed with the familiar tones of the tavern owners, coming quickly towards them. Djo couldn't make it to the stairs faster, and instead bowed their head to cover the sight of the doorway with their visor, and clutched the tankard possessively.

The voices paused at the top step. Djo didn't move. They sensed some kind of movement, and potentially a silent conversation above them.

"It's alright Djo," the light, almost lyrical inflection of Rephuen called to them. "We know you mean no harm."

Cautiously, Djo raised their head, and before them, among

the familiar bat faces of the owners, was a towering figure in a long, hooded cape. Their white plumage capped with lustrous gold shimmered in the torchlight, and their massive frame was made even more imposing by the wings gently flexing behind them. Djo had never seen an eagle with such striking features before. As they tracked their vision back to the creature's feet, they realised that they still hadn't.

Paws. It was a gryphon.

Immediately they froze again, save for a slight, nervous shuffle. Vune, a slender bat with a hint of purple in her grey-brown fur and painted tattoos in her ears, swept down and gathered a wing around their shoulder. "Come, sit with us. It's about time we treated you to a gathering."

The gryphon bowed their head in curt greeting to the pangolin, and descended the steps to the gantry. Djo watched them pass and head to the suspended bar, in silent awe at their sheer size. They followed quietly behind, and scooped themself up onto one of the upright stools surrounding the table's edge, while the bats clung to the railing above them and Vune climbed behind the bar to start pouring drinks and distributing small snacks.

The position was always unnerving for a very ground-based creature. Djo wasn't afraid of heights, but didn't exactly enjoy them, and found it hard to relax when so close to an edge that led directly into darkness, even one so familiar. The gryphon claimed a stool nearby. Djo turned the battered tankard over in their claws.

"You need not be nervous," the gryphon spoke. "I understand you did not mean to be here, but you are trusted by my hosts, and by me in extension."

Djo rapped their claws on the table. "It's a… constant state of being, really. But I appreciate it. I promise to keep your, er, self, secret."

The imposing guest raised his own tankard to his beak and took a long, slow drink of its contents. "I imagine you have your own sense of being under scrutiny, being as you are a rare enough species in yourself."

The pangolin shrugged. "It comes and goes. Mostly I keep to myself but… sometimes it does make things odd. I'm lucky to have support."

"So should we all hope for," the gryphon replied, staring into his drink for a few seconds. His stare was hard, like honed metal, but not cold. Under the piercing red of his irises lay memories upon memories, almost as if they all played out somewhere distantly that only he could see, ever-presently. Then, he turned to Djo. They jumped a little, almost dropping the tankard down into the darkness again.

"I am expecting a guest at some point during my stay," the gryphon said. "If you would not mind showing them to my room, it would be appreciated. He is a fox, from Xayall. He will ask for Osiris. It may be as early as tomorrow, depending how long the journey back from the Senate takes."

Djo nodded affirmatively, and to their relief Lumo took the tankard from them and handed it back to the bar; Rephuen laughed at the state of it, and placed it on the tray to be taken to clean for the next morning's opening preparations.

They sat for some time: Rephuen and Lumo prepared snacks, which they ate casually but completely finished, while Vune played some soft music on a hollow wooden box with sprung metal tines mounted over its chamber. She plucked them in gentle rhythm, and the sound was akin to how Djo imagined raindrops would speak to each other. Osiris mostly listened to the stories from the bats about their relationships with each other, or news about Andarn generally. Nothing particularly noteworthy came up; Osiris offered an occasional gnarled remark at a sniff of corruption or dangerous development, but largely seemed disinterested in the larger events of the world. Djo quietly slipped from the stool and gave them all a bow. "I think I should head home," they said quietly. "I don't wish to impose, and it's getting late for me."

The bats all bowed respectfully, as did Osiris. Before turning to leave, Djo addressed the gryphon specifically. "You are a very grand creature. I hope you are always treated as such."

Osiris swirled the dregs of his drink. "You are a noble creature to wish such. I will be treated as I have treated the world. I do not much care for compliments until I feel they are deserved." He paused, and seemed to rethink himself a little. "But it is always heartening to know there are creatures to whom kindness is their guidance. Even if it is not my path to take any longer, it will always be in need. May you be treated even better than I."

Djo bowed their head again, and descended the stairs. They considered looking back up at the stoic gryphon but decided against it, fearing it may look conspicuous. Instead they gently latched open the door and made a quiet exit, before treading the streets back to their home.

Andarn was not a friendly place to begin with, and it was less so in the dark.

Inmate's Gulley, the street that passed over a subterranean section of the Andarn prison, was not a pleasant place on the brightest of days, let alone at night. It was left open for citizens to mock or gawk at the prisoners, and was guarded at all times of the day. Night was somehow more unpleasant; the quiet streets hid far less of the torment the prisoners were kept in. Djo lived near but always skirted around, unwilling to become an accessory to a piteous display of cruelty. Andarn was, however, nothing if not a slave to its money and authority, evidenced in the way it treated those who showed deference to neither or fell victim to both.

They made it back to their modest house, a small single-storey buildings of stone and thatch in the city's outermost ring, where the pathways were warped and ragged, and stones jutted out at odd angles where the drainage was insufficient, caused by overbuilding in new areas towards the centre of the city. Once through the doorway the house was divided into two halves. A small table with a set of stools lay on the right, with a workbench beyond it, and on the left a long wooden partition that separated the sleeping area, which for them was a large cot of blankets and moulded wood.

They found the small lantern in the middle of the table and took the matches by its side to light it, then sat at the workbench. Small blocks of wood, of varying sizes, sat in small piles against the back, and above it hung knives, chisels, and various delicate woodcarving tools, as well as a series of dyes and paints on a shelf mounted to the wall.

They skirted a claw over the ends of the wooden blocks, feeling for softness and judging for size, then picked out a squarish block, laid it on its side, and with a stick of graphite began to draw out the shape of a wing onto its grain.

The next day's walk was slow. They had been up for a good amount of the night; the desire to carve had kept them from sleep. The small cloth bundle tucked into their belt swung gently, and occasionally they placed a claw over it to stop it from bumping around too much. They began their work a little after mid-morning; there hadn't been much point coming in earlier with only one guest to entertain.

The usual guests were milling around, except in more modest numbers today. The Senate meeting being over meant various delegations were making their way back from Sinédrion, or had already returned. More politicians back in Andarn always meant more drinking, for better or worse.

Djo pushed open the door and glanced up, seeing the soft lantern light bathing the ceiling in a warm glow. The shutters were closed today, so the sunlight only peaked through in narrow slits of blue-white, and the curtain across the upper balcony had been drawn, leaving the upper section in a warm, familiar darkness.

There was no sign of the gryphon. Probably staying in his room if privacy, or secrecy, was of his greatest concern. Djo gently ran a claw over the pouch at their belt, then set to work turning out the lower floor's benches and lighting the lanterns around them.

After a short while, they heard the main door quietly open, and shut gently on the latch. Over their shoulder, they saw a fox had entered, wearing crisp robes of green, gold and black, with silvery eyes that seemed almost metal, but glancing around with an unnatural acuity. Djo turned and approached them, giving a welcoming bow.

"Welcome to Cauldron's Rest," they said softly. "Can I help you?"

"I'm here to meet someone," the fox replied, with a hushed undertone. "I'm told he's to be waiting for me upstairs."

Immediately Djo recognised the request, and nodded. "Of course, please come this way." They led the fox up the stairs and gave a polite wave to the owners, who glanced to each other briefly to acknowledge the fox's entrance.

The wide hallway that housed the bedrooms was made of dark-stained wood with red-pillars; in the lantern light the almost-black wood seemed to look like darkness, and the pillars as strange trees against a smooth, inky void. The doors were slightly lighter, and had unique wooden plates with their numbers carved on them. The gryphon had been roomed in the corner suite ahead, one of the largest, and one with the most distance away from a window within its space.

Djo rapped quietly on the door. A low, heavy padding sounded from within, then the door clicked open on its chain. A hooded figure cast a deep red eye through its gap.

"Yes?"

Djo bowed respectfully. "Your guest is here."

The door swung closed briefly to allow the chain to retract, then swept open while the hooded gryphon whirled away.

"Hurry," Osiris growled. The fox moved inside quickly, and as Djo was about to close the door, they slipped the pouch from their pocket and dropped it into the chair by the inside wall, and hoped it would be enough for them to notice.

Dutifully, they closed the door and made their way back towards their post on the ground floor, passing by Lumo, who was waiting by the hallway's entrance to ensure nobody lingered too long outside the bedroom doors.

An hour or so passed – Djo wasn't sure exactly how long it was, but time enough that guests had arrived for lunch – and they saw the fox softly padding down the stairs, looking somewhat shaken down. Djo went to greet him and seemed to almost startle him upon their approach. They gave a tired smile, but produced from their paw Djo's small pouch, now empty.

"He said thank you, it was beautifully carved. He hopes he may get the chance to tell you himself before he leaves, but isn't sure how long he'll be here, or where he'll be needed."

Djo gestured to a table, feeling a little unnerved by the fox's tone. "Would you like to stay? We have plenty of room if you need rest."

The fox gave a thankful, dismissive wave of his paw. "Thank you, I… need to get back to Xayall. Be safe."

He left, and Djo gently tucked the pouch under his belt.

Almost a week later, Djo had seen so little of the gryphon that they weren't even sure he was still here. New guests had arrived, left, and they had seen nobody come to the upper bar after hours as he had on his first night. If he was laying low, he was doing a good enough job of it that Djo wasn't even sure if the stewards upstairs knew he existed.

There had been a strange, disquieting buzz to the city in the days after the Senate meeting. Lots of talk of refugees and conflict in the South, centred around a city Djo hadn't much heard about before. There were whispers of invasions and sieges, and equally disconcerting vehemence to deny it would affect anyone in Andarn, that it should remain business as usual and to ignore such scaremongering.

It was closing time, and Djo was lifting the final benches onto the tabletops to sweep the stones underneath them. The tables' wooden surfaces glistened with the fresh wipe of their cleaning cloth, which now hung over the edge of the wooden pail placed just under the edge of the awning, out of the way of moving furniture.

As they carefully swung one of the final benches over and up, a loud, desperate banging rattled the door behind them. They spun, clutching the bench. Another wave of impacts shook the door. Above them, they heard the bats moving around; at least one of them was coming down to investigate. They reached the double doors first, though, and flicked open the small hatch that lay at head height on the right-hand panel.

The fox's silver eyes, almost glowing with urgency, met theirs.

"Please, we need help."

Djo glanced past him to his companion. Supported by the fox was an ocelot; emaciated, pale, with patches of dried blood in his fur, and barely conscious.

Just as Rephuen appeared behind them, Djo opened the door and the fox and ocelot spilled inside. Rephuen quickly closed the door and called for the others, who descended immediately from the bar on their wide, membranous wings. Together they supported the ocelot to a bedroom, while Djo hurried to grab water and towels for them both. Along the way, the injured feline kept trying to protest the group assistance, but was either ignored or hushed by the fox, who seemed about as exhausted himself, although physically unhurt.

Once the ocelot was into a room and the bats were tending to him, the fox marched purposefully to the gryphon's door, landing heavy knocks against it with his paw. With his other, he rubbed his eyes. His ears twitched in an odd manner, as if inflamed, or irritated.

The door burst open, almost wrenching the chain free as it barely held the force of Osiris' ire at the interruption. The same eye that greeted the fox before took a second to recognise him, and as soon as he did, he released the chain.

"Kier? What happened?"

The fox was breathing heavily, trying to recover his energy. "They besieged Xayall. I got to the city just as they attacked, and pulled Bayer out. But Faria… we lost her, we don't know where she is."

Osiris froze, radiating a sudden, visceral coldness in his stony, grave visage. "How long ago?"

"Four days."

"Where's Aidan?"

There was a long pause of horrific realisation. Osiris let out a long, steadying, but very, very dangerous breath through his beak.

"Stay with Bayer. Once you're rested, alert the Andarn generals and lead whoever you can back to Xayall. I will scan the city for signs of Aidan."

Kier nodded. His left eye closed and he pressed a paw to it, grimacing through a wave of pain. "What about Faria?"

Osiris sighed, more of a growl. "We will have to leave her till we can regroup. Aidan is the priority. He has to make it to Skyria."

"But he wanted—"

Osiris loomed over him. "The orders he gave you are now null in his absence. We cannot search a continent for her until we know where Aidan is. Aidan will strive to get here as planned, and I will wait until he does, or does not," he growled. "He may not even be aware the siege has happened if he is en-route, as he *should* have been days ago when he sent *you* instead. Once we know his status, we can set about a plan for the city and Faria."

"Aidan would rue you for being so callous," Kier bit back.

Osiris' face grew dark. "Aidan is not here. Neither is Faria. Right now Aidan holds the key to a matter far deeper and more dangerous than any single one of us. Grandstand your moral absolutions if you insist, but I will not let us descend into extinction again."

With great protest in his face, Kier turned and entered

Bayer's room, brushing past Djo, who looked anywhere but at the ferociously powerful Osiris. The gryphon said nothing more but swirled the hood over his head and strode down the corridor, heading towards the balcony. There was a distant sweeping of the curtains and a creaking of boards, and the sounds of Andarn's city beyond crept into the hallway. Djo slowly turned to look back into the room where Bayer was being tended to. The three bats had applied bandages and cleaned wounds, and were now making plans to keep him safe and hidden. Vune held out a claw to Kier, who shook his head and sat heavily on the bed opposite. Taking the cue for some peace, Vune gently touched the other two on the shoulders, and they both finished their current care tasks and quietly left the room. Djo watched them all leave, and stood in the doorway for a second, wondering what they should do.

If what had happened couldn't be undone, they could at least protect them now, in whatever way they had resources. They reached to their waist and took a small blue-leather cask from it, gently approaching Kier as he hung his head.

They held it out to him. "For you."

Kier didn't raise his head but looked to Djo with tired, pained gratitude. "He needs it more."

"You can't protect him if you don't maintain yourself, too."

Kier took it reluctantly and twisted the stop off, staring at it but seeing something different than what was in front of his eyes.

"I don't want to rest," he said quietly.

Djo wrung their claws. "I imagine not. I'm... sorry. For what you've been through."

He shrugged. "It's not even so much for me. Others have lost more. And I... need to get back. Try and save them if I can."

"That's… a lot to do by yourself."

He clenched his claws. "I… it… it shouldn't have happened. I'm still here. And I have to do something." He looked to Bayer, who had now drifted into a light, uneasy sleep. "I should have been there."

Djo looked between the two, and at the silver tears slowly forming in the fox's eyes. They wrung their claws together. "It is an easy thing to wish, that no harm be done. And it should be an easy request to make of the world," they said quietly, shifting from foot to foot at a speech they worried was an impropriety. "But a world is a big thing to change. I would, um… I would do what you can. I might only clean at tavern, but it's… my little bit of the world I can make better, It makes those I care for happy."

Djo pointed to Bayer. "I-I don't know you, but you saved him, and brought your friend a message. Those, it sounds like, are, um… very important things that the world needed."

They indicated the cask again with a quick flick of a claw before holding their hands back together again. "So drink… please. I'll bring more, and some food. And I'll stay for anything else you need."

Kier nodded thankfully, and cleared his throat, taking a moment to wipe his eyes.

"Could you… could you bring a cold towel, for my eyes?" he asked quietly.

Djo bowed their head. "Of course, immediately."

They quickly padded from the room and to the bar, where the bats were waiting and talking among themselves in hushed tones. Djo carefully moved through them to the sink and doused a small towel with cold water, before making their way back. Lumo gave them a cautious look.

"Are they alright, Djo?"

The pangolin gave a thoughtful tilt of their head. "I don't think 'alright' is accurate. But I am doing my best to make it less painful. Maybe, at least, they can sleep."

Lumo nodded. "Osiris; did he leave?"

Djo frowned. "I believe so."

"He will return, I'm sure. Please let us know if you hear anything, although we may be beyond the realm of his priority right now."

The pangolin bowed and returned to the bedroom, where Kier was kneeling by Bayer's bed, with a paw on top of his.

"I'm here if you need me," Kier said quietly.

"You always are," Bayer replied, barely audibly, before his breathing settled once more into a pained sleep rhythm.

Kier looked round and stood, taking the towel that Djo offered, and placing it over his eyes.

"Thank you," he breathed. "I think… I think I can sleep now."

Djo bowed again. "I'm glad. I'll be just outside the door should you need anything." They turned to leave, and gently pulled the door closed behind them.

HEART OF STEEL

Chapter One

The wind roared. The giant trees of Skyria rumbled and shook; branches whipped violently, some were snapped clean from their limbs to disappear into the grey beyond or crash to the shelters below.

Many families had moved to the buildings at the base of the trees, wary that, even for how diligently the trees were cared for, that this would be the disaster that finally felled them. The purpose-made shelters, and many of the storehouses and trade posts, were filled to capacity by people wanting to stay out of harm's way. Some felt obliged to stay among the upper levels however, to ensure that any of those who weren't able to move by their own efforts would have some means of assistance. Nowhere was this more true than in the tree which housed one of the children's hospitals, towards the edge of the island. Physicians and volunteers roamed the halls, checking on patients or taking turns to deliver supplies up and down the tree.

A small nursery adjoined the hospital. One of the volunteers' elder sons, a raccoon, was supervising the young ones there. He was regaling his charges with energetic stories of mischief, or legends he'd heard told between soldiers on patrol, and they were enthralled.

The rain increased; the wind whistled and groaned like an enormous, forlorn sea creature trying to bash its way inside. Some of the children whimpered. Lightning flared and flashed with heightening frequency. The raccoon looked about cautiously.

"Hey, why don't we—"

The walls flashed bright white; a deafening crack split the air and shook the room. Shards of wood exploded everywhere. The raccoon felt something scratch his left ear, knocking him to the ground.

Dazed and deafened, he rolled his head to the side. A deep red glow throbbed in the tree's side wall. Smoke began to spread. The children around him were screaming. He hauled himself up in a daze, and tried to shout for them to leave, now. His voice sounded distant, muffled in his head, and he wasn't even sure if he'd spoken.

The nursery's entrance had been distorted, trapping the door at an angle. He tried to wrench the door free; it was stuck solid.

The room began to fill with smoke. He clambered up the frame to the circular window which had once nestled in its arch and threw his fist through the remaining shards, clearing a space big enough to start lifting the younger children through it. Some crawled through in a blind panic – one scurried off for help.

He kept lifting the youngsters through, mindful of the ones who'd been hit with shrapnel or were disorientated from the blast, as the fire crept closer and the smoke billowed overhead.

He looked around purposefully. The heat from the spreading fire burnt his eyes, the smoke made his chest thick and heavy. He raised a hand to check the scratch on his ear, from which he could feel blood pouring.

It was missing.

His paws started to shake. He turned back to the door to see people coming to help, bearing axes and blankets. He stepped away to allow them room to break the trapped barrier and knelt on the floor, trying to keep out of the smoke swamping his vision and slowing his movements.

A series of thumps and cracks resounded above him. He glanced up. Through the smoke he could see one of the support beams had been split in the blast. The rushing fire and buffeting winds were eroding its strength. It fell. For a second he felt sharp, intense pain in his head and arms, then…

…nothing.

Chapter Two

The water lapped at the Skyrian docks; once-moored ships creaked and snapped against each other with the gentle swell of the water, swept against the shore by the previous week's harsh tides.

A meerkat guard knelt down to the small boat that slid alongside the pier, and quickly lashed the spring line to the thick wooden post next to him. He held out his hand for the passenger at its aft, a slender wolverine in a dark leather jacket and gloved claws that twitched erratically. Behind the guard was Irien, the red panda who was Skyria's Representative, standing humbly with paws laced in front of him.

The wolverine hesitated for a moment at the guard's offer of assistance, his right claw poised in a way that almost inferred disgust, but a second later he took the aid and strode onto the pier. Irien gave a polite bow.

"Thank you for returning, Talos. I know we have not been on the best of terms."

"Opportunity is transient; I care less for feelings if there is a task to be completed." Talos said curtly, thrusting his hand into his cavernous pocket. "It appears you had quite a storm here."

Irien shook his head. "One of the worst in living memory. We had substantial injuries, some fatalities. A fire started in our north-eastern hospital. That's where most of the damage was."

Talos' lip curled. "Sounds careless to have a fire in a storm, in a hospital, of all places."

Irien sighed. "A lightning rod had corroded and snapped just above the nursery level, caused by a drainage issue further up. It only took one strike, but it discharged at the break point and caused an explosion. The damage wasn't restricted to that room, but the young ones were trapped for a time, and we suffered secondary fires in our silos…"

He hung his head slightly.

Talos glanced over his shoulder to the boat and clicked his fingers. A gaunt young ferret gently clambered onto the pier and stood behind him, holding a sturdy leather case which rattled with myriad sounds as it moved.

"I presume I am asked to attend to the children."

"Fortunately, many have only minor abrasions or hearing issues from the blast, at worst a broken limb. There is one, however, who is much more severe. He helped evacuate the nursery, and took the worst of the impact. He… well, you'll see when you get there."

Irien took Talos and the ferret directly to a waiting open-top carriage, drawn by two Anserisaurs. Once aboard, the reptilian steeds lurched into life, bringing them rattling towards the hospital at great speed. Debris lay in piles along the sides of the pathway. Sounds of great saws being raked across giant tree limbs scraped the air, mixing with the hammering of construction and busy cries of workers, volunteers, and supervisors.

The pathways and structures surrounding the hospital tree were relatively clear, but immediately Talos could see the area which had been struck. Monstrous tears streaked down its sides, bark and splinters had been blown from its walls, with some of the rifts deep enough to see inside the rooms. Black needles of soot had been scorched into the wood by the smoke billowing from the narrow slits, and some of the leaves still bore shades of ash. The lightning bolt's explosive path could be followed to where it discharged, and below that where its remnants tracked down to the roots. Were the tree itself not thick enough to house an entire hospital wing above many other structures, it would have been entirely obliterated.

"We're not sure whether to repair or demolish it." Irien wore the fatigue of many difficult decisions. Skyria's trees were unique in the world. Even if there was no practical opposition to removing an element with such historical importance, the personal battles were just as troublesome.

"Nature has its limits," Talos mused. "We are all bound to it. But, there are ways forward…"

Irien gave him a sober look.

"You know what I do," the wolverine returned. "You would not have summoned me otherwise."

The ferret gripped the bag tightly. She had been silent for the entire journey.

"Are you alright?" Irien asked her quietly.

The ferret glanced at him, then huddled into the bag.

"Her name is Feith," Talos replied, almost dismissively. "She is my assistant, newly adopted from a workhouse in Balasso."

Irien frowned. "There are… many orphans in Balasso."

Talos let out a quiet snort. "She's not an orphan, she was just one of too many. But she'll serve a greater purpose with me than she will dying of pneumonia. Right, Feith?"

Feith nodded, still burying her chest in the bag.

When they disembarked at the hospital, nurses were already waiting for them, and ushered them quickly upstairs. Talos's eyes scanned every scorchmark and split in the structure still being repaired by diligent workers. Many rooms were empty, but some still contained patients too sick or injured to move.

The nurse that led them upstairs, a red squirrel, knocked softly on a door to a small, private room. It shifted open, and they quietly stepped inside.

Two raccoons, male and female, stood to greet them. On the bed lay their son, supported to a recline by a bank of pillows. His breathing was steady, his head half obscured by thick gauze and heavy bandages. His arms were bandaged from bicep to elbow, below which there was no more limb to cover.

The parents bowed deeply to Talos and Irien as they moved further in.

"Taban, Zia," Talos said politely.

Zia clasped her hands at her stomach. "Thank you so much for returning. I know we haven't often crossed paths, but we didn't know who else to ask."

Talos nodded, regarding the kit. His hands twitched and flicked in his pockets. "I can see exactly why. So, this is…?"

"Tierenan," Taban, his father, said quietly. "He volunteered to supervise the nursery and was… was caught in the blast."

The wolverine slid a stool to Tierenan's bedside. "Tierenan, can you hear me?"

Taban gently touched his son's shoulder. The raccoon shuddered awake with a sharp breath.

"Pardon my interruption," Talos said quietly. "My name is Talos. I'm going to mend you, if you'll let me."

Tierenan nodded, forcibly blinking his eyes into working

order. After a few seconds he greeted the surgeon with a smile. "Nice to meet you," he croaked. He looked about, and saw Irien, who bowed his head politely. Standing slightly behind him, Tierenan saw the small, shy figure of Feith. She shifted the bag to cover her chin, but her gaze kept flicking back to him and his bright expression, shining even under the injury and surgical cloth. Tierenan's smile softened and grew. He gently swayed what remained of his right arm at her.

"I can't move much," he said, "but that's me saying 'hi'. It's more of a wiggle than a wave right now."

Feith looked away, but flexed three pawfingers from her grip of the bag to respond. Tierenan's smile grew again. He turned slightly to Talos. "So… what are you gonna do to me, Mr. Talos?"

Talos withdrew his paw from his pocket with a dismissive glint at the raccoon's tone and tugged the glove gingerly away. He presented his claw, twitching and flicking in almost constant movement, to the young raccoon. "I built this," he said firmly. "And I will do the same for you."

Tierenan's brow furrowed. "You… built… your paw?"

Talos flicked his claw and Feith leapt to the bedside, snapping open his physician's case. Surgical tools lined pockets around the edge, and inside were several metalworking tools, wires, lenses, and devices Tierenan had never seen before. Talos whipped a knife from a pocket and pressed the blade to the back of his right thumb. A drop of blood trickled down the fur. Gently, he squeezed apart the slit, to reveal a gleaming metal surface within his skin.

"My hand was distorted, almost unviable, from birth, so I learnt to build a new one. There are things in this world we are often denied access to, but living to our potential should not be one of them. If you are willing, I can give you new arms. It may take a while, but you may be what we need to allow this process to save the futures of many like you and I in this world."

Tierenan's eyes were wide. He looked to his parents. "Is that okay? Would you mind if I had metal arms? I promise to be careful with the curtains and things."

His parents' faces were a mix of emotions; Taban's eyes glistened, and Zia rubbed the base of her neck while a hesitant smile bloomed on her face. "We trust you, Tierenan," she said softly. "Whatever your choice is, your body is yours. We will love you always."

Tierenan smiled, and gently patted his gauze. "I have a request, though."

Talos raised an eyebrow. "I think… I think my ear is missing. Can you make me a new one?"

The wolverine laughed. "Child's play."

Tierenan puffed up his chest, resulting in a cough that he tried to suppress. "Then I accept this mission," he said proudly. He beamed at Feith. "Then I can give you a proper wave."

She hung her head to look in the bag, but her ears flushed, and a hint of a smile brushed her muzzle.

Chapter Three

Talos had set to work almost immediately, taking dozens of detailed measurements and examining Tierenan's injuries with intricate care. The raccoon was lucky that the beam only grazed his head, otherwise there would have been little left for anyone to communicate with. Along with his missing ear and most of his arms, he'd suffered considerable burns on his head where the beam hit him, and Talos promised to address all of these in time. While the two were very different in their manner of socialisation, with Tierenan's chirpiness and Talos' perfunctory stoicism, they managed to develop an accord for their patient-doctor relationship. When he could, Tierenan directed a lot of his conversation at Feith, who took to focusing on the duties that Talos prescribed her to, with minimal response unless Talos instructed her to give an answer. Even for her relative unresponsiveness, Tierenan was persistent in his encouragement, and any reply she gave was met with unbridled enthusiasm for continuing conversation. When he was too excited sometimes she would withdraw again like an anemone, and he would subdue himself to try and coax her out of her shell again. But even with the ripples in conversation between the three, with Tierenan unable to do little without considerable assistance, he was intensely amenable to company.

Other young survivors from the nursery and their grateful parents often came to visit him and bestow thanks, and in these moments Talos either left or slunk into a corner to pore over a worn journal filled with diagrams, notes, and concepts. The wolverine was not necessarily an unwelcome presence but apparently a contentious one, judging from the glances some of the older visitors shied his way. He spent a small, cursory time inspecting other patients' injuries and performed some procedures to placate those who whispered that he was there on some duplicitous or sinister favour, but thankfully Tierenan's demeanour silenced much of this whenever he was asked about it.

"I trust him. I mean, I don't really have a choice, but as non-choices go I think he's a good one," he'd said, perhaps a little too brightly for some, including Talos. The wolverine paused in his note-taking, flicked his ears, then went back to focused scribbling. A few minutes after the visitors had left, he flipped his notebook shut; the worn leather cover hit the old paper with a sharp slap. He thrust it into his bag and lifted the case in the same motion, startling Feith, who had been quietly staring at the tools inside.

"I believe I have everything I need to begin," the wolverine clipped. "I'll be in the workshop for a few days. It will be a detailed construction, so I'll need my focus, but I'll send Feith up to relay additional measurements and communications." He turned to his assistant, who looked away sharply. "You can stay here while I set up my workspace, but I'll need you with me after an hour or two."

Feith nodded once, clasping her paws at her waist.

Talos gave a curt bow of his head to Tierenan and whirled out of the door. The click of the latch finding its place echoed in the padded silence they were left in. Tierenan looked around idly, while Feith kept massaging her paw pads, looking towards the floor.

"He seems nice," Tierenan whistled, after a few pregnant seconds. "But grumpy. Maybe it's just concentrating."

Feith shifted on her stool and shrugged, looking to the floor.

"I mean, he's nice to *me*," he said, a little quietly. "But I guess he has to be. Is he good to you?"

Feith shrugged again. "He's… fine." She whispered.

Tierenan shuffled himself forward a little in his bed. "Hey, what do you like doing? I know you're here to help Talos, but I can always ask someone to bring in some games, or books, or something fun for you to do."

She glanced about the room, everywhere but at him, gripping her fingers tightly. She mumbled something, then accidentally caught his gaze, and looked quickly back to her lap.

He wriggled his legs as much as he was able, still fairly stiff from excessive bed rest, kicking the blanket from him to perch on the end of the bed and be closer to her. Her right leg began to jostle up and down rapidly. He leant back, trying not to crowd her too much.

"I promise I won't hurt you," he said quietly. "It's okay to be here." He looked at where his right arm was, and slowly, with a grimace at the pain, leant it towards her. "This is the best shake I can give you. I wish I could do more, but… well, that's what you're here to help me with. Thank you."

She looked up, and even though it was shaded with pain, the smile he gave was still sincere and bright. She held her left paw up and, incredibly gently, laid two of her fingers on the bandage. Tierenan's smile grew even wider, and the look of pain was completely erased.

"But even if you can't fix them," he beamed, "I'd never want to scare a friend away."

"It… it hurts?" she said quietly.

He nodded. "It comes and goes. I can take it," he replied, his smile a little enervated.

"Did you know that it would hurt, when you saved them?"

He shook his head. "I didn't think about it. I mean, it's not about what could happen to you, it's about making someone safe. I wish…" He paused for a second, and swallowed. "I wish it hadn't hurt, but if I changed it now, I might not have saved everyone." He swallowed again, his eyes glistening. "My friends are important to me. I'm happy if they're safe."

He gave another smile, and a tear rolled down the side of his muzzle. Feith wrung her hands, then softly stood and walked to the side of the bed to fetch a napkin. She returned to Tierenan's side and held it out to him. He looked at it for a second, then back to her.

"Oh," she squeaked, hands shaking. "S-sorry."

He shook his head and laughed. "It's okay. I still forget too, which is why I have to scratch my face like this:"

He threw himself backwards onto the bed and rolled onto his right side, rubbing his face up and down the bedsheets with rigorous, exaggerated grunting. His tail flicked erratically in the air, and he pushed himself far enough up the bed that his head vanished underneath his egregious slope of cushions, where he stopped, his back rising and falling heavily with exhausted breaths.

"And then I'm good," came his muffled reply. He twisted round to poke his nose out from under the side of the pillows, and stuck out his tongue.

Feith's eyes were wide; she stood stock still at the spectacle of this hyper raccoon boy slithering around the bed. A smile crept across her cheeks, and she let out a tiny, soft laugh.

Small as it was, he heard it and, using his legs as a counterweight, swung himself upright immediately to see her face. The pillows toppled and slid off the other side of the bed. She was holding her hands close to her chin, head slightly tucked, and in her eyes was the first flicker of unrestrained happiness Tierenan had seen since she'd arrived. He bounced excitedly in place on the bed.

"Yay! So, what do you like to do?"

She held her hands to her sternum, still worrying her thumbs. "I like… birds."

He looked around and spied the window adorning the wall behind his bed. It was a little high, and out of the way for either of them to view comfortably from the floor. With a click of his tongue, he kicked both of his legs out and arched onto the floor, then strode around bed to lean his back against it. The foot end of the bed scraped and groaned in a wide circle as he pushed it slowly around, displacing the cabinet that had been next to it and further spreading the pillows about the floor, until the bed was flush against the wall. He gave her a satisfied nod and clambered back onto the bed, then gestured for her to sit next to him. Gingerly, she climbed up and together they looked out of the window.

The hospital tree was moderate by Skyria's standards, but still impressive for those who had spent most of their time around ones that were too small to have different weather systems between their base and summit. As Feith brought her face to the window, the leviathan forest came into view, with enormous trunks tens of metres across ascending into a labyrinth of branches and leaves. The closer she looked, the more intricate the living city became, and when she turned her eyes to the canopy she saw even more creatures flying and jumping between the limbs.

"We get more birds on the coast, but there are some pretty ones that live in the trees and eat bugs and things. I mean, the smaller ones, that don't talk and wear clothes and things. We have those too, but I guessed you meant the *bird* birds and not avian people."

Feith said nothing, but pressed her face to the glass. Her ears flicked and her tail twitched, and her expression was agape in wonder.

Tierenan smiled.

A short while later, the door creaked open. A young sable poked her head through the crack.

"Miss Feith, Dr Talos has—oh, gracious."

The two young ones looked from the window, to each other, and then to the mess. Feith immediately clasped her hands to her chest in alarm at being in potential trouble.

"We wanted to see out of the window," Tierenan beamed.

"Well yes, I can see that," the sable sighed. "I can't believe you're still capable of making such a mess in your state."

Tierenan puffed out his chest. "I dream big."

Feith slid from the bed with her head down and slunk towards the door.

"Oh yes," the sable nurse continued. "Feith, Dr Talos has asked for you, do you need me to take you?"

Feith shook her head, but glanced up at Tierenan and gave a shy, silent wave, then slipped quickly through the door.

The raccoon looked a little crestfallen, but kept his focus on the world outside as the nurse swept the pillows from the floor and piled them behind him.

Chapter Four

Tierenan saw very little of Feith for the following week. She would slip into his room, take a measurement or two, and then leave. He'd try to trap her into conversation but she'd hurry away again as soon as her work was done. The few times he managed to pry dialogue from her, she immediately excused herself in a panic and darted away. He knew there was likely a lot to be done, but his determination to forge a stronger friendship with her was all but indestructible, and it eased his loneliness, too.

The door opened like it had many times before, but through it now strode Feith and Talos, followed by Irien, his parents, and a group of others. Talos carried a large bundle wrapped in blankets, and Irien a smaller, triangular one.

Tierenan's eyes widened. "Just as well I moved the bed," he chuckled.

Talos stepped forwards as the group formed a circle around the young racoon. "Thank you for your patience. I understand you must be eager to get moving again, and I hope this will be the first step towards a great and exciting future for you."

The wolverine pulled the blanket from the bundle,

revealing a set of steel-plated forearms, their clean, smooth metal glinting in the light. When Irien unwrapped his, it unveiled a sleek raccoon ear shaped in steel. Tierenan's eyes glistened.

"They're… amazing! Can I wear them now?"

Talos recoiled slightly. "There are several things we must do to ensure they work properly, and you must be ready for them. The first will be fitting them for size. The next will be more unpleasant and arduous – placing the wires within your nerves to ensure conductivity to the new limbs. Your ear, unless you want straps over your face for the rest of your life, will need to be attached to you directly."

He flicked his claw towards Feith, who was carrying a large, ancient-looking journal bound in leather, adorned with carvings of gryphons and foxes. A slate blue feather, about the length of Feith's forearm, stuck out from between two pages.

"Using research from Skyria's vaults I have developed a means of securing metal to your body without subsidiary infection or rejection, but I can guarantee these operations will be painful, and intricate. Are you willing to proceed?"

Tierenan looked about him; to his parents, to Feith, Irien, and the scholars and nurses he barely knew. "I've come this far," he said quietly. "If I turned back now, it'd be a boring story to tell. I can't encourage others to be brave if I haven't been. So… I'll do it."

His parents hugged him, and Talos moved forward to present him with his arms. He carefully slipped Tierenan's stump into the prosthetic socket. It fit perfectly. He tried to lift it but without any securing structure, it just slipped free and slumped onto the bed.

Talos' eyes widened in awe. "This is the first time I have seen a full articulated prosthesis on one other than myself. You are opening us up to a world of possibilities, young Master Cloud."

He took the ear from Irien's paws and held it to Tierenan's head, roughly angling it in symmetry to his remaining one. "It may not be enough to simply have this rest here. We shall see what other work shall be done, and maybe even make this mobile." From this close Tierenan could see flashes of thought dash across Talos' vision. He seemed to almost salivate at the precision and care he took at this. Quickly he set the ear down and began leafing through the old journal, carefully peeling the pages away from each other. They looked older than Skyria. He appeared to mutter and grumble under his breath, occasionally flicking Tierenan analytic glances, then consulting the stack of his own papers and flitting between them and the aged tome. Irien gave Tierenan a bow and ushered the rest of the guests out, save for his parents; apparently the presentation was both a spectacle and somewhat guarded knowledge. Talos seemed to pause as they left, looking askance as if someone were about to address him on their exit.

They did not.

While Talos pored over the journal scraps and sketched, the young raccoon shot Feith an optimistic smile. She looked away, wistfully gazing out of the window.

Just as he was about to tell her about a really noisy sparrow he'd had a shouting match with earlier, Talos shut his journal with a loud *snap*. On cue, Feith scooped her arms under both covers of the old journal, and gently laid the open sections together till it shut, then held it to her chest. As she lifted it, Tierenan swore he saw a streak of metal under the neckline of her tunic.

Talos gathered up Tierenan's prostheses. "Are you ready? I cannot work on them here."

The raccoon jumped. "You mean, I'm going outside?"

"It's time for your treatment to move to my workshop. Your legs appear normal, so I suggest using them."

A little bewildered, but significantly excited, Tierenan didn't even wait for his parents to assist him before thrashing off his blanket and leaping to his feet, tail whirling in a circle behind him to keep his balance. He wavered a little, moving perhaps too quickly, and swayed enough that his mother caught him under his arm. He thanked her with a smile, then beamed at Talos.

"I am ready to be im-paw-tant."

His parents groaned. Talos did not react, and simply pulled open the door. The raccoon looked a little put-out but marched across the threshold of his room and followed the wolverine and Feith along the hospital corridors.

His stride became less confident as he moved. His legs were weak and shaking, but more unsettling to him was the environment. Hospitals could be harrowing at the best of times, moreso when you're young, and with several kits still ailing in bed for reasons not even related to the storm he wanted to be able to help or comfort each that he passed. He gave a small wish that they would be granted the same fortune he had. He focused on each unsteady step he took, growing quieter along the way, his head hanging a little lower with each patient.

He felt his mother's paw on his shoulder; he gave her a brief, distracted smile, then looked ahead as they approached the hospital's main entrance.

"I'm okay," he said, pre-empting her look of concern. "I just… want to be strong. For me and anyone else who needs it."

"You already are, love."

He wanted to tell her that it was more than that, but knew better than trying to undermine someone else's comfort so he nodded instead, just in time to pass into the sunlight of Skyria's outdoor sky bridges. He couldn't raise a claw to shield his eyes anymore, so instead he kept his head angled down. The wood was nice, but not what he wanted to see. Eventually, as they traversed a set of carved wooden stairways covered by delicate archways of ivy and climbing vines, his eyes had adjusted enough that he was able to look around, and once more be impassioned about the landscape he loved so dearly.

"I'll be able to go climbing again!" he squeaked. He caught up with Feith, who had been walking next to her keeper, and nudged her gently with his left stump. "You can climb all over these trees! Technically kits aren't allowed past a certain height, but next year I'll be able to climb all the way up, with supervision! I've seen from the inside what the view of the land looks like, but the air on your whiskers and the rush of the sun against you feels so good!" He rounded in front of her, eyes gleaming. "You'll come too, right? You'll break through the canopy with me and watch the clouds?"

She blushed a little and looked away. "I'd like to," she said quietly.

Talos shot him a brief, austere glance, which Tierenan chose to ignore any potential implications of.

"You should! I'll take you up there, and point you to all of the parts of Skyria. You can see the sea, the farms, the bridges to the other islands, the shoals of fish, and sometimes whales!"

He trailed excitement and tales of beauteous landscapes all the way down, past quiet onlookers who weren't used to seeing an amputee kit walking so brazenly through the main thoroughfares. He waved at anyone he noticed, and a couple of times stuck his tongue out at young ones he wanted to make laugh, but quickly realised after one started crying that it could be ambiguous as to whether he was being rude or not, and surmised that many who didn't understand the nature of disability may not want an exuberant, limbless raccoon coming towards them, even in overcautious apology. He would just have to be friends with as many as people as possible. Then they couldn't complain about how he looked.

They came to a stone building by the dockside, with a squat chimney softly pluming smoke upwards. The sounds of lapping waves caressed the air, and seabirds called on the northern rocks. The building looked weather beaten and not particularly fit for purpose, but it seemed that this was the safest place for Talos to have the necessary fires for his metalwork, while still being away from the distractions and traffic of the larger forges away from the forests.

He held open the door for Feith and Tierenan to enter. The raccoon looked back to his parents, who waited apprehensively at the doorway.

"He won't be harmed," Talos said, somewhat brusquely. "I cannot guarantee a lack of pain, but that is an inevitability of his procedure."

Tierenan stepped back out to the door. "I'll be fine. I promise."

Zia frowned. "I trust you, Tierenan." She gave a stern look to the wolverine. "You've done a great deal for him, but don't push him. You don't know what he'll give if asked. He's generous, sometimes against his better interests. Don't take advantage of that. He needs to remain in control. I know your reputation, and why you were made to leave."

Talos stiffened. "I know what I'm doing. Rest assured, nothing I do to him will be beyond his capability. Now please, I must work."

Tierenan's ear flattened a little at the tension between them, so he gave his parents a hug. "Love you both. Please don't worry."

They hugged him back, and withdrew cautiously. Taban gave a terse sigh. "We'll be here, if you need anything at all. Call for us."

Tierenan nodded, and gave them a brief salute as he entered the brick hut, and Talos closed the door behind him.

The room was barely lit – all of the windows had been covered with canvas or wood, and aside from a strange glass apparatus at a gurney in the centre of the biggest room, everything else was lit only by small, almost-depleted candles in sconces around the walls. Talos brushed past and laid the metal arms directly on the gurney, then turned to the strange glass equipment by his shoulder. He spun a dial on the side of a small glass ball and a spark fizzled into life at its centre, casting a bright white light across the space. All around the walls were wooden arms on hooks and stands, and between them were long lengths of different coloured yarn, all coalescing at a strange metal platform in the middle, which was adorned with multiple rows of buttons and levers. The yarn was tied to individual spokes that protruded from square chips of metal which held a strange green-blue iridescence to them. On the table were several more versions of these squares, except much smaller, and glinting with the same bright blue-green at their hearts. Tierenan gazed around at everything in awe, but stopped short of asking questions, as Feith and Talos were immediately preparing the gurney and carefully unthreading the yarn from all but one of the arms, which looked most like the ones presented to Tierenan. Instead he sat on a stool by a side room and followed the trail of yarns like a puzzle.

Eventually, when most of it had been cleared and it was

safer to walk around without it catching on ears or tails, he risked speaking up.

"Is this how you'll attach my hands to my head?"

"In a manner of speaking. This is a figurative representation of the pathways that must be completed in your body for the augmentations to work."

"Ah. So… what will you need to do to me?"

Talos gestured to the gurney, which was now clear. Feith and Talos helped pull him up, and he nestled into the strange divots that were probably meant for body contours, but just seemed to deepen a sense of overall discomfort. This was not helped by Talos pulling a rickety wheeled table over that was covered in sharp instruments, a shallow, wide bowl, and a lot of towels.

"My input should be minimal; grafts and attachments are not difficult. What will require more effort will be refining the controls and communication between the prostheses and you. Now, if you are ready?"

He tensed. "As in, immediately?"

Talos uncorked a bottle of something that smelt foul, and made Tierenan feel dizzy.

"We have a lot to cover."

He poured the weird, awful liquid onto a towel and held it to Tierenan's nose. He turned away at first, but his legs quickly turned cold and heavy. It felt like his body was melting below his neck. He tried to say something, but all he managed was a tired half-laugh, before the room spiralled into black.

Chapter Five

His arms ached. Painful throbbing shook his body, across his shoulders, in his neck, down his arms, and into his…

…claws.

He tried to open his eyes, but it was like trying to push against a blanket with his eyelids. He couldn't move. He guessed he'd been on his side for a long time, because his left hip had a sore that felt the same as when he accidentally fell asleep on the stalwart hardwood of his old bedroom.

Something kept jostling him, but he couldn't tell where it was touching him. Maybe below his elbow? It was tugging and twisting his right arm, occasionally wrenching his shoulder. He was still dizzy. If he wasn't so tired he felt like he would throw up. Maybe he could sleep a little more…

There was a loud whirring noise, piercing enough that it made his eyes shake. He flinched as something touched the left side of his head. Then that smell was there again, and he slipped back into unconsciousness.

It wasn't the stone underneath him anymore when he next woke. It was a bed. Probably. His eyes flickered open; the room was intensely dark aside from a small candle flame dancing on a desk opposite him. He drifted in and out of awareness for a short while, until the discomfort at his groggy, heavy body was too much and he tried to roll over. Two unfamiliar weights hung below his elbows, and a strange coldness sat on the left side of his head. He tried to raise a stump to touch it somehow, but the weight pulled at his arm and hurt, all the way down to his wrist. A strange sense of alarm flooded him as the realisation of the pain wasn't as familiar as the phantom sensations he'd experienced before, and he tried harder to sit up.

Something resisted him, put a soft paw on his shoulder.

"Don't," Feith said. "You need time."

He calmed a little, but still tried to crane his neck down to see his body. Trying to move at all made him incredibly nauseous and his head hit the pillow again.

"Where am I?"

"The bedroom next to the workshop. Master Talos is… out."

He heard some rustling, followed by a series of light thumps and scratches, then a shaft of light split the room. It took him a few minutes of squinting to adjust to it, a shade of sunlight he immediately knew as Skyria's midday glow.

He shuffled backwards, wresting his shoulders upwards until he was leaning somewhat against the pillow and the bed's tattered headboard, then was able to look down at his body.

Two metal arms glinted in the light. *His* new arms. The base of his forearm throbbed, swollen, feeling sensitive to every movement he made. He tried, gently, to squeeze his claws. A shock of pain rushed up his arms, but his eyes were still wide and full of wonder at the way his claws shone. He rolled his arms delicately from his shoulders, and watched the reflection dance around the ceiling.

"Feith," he whispered. "I have claws again."

She nodded, holding her left arm. Tierenan looked over to her, grinning, and noticed once again the metal on her own shoulder. It was more visible this time, a little trough with a handle sticking out just above her clavicle.

"What… what's that part of you?" he asked quietly. "Were you hurt too?"

She shook her head and looked away.

"Has he… did you want that?"

She shrugged. "I wanted to be useful," she said quietly.

He watched her for a second, then tried to swing his arms to shift himself sideways. They still felt heavy, but not as cumbersome as he expected. Their uneven, uncoordinated weight was the biggest hindrance, combined with the stabs of pain at the sensation of them being newly attached to raw nerves. It was the breeze carrying the cold through the metal, touching where they attached that felt the most alien. The strange, quiet chill sent a wave of cold up him. Not an unwelcome one, but… one that would take getting used to.

He scrunched his eyes a few times, trying to blink away the tiredness. Something new and heavy pulled at the left side of his head, but he couldn't lift his arms high enough to investigate it.

"I…" he began, swallowing down a wave of nausea. "…don't be just 'useful'. You're more than that," he said, catching her eyes with his when he could eventually open them without the room being a blur of semi-dryness. "Because everyone has their own ideas on what that means. You have to be the one who decides what's useful to *you*." He looked down at his claws, and the increasing quiver in them with the strain of holding them up. He managed to turn them over, and gave a jerky, uneven gesture for her to approach him. She did, tentatively, but rubbed her claws together and mostly looked at the bed sheets.

With a grunt of exertion, ignoring the discomfort that rolled up his shoulder and neck, he gently touched his claws to hers. "I mean… I know these make me more 'useful'. But, well…" He desperately wanted to scratch his head. "Yeah, being useful or helpful is something that makes me happy, but *I'm* the one who decides it. Some people wouldn't, and don't have to. They use their voice or eyes or ears for what makes them happy – you may not need paws at all if you were a storyteller or singer. But…" he looked out of the window, and the golden sunbeams lit his muzzle. "…it made me sad when kits told me they were worried injuries would make them not be loved anymore." He looked down at his claws again. "Their hearts didn't change. Nor their minds or stories or games they liked. But they were worried they'd get treated as broken. And you're not. Or… even if you were, it wasn't your fault."

His claws twitched again as he tried and failed to close them. "So I promised I'd do everything I could to make people happy. To love who they are, or want to be. Because… yeah, I'm not very old and I don't know a lot, but this world is amazing, and the creatures in it make it even more beautiful." He gestured to the window. "Not just creatures, either. We made those trees grow that high, years ago. If we all looked after each other that way…" He wore a wistful, hopeful smile. "…the world would be even *more* amazing."

He looked back to her with a sternness that hardened him with passionate resolve. "My parents always told me one of the very first rules is: my body is mine. Same goes for you. Don't let anyone else make decisions about it for you."

Feith's eyes widened, and glistened.

"If anyone ever tries to do that to you, I promise I will

protect you."

She nodded, and rubbed her throat, looking down and making small noises as if to hide a cry.

"I…" she croaked, "I was unwanted. So I want to be needed. I like what I've been taught. It's detailed." She pointed at his claws. "Some of the connections in there, and in your head, were put together by me because my hands are steadier. But I… don't know how to make friends. Not really. Being around people isn't enough."

Tierenan broke into a wide grin. "I can help you do that!"

She blushed. "I… it seems hard."

They talked for a few hours. Tierenan gave emboldened speeches about adventures he'd had that taught him things about others, and Feith mostly listened, but became more lively as the conversation flowed. She began talking about the places she'd experienced, the people she'd met, and a little of the place Talos had taken her from. But she kept looking over her shoulder as if to guard against a hypothetical someone in the next room. Tierenan inferred that talking was purely functional where Talos was concerned. Feith needed more than just duty to someone else's commands.

Sometime later the door to the workshop opened; they heard the heavy wood clash against the brickwork, and the swift footsteps of Talos marching across the dust. Feith pulled away to stand beside the bed. Talos pushed through the curtain that separated the rooms and immediately steeled his eyes on the raccoon.

"Good. We can start."

He whipped a leather roll of tools from his pocket and unfurled it across the bed; before Tierenan even had time to protest he had clipped open a panel on his wrist and was watching the cables and pistons pull.

"Feith and I talked a lot," Tierenan said, pointedly. "She's looked after me well."

"She is diligent. Ball your claws," Talos commanded. Tierenan tried to do so, but they twitched and flicked; he grimaced as it sent a feedback wave through his arm. Talos seemed uninterested in his reaction, and more in the results offered by the claws. He prodded a few cables, then clipped a small extra wire to one of them, and whipped it over Tierenan's ear to something on his head. He felt a slight cold tightness above his left eyebrow, and a strange sensation of soft current down both his arms.

"I could take her round the island if she hasn't seen it yet."

"Concentrate, please. Again."

He willed his claws into fists, just as he would have before the fire, and they slowly, steadily, shakily, began to curl over.

Talos licked his teeth. "Good."

Chapter Six

The wolverine sat with Tierenan for hours in this way, devising exercises for him to do, then making constant miniscule adjustments wherever needed, and avoiding any insistence at Feith's inclusion or discussion. Sometimes Talos completely detached portions of the arm, or a finger, to rebuild or rewire part of it, and built it back in place later, all with the same analytical coldness. It was exhausting, but Tierenan was determined. If he could succeed quickly, maybe he could have more time to talk with Feith alone, but once Talos knew Tierenan hadn't rejected the grafted cybernetics, the wolverine was always within earshot. Even when Tierenan's parents visited and he was able to show the marginal process he made, Feith would shy away and bury herself in organising at Talos' whim.

At night, when the experiments and calibrations finally ceased for a reluctant rest, even though Talos tinkered away in the workshop for long into the night afterwards, Tierenan would admire his claws, and try to make his own progress with exercising his mind and body to its new limbs.

Despite all they'd done so far they were very slow to respond, sometimes barely registering any movement at all until he felt like he was screaming at them, at which point they might close and lock up completely. Talos rarely vented his frustration verbally, but would frequently tear wires from their place with vicious precision and force them into new configurations with staccato physical ire. The only place he had complete focus was at the chip, where he used a small bird-like device with a finger trigger to configure the crystal array via sounds and vibrations. He had said, briefly, that this changed the shape of the tiny glowing fragment, but it would only work this way because the shard was so small, and its frequency light.

Tierenan didn't really understand, but hoped he would someday, so he could tell his parents about it in greater detail than Talos was likely to reveal. The engineer-physician seemed protective of all information, even sometimes of Tierenan himself, as if this was all *his* domain to reveal and control at his leisure, and never before he was ready.

After a time, Tierenan felt the exhaustion of the new limbs begin to ebb. The strain on his body reduced enough to get him out of bed and walking to the window without feeling that the world would dissolve into sudden sleep and dizziness, and the dull pounding in his head was far less constant than it used to be. He flexed his claws and paced the small stone room, and threw back the curtains with hunger for a reprieve from the same dusty dim light of his quarters. There wasn't a huge view; no sprawling landscape or tree-filled vista for him to lose his imagination in, just more of the same stone and mortar buildings, with regular foot traffic from dockworkers and supply carts. At one point someone had parked a tall cart laden with barrels in front of his window, and he'd managed to get the driver to move by pretending to be something inside one of them, clumsily rapping his metal claws against the barrel's steel rings.

But he yearned for more exercise. Talos was strict, and he knew his duty. But he also knew that healing didn't come from isolation and his soul was too strong and bright to be bound within a concrete shroud, so he absorbed as much of the outside as he could from the window when Talos wasn't around, and conducted his exercises with enthusiasm that it may grant him freedom before any indeterminate threshold that Talos refused to identify.

He saw Feith almost daily. That was his greatest source of excitement, and it remained his constant mission to enliven her reactions and brighten her eyes with a spark of happiness, which she was still resistant to show.

One such afternoon she arrived with a box of metal scraps, wires, and some other strange intricate fittings, and he had been waiting by the door to greet her, albeit halfway stuck inside his shirt. It had snagged on one of his claws and he couldn't reach round far enough with his other arm to free it, so he loomed in the doorway like a distressed scarecrow.

"I require some assistance," he pouted, only the very end of his snout visible over the fabric, while his trapped arm was above his head in a strange S-shape.

Her normal shy demeanour softened when he was nearby, and he appreciated that she had opened up even this far to him. She stifled a grin, and gently extricated his arm and helped him slip the shirt down. He tilted his head as the neck hole slipped over his face, and he gave a relieved smile, letting his formerly-restrained arm drop, easing away the tiredness of its unintended suspension.

"Thank you, Feith," he said, brightly and warmly, enough to make Feith look away and clutch the box she was holding more possessively. Her normal shy demeanour softened when he was nearby, and he appreciated that she had opened up even this far to him.

"New pieces for me?" he said eagerly, peering over the edge of the small wooden container. She withdrew them slightly.

"Maybe. They might be for others," she replied, taking them out and sorting them into trays within Talos' rolling chest filled with dozens of divided sections. Tierenan had been warned against touching it; the temptation to defy that order was immense. He slowly reached a shaky claw over to try and poke the box from under Feith's peripheral vision, but it rattled with the fatigue of his muscles and she immediately snatched the piece into her paw, giving him an admonishing look.

"He'll get angry."

"He's not here! And he's…" he scrunched his muzzle, arcing his whiskers to look like an angry spider, "he's not very kind to you. Does he ever let you be… you?"

Feith looked down at the box, rocking a small metal ring under her claw. "I'm here because of him. So I'm me… because I'm here."

He looked disheartened. "No, I mean… it's not enough just to exist."

She gave him a somewhat bitter look, the first time he had seen a shade of resentment, and he realised he may have discovered the limit of her patience. "You don't know how hard it is," she said coldly. "I know what others get to do, and you've told me what I *should* be able to do. I'm just… not part of that. So I am useful instead."

Holding out his claw to her, he gave a pleading look.

"Just a walk. It's gorgeous outside."

Tentatively, she sighed and nodded. The door creaked open with a cloud of dust flashing in the sun like tiny stars as they stepped out. Despite their molecular marvel Tierenan barely noticed, focused as he was on the sun beaming down and the gentle warmth that began to blossom through his fur. He spread his arms as wide as he could, and let in a deep breath. The fresh air, devoid of the stony must, refreshed him from nose to tail and he bristled with energy. Eyes gleaming, he turned back to Feith, and although he looked like he could burst with how alive he looked, he politely bowed, and gestured for her to enter the street.

With shy steps she followed, but pulled her ragged jacket close to her shoulders.

Skyria's dock was always busy. Tools and materials from the mainland, crops and fruits, an abundance of fish, cultivars, and medicinal supplies leaving, along with barrels of salt and sea minerals. It was an energising smell (aside from the fish) and it made Tierenan bristle with passion for his home.

"See? Isn't this lovely? If you're going to exist, it may as well be somewhere the world can see you."

Feith wrung her paws. "I'm not sure I'm wanted… to be seen."

He abruptly turned, scowling. "Anyone who told you that should have their mouth removed."

He stepped forwards and puffed out his chest. "*I* want you," he said proudly, "to enjoy this walk with me and I want you to want to be here."

He remained puffed up like some kind of defensive creature, giving the air of intimidation but none of the gravitas. Feith being almost exactly his height wasn't helping his case, but actual threat wasn't his aim.

She shook her head and looked away. "Show me where you walk," she said quietly.

With glee, he took her on a parade of the dock, waving to the people loading and offloading, carting materials around, and staying to chat to some fisherfolk along the quays. Tierenan held his claw out towards the fish and made a mock grabbing motion while aiming down his outstretched arm like it was a cannon or arrow nocked onto a drawn bow.

"You think Talos could add some kind of rope or net to it, to catch the fish? He could make my arms really long if he wanted to."

She picked at her claws. "I think they'd be too heavy," she remarked.

He posed, stamping his paw on a nearby fishing stool and flexing his arms above his head. "I think you'll find I have the strength of a bear underneath this athletic physique."

"Only the strength of its stomach," she retorted.

He froze. She immediately looked away, cheeks flushing.

"Did you… did you just make a joke?" he stammered. She shrank away.

"I, it was—"

His eyes widened yet again and his grin looked like it would escape the confines of his face. "Yes!" he yelled gleefully, jumping so hard that the stool rolled over the pier and tumbled onto the rocks below. "I knew you had it in you!" He grabbed her paws and danced the two of them around in a circle, laughing. "That was a good one, too!"

Feith tensed but was kept in swing with his motions, unsure where to look but unable to break from his contagious smile and radiant energy. She smiled too, nervously at first, then wholly, as the world spun around them. Even after he stopped spinning, the smile warmed her face, and he gave her a thumbs-up.

"Your smile is lovely."

As the rush of the impromptu dance faded, so did her confidence, and the smile disappeared again. She immediately began looking around, then down, as if it had been too much, or some invisible scold was being broadcast to her from an unseen presence. Tierenan stood by her, and gently nudged her arm.

"It's okay to take time with this. But don't think you don't deserve to be happy."

"We should get back," she whispered.

"There's a lot left to see," he said softly, indicating the quay's curve around the island. "We could make it all the way round in not much time—"

A pained glare stopped him. "It's not about *time*," she hit back, bitterly. "It's… I'm not part of this place. You dance, and sing, and laugh, and… They're… they're too much for me." She held her paws tightly to her chest, pulling her elbows further in. "It hurts. I don't…" she looked at him, almost ruefully, but with more a pointed sense of longing than anything else. "I don't understand how you do this so easily."

He looked down at his claws. "I haven't changed. I've some metal parts now, sure, but—"

"It's not about you," she snapped. "You've always had a family. I had none. For years I was nothing but the cautionary remnant for others to warn their cubs about. I've seen the way people look at me, and now… how they'll see you when they've decided your injury is more important than your individuality. Not everyone has the strength to push through it the way you do."

She slid a hand up to her shoulder, where the metal perch had been carved, and wires snaked in a braid up her neck to behind her right ear. "When Talos chose me, I took that chance to be useful. Because I could hide from what *they* wanted to reduce me to, and what they said about me." She looked back to her balled claws, and opened them slowly. "If

I'm to be invisible, I will at least be useful. Not everyone has your happiness. And it hurts to see. So I don't even know if I want it."

Tierenan sank, and his ear folded back. "Happiness shouldn't hurt," he said quietly, his claw instinctively reaching for his other arm to hold it. "I'm… I'm sorry that anyone made you feel that way. That things aren't… different."

They stood there for a few seconds, together but apart.

"I'm sorry for hurting you," he said softly.

"You didn't," she replied, still not looking at him. "I was already hurt, thinking about… what's to come."

He began to walk back to Talos' makeshift workshop, and felt a tug at his shirt. He looked back round, and Feith's paw was clutching it.

"But one day… I might not be" she whispered. "And I'd like… I'd like to walk with you then."

Tierenan nodded as a gentle smile crept back across his face.

Two days later, Talos had woken Tierenan by roughly thrusting a long piece of parchment onto his lap, with a scrawled list of exercises to do, with notes on how to combat feedback within his own thought processes, then disappeared, citing that he needed to 'make important arrangements for security'.

Feith had been taken with him, apparently.

Tierenan faithfully conducted the exercises, and in-between sessions laid back in his bed or wandered the docklands immediately outside the workshop.

People were used to basic prosthetics in Skyria, to an extent; usually in rare circumstances, but not to the degree or style that Tierenan had, apparently. He knew Skyria were advanced medically, but a great deal of their focus had been on creating living conditions, safety, and medicine that prevented such things from being necessary. So it became a sort of forgotten essential, as Talos put it, bitterly. Tierenan wondered how he knew so much, and Talos had not been forthcoming about his history within Skyria, other than he left due to conflicting ideals of ideological pursuit.

It wasn't a comforting situation to be at the centre of, but Tierenan steeled himself with his kind heart and determination to do well enough that people's misgivings wouldn't matter, and perhaps he could bridge the gaps between suspicion and past that kept people separate.

He kicked some small pebbles into the waterside and watched a fleet of small fish swirl around them with interest, then vanish. He desperately wanted to put his claws in the water and try to play with them, but he was terrified his claws would damage them, or that he'd break the mechanism and have to start from the beginning again. Becoming acutely aware that he didn't know the durability of his claws, he returned to his room and continued his routine, stopping only to eat with his parents, who returned home as it began to fall dark.

It must have been about an hour or so after that when he heard the door once more swing open. This time it was quieter, and the footsteps that entered more discreet.

Talos stepped through the door, looking urgently at him.

"Tierenan, it's time for something very special."

The young raccoon's ears pricked.

"We are running low on resources here, but with an appeal to the Senate, with you as an example of what we can bring to the world, they may grant us more access to materials and better engineers. We have to leave quickly as they meet in a few days. I have already notified your parents."

"Wait, we're already decided? Even while my arms aren't

ready?" He looked around quickly and clumsily grabbed at the clothes his parents had left for him.

Talos gave a dismissive wave of his paw. "I already know the changes to be made. I have discussed it with a panel of other interests whom I saw today. We'll fix everything once we get there. It will be simple, and you'll come home even newer and stronger than you are now."

Tierenan shuffled nervously. "Can I say goodbye to them quickly?"

The wolverine flashed with anger for a second, then let out a long, shaky breath. "You're a credit to your family, but they're aware of the rush. They send their love and wishes for a quick return. The quicker we leave, the more guaranteed that will be. And you won't be alone either. Feith, and some other kits from the hospital, will be there too."

Tierenan resisted as Talos took hold of his upper arm. "Wait, this isn't right."

For one of the first times since he'd met him, Tierenan saw Talos lose his composure and a blaze of anger flashed across his face. "There's no time for this! It's now, or never again, and all those you wished to help shall remain forever languishing in their torpor of uselessness."

"Nobody's useless," Tierenan said firmly.

"Not everyone is useful, either. Especially if they choose inaction. You wouldn't be here if you had walked that path, Tierenan. You know your purpose. This will change the world for them and for you – forever, if you allow it."

All of the lights were extinguished, and he gathered up every single one of his tools. The journals were already gone.

Feeling the darkness closing around him in the rush and uncertainty, Tierenan slowly nodded his agreement. Satisfied, Talos pulled him outside by the shoulder.

They swept along the dockside, past each of the quays, and had to navigate to a strange part of a shale beach head, where a rowing boat was waiting for them. Talos leapt in, then reached out for Tierenan's hand, all the while looking around into the distance. Already inside the boat at the oars were two large creatures with folded wings. Dragons.

"Uh, I don't think—"

That horrible smell filled his nostrils again as a wet rag smothered his face. He felt his head hit the side of the boat, and then the rush of the oars through the water carried him into a deep, dark sleep.

Chapter Seven

The convoy of dark carriages rumbled across the Dhrakan landscape, heaving and jostling over the uneven terrain. Left behind was the wide but treacherously craggy bay, in which lay the galleon they had just unloaded their living cargo from. It would rest there for the night, before returning to its port on the other coast of Dhraka's lands.

Riding atop the second carriage of four was a small creature wrapped in a cloak, with a cloth mask tight to her muzzle. Next to her, Talos's whip flicked and quivered in response to the quickening pulses in his hands. It was his only tell; the anticipation of arriving was building. Feith pulled her cloak closer about her, and ran a claw under the edge of her mask to alleviate some of the pressure. She could feel her fur rubbing away from the welts it created.

"You can take it off now," Talos instructed, staring ahead. "You shouldn't breathe any of the sedative from up here. Just be careful that it may dissipate from the wagon ahead."

She shook her head, still wary of the anaesthetic's strength. They had used it repeatedly on the children from Skyria over their five-day sail to the northernmost coast of Dhraka and the whole cabin had reeked of it. It clung to her clothes, felt like it was soaked into her fur, making her dizzy and nauseous. She pulled down her hood and felt the cool air wash over her. She wrinkled her nose a few times under the mask to shape it back to what felt like a normal state and caught a sideways look from him that intimated both indifference to her discomfort and a privilege of size making the smell affect him much less.

She watched the ground as they passed, surprisingly verdant for the stories she'd been told about Dhraka. Short, soft grass, and plump leafy bushes carpeted from the undulating lands to all the way up the mountains nearby. She had never seen such a striking consistency of greenery, nor as many mountains in one area. She'd heard Dhraka was nothing but volcanoes and ash, and this was a world away from it.

The carriage hit a large mound and reared up; she slammed her paws down to the wooden seat and gripped it, trying to keep her balance. The wolverine swayed, and laid out his hand to keep from falling off. Once steady, he flexed his claws while muttering a string of low curses, inspecting his erratically tremulous hand for damage.

She looked back at the carriage, trying to listen through the sound of the wind for noises of their cargo. She thought she heard a muffled cry, only once, and strained to hear further.

"They'll be fine," the wolverine snapped. "We have plenty to repair them with. Children mend easily, as you well know."

"You lied. They didn't give permission for this."

Talos snarled. "They don't know what they want. Idealism is fine when you're under the protection of pandering parents or coddling nurseries, but there is a deeper, darker world they will never be prepared for if they're not forced into it."

Feith balled her claws in her lap. "The world is only darkened by people who think that way."

Through eyelids narrowed by scorn he pierced her with a

glare. "I taught you better than to be so naive. That Tierenan is a poor influence, indoctrinated by his bleeding heart parents. But his malleability will make him a useful vessel."

She hadn't looked at him while he talked, still listening to the wagon behind her for signs of movement or distress. Even after he turned his attention back to the path ahead she kept her head half-turned for some time, not sure whether silence was a blessing or an omen for their unwilling passengers.

"Why are we here?" she asked quietly.

He gnarled his muzzle. "I always wondered why the Skyrians were so secretive. I had to develop my hands using the tiniest scraps of knowledge I could get from their libraries, and the rest of the work was my own. But they had knowledge and kept it from me. An ancient book detailing mechanical limbs from thousands of years ago. I could have done more years sooner. As soon as I found it, I let the council have it about how much more we could do. They refused. They said it was 'perpetually dangerous'. They barred me from ever accessing it again. After a humiliating inquiry into my 'illegal' access of it, I was forced from their insipid overbearing daycare of an island, and found Dhrakan metallurgists who had the same drive for progress that I did. Eventually they invited me to view something… immensely interesting, and gave me everything I needed if I agreed to help them with it. But they needed something from me first – greater success than on my own body, and something strategic for their expansion efforts. When Irien sent his message about the fires, it was the perfect opportunity. And they finally gave me access to that wealth of ancient knowledge. All for the sake of their precious raccoon boy." He gave a derisive, spiteful suck of air through his teeth. "Goes to show there is equality for some, not for all. But no longer. I'm setting the world straight."

Feith gripped the bundle next to her with incredible force, knowing her life was forfeit if the journal was even slightly damaged.

"Smuggling that out was a massive undertaking. It's an ancient Aretian engineering log; this gryphon's work was impeccable, and an undeservedly long-held secret of medical technology."

Feith looked into the darkness ahead, through the small torches that lined the roadway. "Are the Dhrakans good?"

"Good for me, good for a stronger future," Talos smiled. "Your morality is too blinkered if you think only in terms of what's polite. The Skyrians lived in fear of their potential till they decided who was important to them. It's pathetic. I am living proof of our path to the future, and the Dhrakans know that. You, even Tierenan, can be too, if you let yourselves. Your augmentations are a divinity *we* created."

Feith felt the biting chill in her shoulder as the coursing wind made the metal perch even colder against her skin.

"It wasn't my choice," she whispered.

Darkness again. Even without the nauseating fatigue and acrid smell of that horrible sedative, it was getting tiresome. Tierenan had had vague memories of a boat, some rough, hushed voices, and a terrible headache. But one thing was clear.

Danger.

This was a new place. The stink of the sedative wasn't right by his face anymore. A strange, humid dark, and a dustier, damp-smelling surface surrounded him. A grit floor lay beneath him and irritated his whiskers. He struggled to right himself and reached around, but his arms weren't coordinated enough yet and he slipped with the weight of them, hitting his nose on the floor. It tasted as bad as it smelt, like soot and old grease. A rivulet of blood trickled from his nostril, so he rolled onto his back and tried to shake the sting from his face. Faintly, as the grogginess of the ether ebbed from his aching snout, the swampy ringing in his ears began to clear and the harsh echo of the sharp stone room took its place. An odd shrillness laced the ambience, punctuated by the distant cries of fearful children.

An unsteady orange light filled his surroundings and he could see, blearily, that he was right. His 'room' was little more than a cave with a barred gate. At one edge were two blankets and a pillow, strewn across the floor as if thrown in as a hasty afterthought.

He had made a mistake. No. He'd been manipulated.

Talos was a liar.

"Damn Talos," He groaned, shifting into a cross-legged position on the dirty, damp floor. "I'm going to shove my claws so far up his—" he stopped suddenly, seeing a hunched, hooded figure before him. She gripped a torch with both hands and was staring at the floor.

"I'm sorry," she said quietly. "I'm sorry you're here."

Tierenan shuffled to her, and managed to rise to his feet. "You... you don't want this, do you?"

She looked around furtively, then shook her head.

"He lied," Tierenan said, loudly and urgently. "What does he want with us?"

Feith rubbed her shoulder. A second later, a small, skeletal bird with membrane wings swept down and alighted the perch on her collarbone. Its raw steel frame flickered orange with the glow of her firebrand. Its head rotated as it inspected Tierenan quizzically.

"He wants... you. Mostly," she whispered. "You're an experiment. Just... just like I am to him. The difference is he needs me to help, and everyone else here will end up being tools." She wrung her paws. "I don't know what he'll do, but I hope... I hope I'll still get to speak to you."

Tierenan ran to the caged metal wall and grabbed the bars, the force of his claws bending them. "Feith, if you can get us out, I'll get you away from him."

She shook her head again. "If I left, and you did too, who would keep the others safe?"

His claws rattled against the bars as he shook. "I won't leave a single one of us behind. Not you, not anyone. We have to get out, Feith."

"Even though... even though I was the one who helped get you here?"

He swallowed the lump in his throat. "I'm more the reason we're here than you," he said bitterly. He pressed his face to the cage, his muzzle resting between the cold, damp, rusting metal. "You're not alone, okay? I'm with you. Even in a cage, I'm still here, and if there's anything you can do, I promise I'll be right here to protect you. And I won't stop thinking of a way to escape."

"I'm scared." She raised her eyes to meet his. "And you are too."

A shaky breath left him. "I am. But we can't give up. I can't change... what I've done. But we can change everything from here, now. Please. Please, Feith."

She suddenly stepped back, and Tierenan heard more footsteps approaching.

"I had a feeling you'd be awake by now," Talos said with delighted venom in his voice. "Come, it's time for your upgrades."

Tierenan took as resistant a stance as he could when the dragons entered the chamber, but his kicks and frail whips with his claws were nothing against their bulk.

"You're a liar, Talos! A liar, and a thief! You dare hurt any of these kits and I'll come back and punch you so hard in the face you'll be wearing your teeth as earrings, you stinking fur rag!"

"Admirable strength," Talos said, giving a glance over his shoulder to Feith as they marched him along the torchlit corridor. "You were a good choice."

They entered a room with another gurney, which the dragons strapped Tierenan to, locking his arms above the elbow with thick leather straps. One of them took hold of a saw.

"Be wary though," Talos warned, "your next set of arms will hurt a *lot* more." He turned over a tiny chip in his claws, its heart glowing with the tuned resonance crystal, then flipped open one of the plates on Tierenan's head. "But then, if all goes well, you won't be objecting anyway."

MOON GUARDIAN

(Section cut from original draft of Legacy, then again from Fracture)

On the night of her father's death, Tierenan had stayed with Faria until the early hours of the morning, intent that any flicker of sadness he detected in her was expunged as quickly as possible. It wasn't in ignorance of the situation, or a refusal to allow her to mourn, but a genuine want to help her manage the deepest, most punishing sadness she had ever felt. He'd been fascinated by the crystals since they met, and asked her about their origins to make conversation in the quiet night. He'd listened ravenously as she recounted the story of how they fell to Eeres.

"That's incredible!" he'd gasped. He looked at the staff in her hands with wide, incredulous eyes. "I mean, I knew you were powerful, but you're standing here controlling the *moon*?"

She let out a half-laugh, half-cry. "Heh, not all of it. Just a little bit."

"Yeah, but, I mean, if you had more, you could control all of it, right? It's still the moon!" He gently held out his hand towards the crystal staff that glowed softly in her hands. "You have all this power inside… it must be hard not just letting it explode." He paused for a second, falling quiet. "I think that's proper strength. Like… it's easy to shout at something when you're angry. That's when you've got all this power bursting through you like a sneeze about to happen. But to stop it, control it, and let it out calmly instead…" He gave her a soft, respectful look. "…that makes you strong. And you're really good at that, Faria," he finished, with a quiet smile.

"Thank you," she replied softly.

He clicked his claws together bashfully, eying the staff. "I know you have a lot on your mind, Faria, but… would you mind… if I held it for a second?"

She presented it to him. For a second he flinched back, as if the chance was too much. Carefully, slowly, he ran the smooth backs of his claws against the sharp spearheaded edge of her father's weapon. He made a noise halfway between a squeak and a gurgle, and broke into a smile.

"I'm touching the moon…" he whispered, a brilliant, slightly tearful gleam in his eye. Suddenly, he snapped his hand back and stood to attention, giving her an enormous salute, his chest swelling as far out as he could manage. "From this moment onward, I, Tierenan Cloud, pledge myself to you as the first and very best Moon Guard! I swear to respect and honour the powers of Moon Empress Faria and will protect her and her moon crystals at all costs!"

Tears rolled down her face as she smiled. "So… Mr Moon Guard," she began.

He held up a metal hand, wearing a mock seriousness not dissimilar to Osiris' usual temperament. "Please, your Moon Majestiness, it's Captain Mr Moon Guard."

She smiled again and shook her head. A bright grin lit up his face.

They remained talking for about an hour more, before they fell asleep on one of the long padded benches along the Tor's corridors. Outside, the clouds coursed silently over to tomorrow.

Faria held her new staff tightly on the Coriolis' deck as the small village quay came into view. The memories of that evening played through her mind over and over like a forlorn birdsong. It was the last time she'd spoken to Tierenan openly before Raikali injured him. Almost two years later and he still lay silent, but he was finally on his way to Skyria.

At least, he would be after this Senate meeting. Even if all he could do was convalesce there, at least it would be his home, the place he loved, and probably dreamed of.

She turned back to the sterncastle as the Coriolis drew to a halt, and prepared herself to disembark. A Representative, for the first time. She hoped one day she could take Tierenan inside Sinédrion's immaculately sculpted halls just to listen to his charming but pointed commentary on how lavishly unnecessary it was. She missed his energy, his candid humour, and his ability to be so perfectly supportive in his unique, authentic way.

As the gangplank was lowered and she strode down it to a line of waiting carriages, with Kier close behind her, she gathered a renewed sense of determination. She was here to protect. She was here to be the voice for those who couldn't speak, and deserved to. For herself, for them, for those who didn't even know what the world was keeping from them.

And for him, to build a world that was deserving of him to return to.

"Just a little longer, Tierenan. Now it's my turn to keep *you* safe," she said quietly.

Dear Reader

Thank you for reading *Remnant's Hope*. If you enjoyed this book (or even if you didn't) please consider leaving a star rating or review online. Your feedback is important, and will help other readers to find the book and decide whether to read it, too.

Acknowledgements

'Acknowledgement' never feels like enough of a word, to me. It's a kind of perfunctory term for something that runs far, far deeper. Because support isn't only an encouragement in terms of this book, specifically, but infinite things that go far deeper into making a life that grants me the time, and energy, to continue with projects from the heart like this one.

To begin, I want to thank Mads, the one without whom I would have almost none of this at all; for their patience and understanding, their persistence even in moments of darkness and loneliness, and for a million moments that can't ever be described, but always mean so much.

Nextly I want to thank Cyrus. A kindred soul who, when he approached me about editing his own novel, could not have anticipated how intensely I fell in love with his world, and the characters from within. Without that, that event horizon of introduction, I may still have been struggling to write this book even now. It resurrected my ability to find and tell stories in myself in ways I had almost forgotten I'd lost. A passion, a practice, a vigour for imagination. I cannot ever thank you enough for what you've given me, and the stories that flow so, so much easier now. You gave me a place to fulfil the dreams I had always wanted for myself as me and Archantael, and that is beyond priceless. The crew of the Omega-9 Special Task Force will always be the most powerful and sexiest team I could ever hope to be part of and I hope to make them proud every day.

To Ruby, Skye, Mabel, and Sav: each of you has been endlessly wonderful and kind and if I had the words to tell each of you what you mean to me, I would have a whole book series just of the acknowledgements. To Ruby and Skye specifically, but not exclusively, for giving my gay little fox Cymbel a world to find himself in and complete a side of his story, the affirmation of that is beyond compare. And for giving me a chance to play a battle-worn Branwen who wants to kick more ass every time I think of her. To Mabel and Sav, and the wonderful folks in the RCG Diskorpsd: thank you for helping me find a place to renew an old version of myself I thought I had long since written off. And Sav especially for throwing me (voluntarily) into a slice of your world that turned into a whole one of its own, that just kept getting bigger and bigger and even more full of love and adventure. It has already meant so much to me, and I'm sure it will continue to mean only more in future.

By proxy and directly, thanks and smooches to Sav's wonderful yeen Solace, whose kind companionship and love of puns and torturing and flustering Sav has been an absolute joy.

To Morgan, a kind, loving, wonderfully creative and understanding soul with whom I have shared many adventures, both written, gaming, and personal. Thank you for finding time for me even when I don't have it for myself, and for giving my burly brawling brusque boy Orion a new life of his own, and a world and partner that is absolutely unforgettable.

To Fyger – someone who may not be expecting to be mentioned here but absolutely deserves it, for your incredible heart, wonderful soul, and mind sharp enough to pierce the veil of time. You are a light in this world and I cannot thank you enough for your generosity, compassion, and endless spark of creativity. May the crew of the Cloudskipper (:p) fly eternal in light and love!

To my wonderful Discord and Twitch mod who I haven't

mentioned yet – Melody, who has been both diligent in protecting me in spaces close to my heart but also wonderful presences to help me learn about myself and to be as bold and expressive in themselves as anyone deserves to be. Thank you for all that you do. Even if I am not always able to speak for whatever reason, it is always noticed, and always appreciated so much.

Speaking of my Discord, and realms like BlueSky, to the wonderful kindness of all the folks there: Muse, Salazaar, Xats, Mora, Polaris, xyntoxy, Lyca, dusk, hoofy, Russell, Evo, Claire, Tiggy, Ethel, Lucid, Dusty, DeltVaran, Mac, Cayenne, Ceru, Demo, Ezen, Lucienne, Searska, Kelsey, CryptPik, Josh, Botch, Midori, Laika, Sprocket, Jonie, Alethia, Gordon, Raine: you are all spectacular and each of you has such incredible meaning to me for your support and encouragement, and for making the space as wonderful and kind and colourful as it could ever possibly be. You make the world worth being in. Thank you.

I want to give a special shout-out to aSavageCloud, for being not only a wonderful, incredible and kind artist, but for giving me one of the best pieces of joke fanart I think I will ever receive. You are super fantastic; you as yourself, even outside of any art, are a treasure and I am always wishing for the absolute best of life and happiness for you. Thank you for being who you are and doing what you do. It's what the world needs.

To CeruleanAzura – your memes and fanart and excited conversations over 'Resonance Brainrot' have kept the life going in me and I cannot ever express how humbled I am that it has such a place in your mind. I hope to always be able to do that faith and passion justice.

I also want to give a special shout-out to Quill, an avid supporter, immeasurably kind voice, and beacon of exemplary sincerity and courage. Just wait until Edge of Ascension, I've got something even bigger to thank you for.

I hereby extend my already infinite thanks to Katie Hofgard (Eskiworks), whose work continues to blow apart my expectations and open up a world that I have been aching to visualise for ten years as of writing this set of acknowledgements. Without your work, I would have so much less to show. The writing may make a story, but the cover makes a book. Thank you, from the deepest point of my heart, for being such a huge part of this for me.

The last thanks I think, for this time round, goes to the (although she may not feel it) unstoppable force that is Sara-Jayne, Director of Inspired Quill. Nothing has kept my faith in the publishing industry longer than she has. Even through explicit hardships and an unending current of tiredness, you have been a beacon to follow, an encouragement against all burdens that would otherwise threaten to stop me in my tracks, and a resolve that has kept me holding on throughout this entire journey.

Thank you. Always and forever.

P.S. Also thank you to Aaron, whose obsession over a single line about a bat cafe in *Legacy* prompted the entire 'Last Call at Cauldron's Rest' short story. Djo exists at your kind insistence, and the world of Eeres became a little bigger as a result.

About the Author

Hugo is a British-born author living in North Carolina. They began life as a starry-eyed creature with a fascination for fantastical adventures, heroes, and animals, and invested as much time in their own imagination as they did on animations, video games, and music.

In their spare time, Hugo is heavily involved with the furry fandom, standing as an advocate for LGBT+ rights, mental health awareness, inclusion, and artist/author visibility and fair treatment. They talk about many of these things on their intermittently-updated blog, and occasionally produces their own videos.

Find the author via their social media:
@PangolinFox

More From This Author

The Resonance Tetralogy

Book 1: Legacy

Her power is unmeasured. Her abilities untested. Her destiny inescapable.

Faria Phiraco is a resonator, a manipulator of the elements via rare crystals. It is an extraordinary and secret power which she and her father, the Emperor of Xayall, guard with their lives. The Dhraka, malicious red-scaled dragons, have discovered an ancient artefact; a mysterious relic from the mythical, aeons-lost city of Nazreal.

When her father goes missing, Faria has to rely on her own strength to brave the world that attacks her at every turn. Friends and guardians rally by her to help save her father and reveal the mysteries of the ruined city. She soon realises that this is not the beginning, nor anywhere near the end. A titanic war spanning thousands of years unfolds around her, one that could yet cost the lives of everyone on Eeres.

Book 2: Fracture

The shadows are coming…

Months after the tremors that shook the world, repercussions of battle still lie in Xayall's broken streets. Among the debris stands Bayer, former bodyguard to Faria, Empress of the city state. His position redundant, and his injuries still healing, he struggles to find new purpose.

Unrest between nations is already stirring. A Councillor from Andarn has been murdered, and only a handful realise that sinister machinations are blackening the root of the whole continent. Questioning his duties, Bayer finds himself escorting Captain Alaris on a mission from which neither may return, although their failure may spark a brutal and catastrophic war.

As blades rise, threats both new and old emerge from the darkness and bare their teeth at the world.

Book 3: Ruin's Dawn

"I want to hear everything, Osiris. All that you can tell me."

In the desert town of Mahrae, a young fox is about to discover his power.

A single bolt of crystal energy begins Aidan's journey, one that will test him to his furthest limits and deepest loyalties. The gryphon Osiris takes Aidan under his wing and together they battle shadows and suspicion to bring warring nations to the pinnacle of invention and prosperity – the new city Nazreal.

But not every creature strives for a bright and industrious future.

Conflict is an unsteady foundation for the burgeoning metropolis. The launch of a thousand incredible dreams plants the seed for an immeasurable disaster that even Aidan and his friends do not have the power to prevent.

This is the story of Nazreal's ascension… and the end of the world.

Book 4: Edge of Ascension

When Nazreal falls, resonance ends.

Empress Faria has returned to the Senate to continue and protect her father's legacy, but she is far from welcome. With the ancient city of Nazreal's secrets now in the open, aggressive forces are moving in to stake their claim.

Branded a political delinquent, she walks a knife-edge to guard her sovereign and fulfil the promise of peace, but quickly the blade is twisted and she is forced to fight for her friends, Nazreal, and her life.

A climactic storm begins to rise: the last battle to end a two-thousand year conflict of world-destroying stakes, converging on the beleaguered lost city with Faria as its shield, one final time.

She cannot afford to fail.

Available from all major online and offline outlets.

www.ingramcontent.com/pod-product-compliance
Lightning Source LLC
Chambersburg PA
CBHW030020200726
48283CB00012B/698